AURELIOUS
FORTY

VOLUME ONE

DIANNA BEIRNE

To My Beloved

Chapter One

I like to watch people.

I find people, like you, fascinating. There's something in the way you all act, in your movements, your quirks, and your behaviors, that's mesmerizing to me. You're the most honest with who you are, the most real, when you think no one is watching you. But I only know this because I've been watching.

Let me be clear here, I'm not peeping in anyone's window at night. That's just too creepy. I watch people in public places doing ordinary things but I always keep a safe distance so no one notices me. I'm extremely observant, often to the point of being preoccupied by my observations, so watching people is rational in my mind. When I've watched enough, I make up stories about the people I've noticed or make notes of my general observations about their behaviors.

Everything I observe gets logged into documents on my laptop. The words on the page are the only dealings that I have with those around me and that's the way I prefer it because although I'm fascinated with people, I don't want to interact with them. My laptop, my one true prized possession, is my only friend. It's been my companion, my outlet, and my shrink ever since I took it out of its box.

I've never felt any kind of connection with the people who have surrounded me in my life. I exist in the same space but that's about it. My life hasn't been easy, it's been lonely, harsh, and perpetually in transition. So it was logical to never get attached to anyone else. It was safer for me that way so I stayed under the radar and made myself easily forgettable. As it turns out, that's something that would come in handy later.

I should mention that my parents died in a car crash when I was eight weeks old. They were young and rebellious and although a drunk driver hit them, they were driving drunk at the time too. Apparently my parents had a history with issues involving drugs and alcohol. I read about it once in my file.

Yes, I have a file because I've been in the foster care system my whole life, except the first eight weeks, of course. And I wasn't in the good side of the foster care system, if there is one. No I was in the bad side. I learned the hard way that the best way to deal with my foster families was to keep my mouth shut and stay out of the house as much as possible. I only got moved to another family when the family I was with screwed up so badly that the social worker felt I wasn't safe anymore. I moved nine times.

I'm telling you all of this because it's part of the story of who I was and where I came from. When I get to the part about how my life changes you'll wonder things like how I could just vanish from the life I knew. You might start wondering why my parents didn't come looking for me, or if my friends missed me. But now you know that no one cared enough to look for me, there weren't any friends, no one is home crying over my disappearance and the change was easy for me because I didn't have anyone that I cared about enough to miss either.

So, let's get to the part about what happens just before everything in my life turned upside down, or maybe right-side up.

The last town I was living in had a center square where there was a water fountain surrounded by shops and a train station. The shops had awnings that were adorned with brightly colored hanging pots of flowers; they offered shade on bright sunny days or refuge from raindrops when the sun refused to poke its head out from behind the clouds. Each store sign was dark green with gold lettering and each store name made a feeble attempt at being clever, like 'The Book Nook' bookstore or 'Delightful Delicacies' for gourmet foods, a place I'd never been in. Benches were placed along the storefronts where people could sit, as long as they didn't sit too long and preferably only if they were getting energized to go and spend, spend, spend in the shop closest to the bench. The town was designed to look like something that would have been there early in the last century if you disregarded the '*free wi-fi*' signs and the garbage cans filled with discarded plastic iced coffee cups. It was quaint and about two miles from my house, which was, as always, in the crappy part of town.

In the center square, people would shop or eat or sit at one of the strategically placed benches with their overpriced designer coffee defining their self worth. This was always a great place for me to observe the local wildlife so on a warm Saturday afternoon in the Spring, I took my familiar post on the ledge around the water fountain and opened my laptop to start my process of being a part of the world.

I was writing about this woman that kept stopping to check herself out in her reflection in the shop windows. Her skirt was way too short and her shirt was way too tight. She didn't look great and, to me, she had this look of desperation in her eyes. I saw desperation a lot so I knew what it looked like. Anyway, I was so engrossed in watching the behavior of this woman and writing my assessment of her that I was totally startled when a man behind me laughed softly, a little under his breath and said, "You're right she does seem like she's trying too hard to find a husband."

I gasped and quickly stood up, closing my laptop at the same time, "What the hell dude?"

"Sorry, I didn't mean to scare you."

I gripped my laptop to my chest as if I needed to protect it, or needed it to protect me, "Did you mean to read over my shoulder? Seriously who does that?"

"You're right, that was rude of me." He held his hand up and backed up one small step, giving me some room to calm down.

"Really? You think this total invasion of my personal space is rude?"

"You just seemed so engaged in what you were doing that I

couldn't help but be drawn in by you." He smiled and coolly tucked his dark, wavy hair behind his right ear like this was actually a normal situation.

"What? What's wrong with you?" I didn't wait for an answer before I started to walk away, my heart was pounding in my chest and sweat was forming on the palms of my hands. I mean I know I'm not wrong here, it's pretty common knowledge that you shouldn't read what someone is writing without an invitation, right?

When I was a safe distance, I turned and looked back at him. He wasn't following me which was good because then I would've had to consider going to the police and that was something I didn't do, I couldn't draw that much attention to myself. He just stood there watching me, his thumbs hooked into his pockets, acting casual like he belonged there, but he didn't.

He looked like he was in his late twenties though it was hard to say, I wasn't great at judging ages. He was wearing a white t-shirt and jeans that were faded enough to look as if they'd been around for a while. His skin was tanned, like he'd been in the sun. This stood out to me because it was too early in the season to be tan, at least around here. As I was turning around again to continue my abrupt exit I noticed that he had silver rings on all of the fingers and the thumb of his right hand. Men in this small, picturesque, suburban town didn't wear rings on more than one finger.

To say that I was distracted for the rest of the day would be an understatement. I was angry that he invaded my privacy but I was also embarrassed. I wrote about my deepest feelings and thoughts, I didn't share them with people. I made an effort for as long as I can remember to not share my thoughts and feelings with anyone. It always backfired on me, it always came back to haunt me in some way, so I put them all into my computer and safely locked them away. Now here was this stranger reading what I wrote. It was wrong, it felt wrong, I felt vulnerable now and that was not something I had the luxury of feeling because the vultures in my life would pick up on that and attack.

I walked quickly with no destination in mind. My cheeks felt hot. I was hyper, completely on edge and constantly looking over my shoulder. I was the one that watched other people that was my thing. But people didn't watch me. I always went unnoticed, until today. What made today different? How did I end up on someone's radar?

I wandered around long enough so that it was late when I got home. This was good because I would just be able to go to bed and not have to worry about doing or saying the wrong thing and causing an uproar with my foster mother. I quietly went into my room, the two other foster kids that I shared it with weren't there, which wasn't unusual. In the silence I opened my laptop to write something about that guy, maybe writing about him would help me make sense of what happened. But, for the first time ever, I couldn't think of what to write.

As I lay awake, willing myself to fall asleep, I realized what bothered me so much. As offended as I was in my head about this guy, there was a part of me that was intrigued by him as well. I understood what he meant when he said he was drawn in by me because, as much as I didn't want to admit it to myself, he drew me in too and the feeling was immediate. I felt it as soon as I looked at him but it didn't make sense because I didn't feel a connection with anyone. Something happened to me that afternoon, something I didn't understand and it made me very uncomfortable.

Chapter Two

I woke up the next morning feeling nauseous. I think it was the combination of a lack of sleep and the hot, dank, stink emanating off my nameless, faceless roommates in the glorified closet we called a bedroom. I shrugged on the same clothes from the day before since I wasn't exactly loaded with outfit choices, slung my backpack with my laptop over my shoulders and headed for the door.

I always tried to get out of this house before my foster mother rolled angrily out of bed. She wasn't a morning person. Actually she wasn't an afternoon or night person either.

There was no breakfast for me here, sometime last year the mother started to get bothered by the foster kids eating the food she bought. Apparently she didn't get the memo that parents are supposed to feed their children. So I worked odd jobs and got my own food with some of the money I made.

Today's work was to unload a week's worth of groceries from a truck at a local deli. This was one of my favorite jobs because it meant that I got my food for free for as long as the job took me. Semi-unlimited free food meant that I could stash some away in my pockets and my backpack for later in the week. Was I taking advantage of the free food for the duration of the job thing? I don't know, probably, but the counter guy looked the other way and I had to survive.

Work took my mind off of my life, including the weird encounter the day before, and put food in my stomach. So when I left in the afternoon I was in a fairly decent mood. But that decent mood was short lived.

As soon as he caught my eye I had that feeling again. The guy from yesterday was walking toward me, he was looking right at me and I felt drawn in.

"Hey, it's good to see you again," he said with a wave and big smile like we were long lost friends. This totally aggravated me.

I put my head down and kept walking. I was sending a pretty clear message that I wasn't interested in a conversation.

"You know I'm sorry about yesterday. I guess that probably seemed kind of odd to you."

He turned and was walking next to me so I quickened my pace and stayed silent. "I'm not from around here but you have a nice town."

"This isn't my town." Oh crap, I spoke.

"You don't live here?"

I walked faster. My heart was beating harder, I was getting out of breath but it wasn't from the walking, it was from him. He was confusing me. This was all confusing. I couldn't understand why he was talking to me. I kept my head down, my eyes focused on the sidewalk and his scuffed black boots, which had no trouble keeping up with me.

But he seemed calm, his breathing was normal, "I just thought that since I saw you in town yesterday and then here again today that maybe you lived here."

I stopped short, my annoyance on full display, "What is your problem? I'm not gonna tell you where I live. Yesterday you were reading over my shoulder and today you're trying to find out where I live. You're new here, good for you, but if you're looking for a friend you're gonna have to look somewhere else. I'm not interested."

I gripped the straps of my backpack, digging my fingertips into my palms and started walking again.

"How about just a conversation then?"

"Are you serious? No, go away, I'm not interested!" I sped up, so did he.

"Yesterday you were sitting alone at the fountain but I saw several groups of kids your age hanging around. Today you're walking alone but just down the street there are kids playing basketball on the town courts. I thought maybe you were lonely and would like to have someone to talk to."

A fat, salty drop of sweat fell into my eye; I blinked the sting away hoping he didn't notice my moment of human weakness. "Not everyone feels the need to hang out with people. Walking down the street and writing private things in a computer are not the same thing as an invitation for some quality time with a stranger. I'm not lonely," lie, "I'm otherwise occupied!"

"In your mind, you mean?" He stated the absolute truth and that caught me even more off guard but I wasn't going to let him know it. "I understand that you have a lot on your mind." His voice was soft, like he actually cared that I had a lot on my mind, like he felt sorry for me that I was alone.

"You're a freak!" I said sounding like as much of a douche bag as I possibly could, maybe that would hurt him. Maybe I could hurt him before he tried to hurt me then he would leave me alone, the same way everyone else did.

I darted into the street, dodging the oncoming traffic and disregarding the blasts from the horns caused by my erratic, risky behavior. But taking on the traffic seemed safer to me than another minute with this guy. I didn't want to stick around to find out what his angle was; everyone I had ever known had some kind of angle.

I ran once I got to the other side of the street. He didn't follow but I kept running anyway. Eventually I stopped trying to outrun him and started trying to outrun my own mind. Rationally I knew that I should avoid this guy at all costs yet, emotionally, I felt like I shouldn't. But that nonsensical realization only made me want to run further.

I thought about him every day for the next two weeks. I replayed what he said to me over and over again. I remembered how he looked, what he wore, how he stood. He was trying to be nice to me. He wanted to talk to me. He thought I needed someone to talk to. That's crazy, I didn't need to talk to anyone, I had my laptop, and I could write about things instead, no talking necessary. In my experience it's been much easier, safer and less disappointing to just write things down.

I made it clear to him that I wanted no part of any interaction, but hidden in my heart I wanted to see him again, I wanted him to be persistent. I wanted him to find me. He didn't make me feel awful or vacant or as invisible as I made the effort to be. And as much as these were feelings I tried not to have, I couldn't help it but I couldn't let him or anyone else know this, so I filled my pages instead.

It turns out he was persistent. On another warm Saturday afternoon, I was sitting on the grass in the park watching a baseball game. I wasn't really interested in the game. I was never all that into sports, likely because I never played any, other than the obligatory game of kickball in gym class. I was there because this was a good place to watch people and write about what I saw.

"You're right, he is observant," a female voice came from behind me, startling me again. Really, what was with the silent entrances and the reading over my shoulder?

"Sorry, we didn't mean to sneak up on you," she said in response to me quickly snapping my computer closed. I looked up at her since I was sitting on the ground and they were standing. The sun behind her was so intense that I couldn't see her face. I shielded my eyes and turned back away to blink out the blue spots that I now saw floating in front of me. If that was the only time I saw her I wouldn't be able to tell you what she looked like because of the brightness around her.

She sat down next to me on my right side, relieving me of my temporary blindness, and the guy, that guy, sat down next to her. They both had the warmest smiles on their faces. They actually made me feel peaceful when I looked at them. But the feeling was out of place so I turned away and tried not to look. I should've gotten up and walked away but I didn't, something inside me made me stay.

"He is lovely," she was talking to the guy but looking at me. Again, someone was looking at me. I was immediately self-conscious. I nervously ran my fingers through my perpetually messy hair and wondered if my clothes gave the illusion of being clean.

"Why do you write about people from a distance instead of being a part of what they're doing?" she asked me.

I guess we're jumping right into another *none-or-your-damn-business* conversation? I casually pulled individual blades of grass from the ground as a way to pretend that I was being nonchalant. I generally fool people pretty well; these two should be no different. I thought about what she asked and mulled over whether or not I should bother answering her. But by now I was feeling very curious about them and figured maybe I could just talk to them for a minute, satisfy their curiosity and mine and be done with them for good.

"Because I'm different from them I guess, I don't really want to be a part of them. People, in my experience, can be pretty disappointing." Crap, I overdid it, I said too much already. What was I thinking? Was I totally inept at talking to people? She was going to make fun of me. I shouldn't have said that.

But she didn't make fun of me, "That's true, some people can be disappointing especially when they're not who you need them to be. And those people at that game, even though you don't know them, you don't think they're interesting or worth getting to know because of your other experiences?"

"No, I guess not. But whatever, it doesn't matter." I was screwing this up. I'd said a few sentences and that was enough. I had to appear disinterested, it was the best way to survive the potential peril of interacting with people. I started to make a move to leave but everything in my body was screaming for me to stay with them.

"Wait," she said putting her hand on my arm. Her hand was warm. Something tingled beneath my skin when she touched me. I pulled away quickly, why did she touch me? I looked at her as if looking was an involuntary reaction.

Her wavy hair was brown and came to about three inches below her shoulders. There was a streak of reddish orange down the side. It was like a flame but it blended in with the brown. It wasn't in the front, where it would frame her face, it was on the side, you probably wouldn't even see it if you were looking at her straight on. Her skin color was just like the guy's, and her eyes were almost orange. Other people would say they were brown but when you looked at them closely, focused on them, you would see the orange in there.

I think I looked at them for a full minute but it wasn't just about the color, she had emotion in her eyes that I couldn't define. I couldn't tell if she was sad, anxious, curious or excited. Maybe it was a combination of all of those things. It was so hard to look away.

She was wearing a t-shirt and old looking jeans like he was, with sneakers on her small feet. She had a silver and gold charm bracelet on her left wrist that was connected to a silver chain that wrapped around her arm all the way up above her elbow. It was wrapped around three, maybe four times from bottom to top and it didn't get in the way of her moving or bending her arm at all. It was like a part of her. She didn't have any make-up on and her clothes weren't fancy or trendy but the sight of her made me lose my breath for a second. She was the most beautiful person I had ever seen.

I had to stop looking at her but it hurt to turn away. My mouth went dry. I wanted to touch her hair, her cheek. Instead I untied and tied the fraying laces on my busted up sneakers three times to keep from reaching out to her. But I wasn't done looking yet. I turned my attention to him.

I didn't just look at him, I had already seen him twice, so this time I studied him. This was when I realized how dark his hair was, it was pure black, so black that at a certain angle it could almost look blue and it was shiny, it held the sunlight in it. His eyes were as dark as his hair, I had never seen eyes that dark before, I couldn't distinguish between his pupil and his iris, it's like they were black but do people actually have black eyes? His eyes showed confidence and calm, he was exactly who he wanted to be. His body was strong without being all steroid-ish and bulky. I noticed the rings again, silver bands on every finger of his right hand, none on his left hand.

I forced myself to turn away, it was weird that I was looking at them like that but they didn't say anything. I was nasty to him, I called him a freak but I was the freak now and they didn't seem to care.

"It's okay, we don't think you're weird," he said.

I looked at him, perplexed, "Why'd you say that?" I hadn't said anything out loud about being weird, which I clearly was.

"You had a look on your face that suggested we might be thinking something like that."

I did? I hadn't realized I was so expressive. You see this is why I didn't like people looking at me. "Is there something that you want? I mean why do you keep finding me?"

"We don't want anything from you, we saw you sitting here and thought we might like to sit with you and talk," he said.

"Talk about what? I mean you realize this makes no sense right? People don't just come up to people and start talking like that out of nowhere."

"I think sometimes they do," this was the girl's response.

"Well, not in my experience," I replied flippantly hopefully disguising that my heart skipped a beat when she spoke.

"Sounds to me like maybe you need some new experiences," she smiled when she said that.

Against my better judgment I smiled back for a quick second, "Maybe I do." Damn it, again I said something I shouldn't have. And I smiled? Smiling was a sign of weakness.

It was time for me to move on. I knew it was time because I really didn't want to go and I was getting comfortable. Each second that passed made the urge to get to know them even more intense and that was not a good idea for me. I couldn't risk talking to these two any longer so, without hesitation, I stood up, once again gripping my laptop to my chest.

"Time to go then?" the guy asked.

"Yeah, time to go," I answered. They stayed where they were. I was going to be the one to leave. I was always the one to leave.

"My name is Brekwyn by the way," this was the guy talking. "This is Anira." He gestured to the girl. I had never heard names like this before, Brekwyn and Anira. Well, I had heard one unusual name.

"What's your name?" Anira asked me.

"Aurelious," I said, "Aurelious Forty."

I waited for the laughter and ridicule. I waited for them to ask me to repeat it followed by more laughter and ridicule, then for probably the first time in my life, none of that happened.

"Beautiful," Anira said which forced me to look at her again. How could she possibly think my name was beautiful? The thought that she might be mocking me actually made me painfully sad, exactly the unforgotten feeling that I spent years avoiding by keeping people away.

"She's telling you the truth Aurelious," Brekwyn said softly, I assume my expression was revealing my emotions again. "Your name is beautiful and completely unique. It's an important name. Far more important than any of these people you write about could possibly understand."

He was being nice again, and she was being nice too. It overwhelmed me. It was too much for me to comprehend. So I did what I always did. I left.

Chapter Three

My last day of finals was on a Friday. I got home early since I only had one test, which was in the morning. My foster mother was there when I walked in and she was not happy.

"What the hell?" She was surprised to see me when I should have been in school by her calculations. I mean come on; did you think she would know my finals schedule and have lunch waiting for me on the table to celebrate the last day of school? Uh, no. She just stood there in the kitchen, all sweaty in the stagnant midday heat.

"Sorry," I said, not meaning it and not making eye contact as I squeezed past her to get my laptop out of my room. I made a point of never leaving it at home but we weren't allowed to have our laptops in school during finals, school policy, so I had no other choice.

"You should be sorry," she said after me. "If it wasn't for your sorry ass costing me so much money I would have a nice air conditioner in my window keeping me cooled off and in a good mood."

"Sorry," I muttered again absently, distracted by the fact that my laptop wasn't under my mattress where I left it. I looked under the other two mattresses on the floor where the other foster kids slept. It wasn't there. Where was it? I looked under a pile of clothes that was in the corner of the room. Where was it? I started panicking.

"Have you seen my laptop?" I went into the kitchen where my foster mother was standing in front of the open freezer with her face shoved inside of it.

"No I have not seen *your* laptop mister money bags. *You* don't have anything, *you* are a foster child, and foster children don't have laptops." She had this obnoxious smirk on her face. I knew she was lying.

Thoughts about everything I had written came flooding into my mind. If anyone read those things I would be a sitting duck. They would be merciless if they knew I had thoughts, I had feelings that they could exploit for their own twisted pleasure.

"Please, it's the only thing I have, please I need it," I begged her, I absolutely begged her, and she smiled and shoved her fat, sweaty face back in the freezer. I stood there, paralyzed waiting for her to say something else, waiting to say she was just kidding or something that would make her seem less cruel. She didn't even know me, how could she be like this?

"I do know where *my* laptop is though."

My heart sank. I literally felt this lump drop down from my chest into my stomach. I knew she didn't have a laptop, I was the only one in the house that did because I was the one who worked hard and saved for two years and bought it myself.

"My man came by today to take *my* laptop to the pawn shop so we could buy an air conditioner."

Fury rose up from my feet to my head, "That was my laptop!" I shouted at her, she whipped around and slammed the freezer shut.

"Excuse me?" she shouted back. "I don't recall giving you permission to purchase any kind of fancy electronical equipment."

"You didn't have to give me permission, I bought it myself!" I continued yelling back at her. This is the most communication we had in the last year and a half, I can't be sure if she even knew what my name was.

"Oh really, and where'd you get the money for it?" She stalked toward me backing me up against the wall. With her fat, sweaty finger she poked me hard in the soft part of my chest just under my collarbone, she knew where she was poking because pain radiated down my arm, "You a thief. That's what you are, a no good thief, no good, nobody wants you cause you a punk ass thief."

I pushed myself away from her moving to put the three and a half legged kitchen table between us, "I worked for that money, didn't you notice that I was working? Where did you think I got the money to feed myself after you stopped letting us eat the food that you needed to shove down your fat throat?"

"What'd you just say to me? That's the thanks I get for opening my home to you out of the goodness of my heart?" She put her hand over her chest and slumped her shoulders acting like she was in some kind of physical distress. But she didn't know me. She didn't know that I spent my life watching people. She didn't know that it was the wicked gleam in her eyes that I saw, the one that wanted to lure me closer to her so she could inflict some kind of bodily harm. I didn't fall for her act.

"Bullshit lady! You didn't take me in out of the goodness of your heart. You took me in for the check from the government, just like you took in all the other kids that you pile into these rooms and fail to provide clothes or food for. You're the thief, you're a thief and a liar, you're pathetic and cruel! You are disgusting!"

"Don't you talk to me like that!" she screamed and pushed the table at me but she didn't push hard enough or fast enough. I jumped out of the way. The fact that she didn't knock me over just pissed her off even more, she looked around the kitchen with frantic eyes, she was crazy with rage. I saw her face change the moment she noticed the sharp, filthy knife laying between two burners on the rusty, broken stove. She reached for it but I was quicker than she was and I grabbed it.

I held it out at her, my whole body shaking, sweat pouring from my forehead, I felt like I was going to throw up. What was my plan here?

She was wondering the same thing, her eyes showed that she was afraid but, just like me, she pretended she wasn't, "Go ahead you good for nothing piece of shit! Go ahead and stab me then you can be a thief and a killer, you're gonna to end up in jail anyway like the rest of these kids nobody wants, so go ahead and kill me!" She started slapping her hand on her chest, just daring me to do it.

Should I do it?

"I hate you!" I screamed at the top of my lungs and with all my strength I plunged the knife deep into the wall right next to her revolting face then turned and ran as fast as I could out of the house for the last time.

I ran hard into town. My lungs were burning by the time I got to the pawn shop. My shirt was stuck to my body with the sweat of the effort it took to get there and the fear that I would not get there in time. Once inside, I breathed deeply to catch my breath but choked instead on the thick, putrid cigarette smoke that hung heavy in the air after it was exhaled from the blackened lungs of the shop owner standing motionlessly behind the counter just staring at me.

"You running from the cops?" He didn't seem like he was too nervous if I was.

"No, I'm looking for a laptop," I said in between fits of coughing while wiping my head and face with my already wet shirt.

"Laptops are popular today," he said without moving from his perch, he didn't look like he moved too often. "But, I just sold my last one, sorry kid. Come back on Monday, I might get one in this weekend."

"But didn't one come in today? It was silver with a small chip in the top right corner. The keys were starting to get shiny from using them so much." I hoped it would sound familiar and he would remember that it was in the back room or something.

"Yeah I got a silver one today but someone was in here looking a minute later and he bought it, no negotiating or nothing." He smiled at his own good fortune revealing a mouth full of empty spaces interrupted only by the occasional yellow tooth clinging desperately to the rotting gum. "Interesting looking guy, talked funny, definitely not from around here." Like I cared what the guy looked like or where he wasn't from, I just wanted to get back what was stolen from me. But there was no hope of that now and I think I died a little at the realization of my loss.

I hated that pawn dealer at that moment. I knew he didn't know what he did but I'm also confident that he wouldn't care if he did know. I hated my foster mother, my foster monster, the fat, sweaty awful woman. All my life I dealt with it, I dealt with having to leave or being left, I dealt with having no one care for me. I dealt with it all just fine, I never complained to anyone. I didn't go crazy, I didn't implode, I wrote instead, and now all that I had written since I bought my laptop was gone. My friend and protector who listened to all of my thoughts, who nurtured my creativity, who hid all of my unspoken fears was gone.

I wandered around for the next few hours until the sun started to set and the heat subsided. I found myself back in the park where I watched the baseball game days earlier. I had nowhere to go, no place to hide. I was, at last, completely alone. And I was terrified.

But then something came over me, this feeling like I would be okay somehow, like this was how my life was supposed to go and it would get better. They sat down on the bench on either side of me, Brekwyn and Anira. We all stayed silent for a long time.

"Have you had enough of this then?" Brekwyn finally asked me.

I nodded knowing that my expressive face must have betrayed me again.

"Come with us Aurelious, you don't belong here," Anira said barely above a whisper.

"How do you know I don't belong here?" I asked without looking away from the nothingness that I was staring at.

"Because you belong with us, and we don't belong here either."

"How do you know I belong with you?"

"It's just a feeling," she said. "Don't you feel it?"

I thought about lying, about walking away from them again, but I was just so tired, "Yes."

So without another word, the three of us stood up and, together, we walked away.

Leaving with them was easy because it was my only option. I pulled a knife on my foster mother today and when I did, I forfeited the privilege of living under her crumbling, neglectful, abusive roof. But it was more than the fact that I had nowhere else to go, it was also because Anira was right, I felt like I belonged with them. I've felt a lot of things in my life but I never felt like I belonged until I met them. The feeling was as awful as it was exhilarating which is probably why it was so confusing. Because now I had something more than my laptop to lose and if the pattern of my past was any indication of my future then I was destined to lose this too. But I would take the risk, wherever I was going had to be better than where I had been.

And thus began my journey.

Chapter Four

I wasn't mindless. Curious? Yeah, I was always curious but I was never mindless. So blindly following Brekwyn and Anira for a solid hour like I didn't have a brain in my head made no sense at all.

"Wait," I stopped short, finally. Anira bumped into my back and my back tingled, "Where are we going?"

As if my survival instinct slapped me out of my complete mental fog, it occurred to me that I didn't ask that before. It also occurred to me that they didn't offer the information either.

"Just north of here," Anira said rubbing her nose where it made contact with my shoulder.

"So where is that, like what's the name of your town?" I knew enough about the surrounding area to recognize a name of a town and be able to figure out about how far we were going.

"We have several more miles to go, it's a bit of a long walk," Brekwyn said from in front of me without looking back and without stopping.

Were they avoiding the name of the town? Ok, so now I really started to think about things like what the hell was I doing? These two are strangers to me, strangers that I had met before but strangers none-the-less. They could be serial killers for all I knew. But they didn't feel like serial killers, they didn't feel bad and bad people usually gave off some kind of vibe. Didn't they? Well, they always did in my experience, and I had a lot of experience with bad people.

As I saw it, I had two options. I could either continue to follow them or I could go back. But honestly, after pulling a knife on my foster mother, I knew that I couldn't really go back. There I certainly wouldn't survive the night but here I might survive it. This path was the better option. And I was able to convince myself that as long as we were walking on the open road, I could make a run for it if I needed to escape. So I closed my mouth again and kept following. But the security of the open road vanished when Brekwyn made a random turn toward the tree line that had been surrounding us for the last mile.

Panic replaced the bewilderment and exhaustion that was beginning to overwhelm my body, "Wait a second, what is this? Why are we going into the woods?" Tiny icicles of fear crept up my neck.

They both looked at me and smiled, in that way that they did when they found me at the park and it evoked the same reaction. I felt peaceful again but the feeling wasn't right, like in my head I knew going into the woods should raise some kind of red flag.

"I know you're weary Aurelious and I know it doesn't make sense to trust us but I promise you that we are not leading you into any danger," Brekwyn said, putting a hand on my shoulder, which I immediately shrugged off. "You're safe with us."

"We're not going to hurt you, this is just a short cut to where we live," Anira added emphatically.

"Where is that again?"

"It's just a little bit further I promise," Anira said and she touched my arm. That warm tingle shot through me again so I immediately pulled my arm away rubbing the spot where she touched.

But my options hadn't changed even if my faith in my own instincts began to waiver. So I continued to walk behind them. The woods became denser with each step we took and the moonlight that illuminated the last hour of our walk was eerily absent here. But they didn't need the moon to light their way, they knew where they were going, and now I was completely lost so all I could do was follow. Helplessly.

I only knew that we had reached our destination when I heard Anira's footsteps change from the vague muffle of feet on dirt to the distinct sound of going up stairs, three stairs to be exact. And that was followed by the familiar sound of a door opening. A couple more footsteps and, behold, we had light. Well, she lit a lamp in what appeared to be a kitchen, which lit up the steps enough for me to see where I was going. I took a deep breath and, somewhat reluctantly, followed Brekwyn inside.

He closed the door behind me but I positioned myself right in front of it just in case he actually turned out to be a serial killer. I mean, at this point anything was possible and I probably should've thought of that before. I immediately scanned the area to search for other exits without getting caught up in looking at too much detail like I usually would. There were small windows but not many of them and they looked to have metal frames so this door was my best option for escape should I need it.

"Is anyone hungry besides me?" Anira looked tired now that I saw her in the light but remarkably she was still beautiful. I looked away so I wouldn't get caught up in her beauty again; I had to stay alert especially now that we were in a confined space. She poured some milk into a small pot on the stove and got right to slicing a loaf of bread. It was weird, the bread looked homemade, it didn't come out of a plastic bag and the milk came out of a pitcher, not a cardboard carton. I wondered if they poisoned it knowing that I would eventually end up here.

"I'm very hungry," Brekwyn said standing beside her, leaving me too much room to escape. Fool. "Aurelious, you must be hungry too, here have some of this bread. Anira made it this morning." As he handed me a plate with two thick slices on it, he took a bite of a slice he had in his hand. I guess they didn't poison the bread. Good thing because I can't remember the last time I was this hungry and I was almost always some level of hungry.

I didn't say anything, I just kept my feet planted where they were and leaned over to take the plate. I planned to eat it slowly but the first bite was so good that I couldn't stop myself from devouring the rest. It was sweet and moist, and a little spongy. I had never tasted bread like this and the milk, in my life I had not tasted milk like this either. Of course I waited to drink it until they did just to be sure but when I did I was so glad it wasn't poison. It was warm and sort of nutty but also a bit sweet and it coated my dry, hoarse throat, and filled any empty spots in my stomach.

Exhaustion hit hard as soon as the food and drink were finished. But it didn't just hit me. I could see it in Anira too. Brekwyn didn't look that tired.

"It's late, I think sleep will do us all well. Tomorrow's a big day," Brekwyn said.

"Aurelious, I have a room ready for you here." Anira pointed to a closed door just beyond the kitchen. "My room is right there." She pointed to another closed door.

"I'm fine here on the couch actually." The couch had an unobstructed path to the door. I couldn't be sure what was in that alleged room.

"Oh but the bed is much more comfortable, you wouldn't even fit your whole body on the couch." She was smiling but she was kind of pleading too, like she really wanted me to sleep in the other room. I refused to trust that even though I felt like I could.

I folded my arms across my chest, tucking my clenched, white knuckled fists under them. I didn't understand their hospitability. They had to have had an angle like everyone else.

"Anira, if Aurelious would prefer to sleep on the couch until he's more comfortable here then by all means, he should do so," Brekwyn said to her. "Please go get him a blanket and pillow to make him more comfortable."

"Don't worry about it, I'm not even sure if I'm gonna stay here," I blurted it out before I could stop myself. It was true, I didn't know if I was going to stay but I didn't want them to know that I was thinking about leaving, I would rather just do it without anyone's knowledge.

They both looked at me, and then at each other. Anira was up-set. He gave her a look like, *'calm down'* and tucked his hair be-hind his left ear revealing a small silver hoop earing that I hadn't noticed before.

"Aurelious, we aren't forcing you to stay here at all. We're just offering you a place to sleep and something to eat while you figure everything out." Brekwyn was looking at me with that smile again, he looked peaceful and I felt peaceful so I looked away.

I stayed silent. Anira went off and a second later was back with a pillow and a blanket. She looked like she was both disap-pointed and worried but I couldn't see any more than that be-cause I didn't want to stare at her.

"Thank you," I said softly, looking at the couch rather than her.

"Well I'll be off to get some sleep as well," Brekwyn said with a wave of his hand, catching me completely off guard.

"You're not staying here?" I asked against my better judgment and squeezed my arms even harder across my chest. This was a strange move for a serial killer.

"No," he smiled and sort of half laughed, "but I'm not far. If you or Anira need me I can be here in less than a minute."

"So it's just me and her sleeping here?"

"*Her?*" Anira's sweet voice suddenly had an edge. I looked over at her. She had one eyebrow raised like she was completely of-fended with her hands perched on her hips. I may have sound-ed a little more offensive than I needed to. "*She* has a name and it's *her* home. You can sleep outside if you're uncomfortable sleeping under the same roof as '*her*', " she continued, clearly insulted.

"Okay, Anira, that's quite enough," Brekwyn said, his smile unwavering. He definitely thought she was funny. I didn't actu-ally mind it either. I was used to people being mean to me but that's not what this was, she was reacting to me being rude. She was more fiery than mean. The color of her eyes and that streak in her hair seemed to match her personality. It was fascinating.

"I wasn't trying to be offensive I was just trying to understand the situation here," I offered. What the hell was the situation here? She was around my age, how does she have her own house? I was starting to create a mental list of questions but I was really tired now, so this line of questioning would have to wait until morning if I stayed through the night.

"It's okay." She took a deep breath and shrugged off any distaste she had for me, "I'm tired and going to bed. If you need me I'm right through that door." She turned and headed in the direction of her room, which was only about eight feet from where I was standing by my get- away position. But before she closed her bedroom door behind her and before Brekwyn closed the house door behind him, she turned and asked, "Will you be here in the morning Aurelious?"

I looked at both of them with my arms still crossed protectively over my chest, longing for my laptop to shield me. I took a deep breath and said, "I don't know."

Neither of them said anything to that, instead they closed their respective doors and left me alone. They left me alone to leave or to stay. They weren't kidnapping me or holding me there against my will. They didn't seem like serial killers anymore because that was definitely not serial killer behavior. Actually, they never really seemed like serial killers or kidnappers. They were just always nice. I'm not sure how I felt about "nice" but I guess I'd figure that out, if I stayed.

Chapter Five

My body betrayed me.

I swear I tried as hard as I possibly could to stay awake in order to decide if I should leave, but I failed. The strength of my resolve was no match for the exhaustion brought on from the raucous physical and emotional experiences of the day. And I didn't just fall asleep; I fell asleep hard, I didn't even dream.

One minute I was fighting to stay awake and the next minute the sun was coming through the windows, casting tiny rainbows around the room as it refracted through little teardrop shaped crystals dangling off the bottom of the lampshade on the table next to the couch. I blinked the sleep out of my eyes, trying to get my bearings, the memory of the day before suddenly flooding through every fiber of my well-rested consciousness. Oh, what did I do? I rubbed my eyes, took a deep breath and looked to my left.

Anira sat in the chair next to the couch, silent, smiling, and staring at me. What the...?

I threw the blanket off and jolted into a sitting position.

She started laughing, "Why do I always seem to startle you?"

I caught my breath and forced my heartbeat to slow down, "Probably because you always sneak up on me."

I tried to seem like I was offended by her presence, freakily stalking me in my sleep, but I really wasn't, not entirely. It surprised the crap out of me but didn't bother me as much as I pretended it did.

"I didn't mean to sneak up on you." She was still smiling. Then she giggled at my perplexed expression. Damn it she was adorable. Look away look away, don't fall for it.

"Well I was asleep so, I think it would be pretty obvious that that's exactly what you were doing."

"Do you always wake up in a bad mood?"

"Pretty much."

"Well, that's good to know. Would you like some breakfast?"

Luring me in with comfortable couches, food, and breathtakingly beautiful girls? I think not, "No thanks," I grumbled and stood to fold the multicolored patchwork blanket that looked like it was made by someone's grandmother.

"Oh come on you have to eat." She was clearly being hospitable again.

"I fell asleep here on accident which probably won't happen again so let's not pretend that since I was here for one night that you know me well enough to know what I need." I tossed the blanket back on the couch and banged my shin on the coffee table as I went to walk away which only forced me to sit back down. She was not impressed by my attitude.

"Well I'm pretty sure you don't need to be such a jerk." She had that eyebrow raised again. She stood up, so I did too, "And I'm not trying to say that I know you so well, clearly I don't know you at all, but food is something everyone needs so I figured it was a pretty good generalization." We stood facing each other, trying to determine who was going to win this confrontation. I had my arms folded across my chest out of habit and security. She had her hands on her hips out of annoyance. Being annoyed made her cheeks pink. I wanted to touch them.

"Maybe I'll eat something if you are." What? Did I just say that? What was wrong with me, why was I giving in so easily? I couldn't let myself get comfortable here. This was just a temporary arrangement until I figured out where I was going to go.

"Good," she said as she stomped off the three feet between the room I was sleeping in and the kitchen.

She banged around some pots and pans probably a little more aggressively then she needed to, I got the point and it was awkward. In my sullen silence, I looked around at the curved walls and tiny metal windows decorated with red and white checked curtains. I looked at the stacks of books on the end tables and the vase of wildflowers on the coffee table, knocked slightly off center when I banged into it. I looked for a television and didn't find one, which was interesting since I thought every house had a t.v. but I wasn't disappointed since I rarely watched it.

The banging lessened as the minutes passed and the awkwardness in the room dissipated as the tantalizing scent of whatever she was cooking filled the air. The refrigerator in the kitchen was half the size of the ones in any of the houses I'd lived in and I suspected it probably contained less mold and bacteria. There was a table big enough for only two people and looked to be carved out of heavy wood before it was painted bright red. The white counter tops flecked with grey specs were clean and uncluttered as was the rest of the house.

If ten people were in here it would have been really crowded and hard to move around comfortably. It was, by far, the smallest house I'd ever been in, but somehow it was the least threatening and the most inviting.

I always liked my silence, I was comfortable in it, I was used to it. I generally preferred not to talk to people but this one made me want to talk. She made me want to ask questions, to pry, maybe even to push beyond the limits of polite conversation into intrusiveness. I wanted to know things that I couldn't find out just by watching her because if I just watched her then I would be far too easily distracted by my growing physical attraction to her. But it was more than just her that I wanted to know about. I wanted to know about Brekwyn and this tiny house and what life was like here and why the hell I didn't feel like the outcast that I'd been my whole life.

"You can sit there if you want," she said breaking the silence and gesturing toward the kitchen table.

I shrugged, absently looked at something else for a few seconds to make the point that I would sit down when I wanted to sit down, and then I sat down like she suggested. But lets be clear, I was going to sit down anyway. She placed a bowl of fruit on the table, plucked a grape and tossed it in her mouth. Then she winked at me to indicate that I should help myself before turning her attention back to the stove. She was pretty nurturing, which could have very easily been irritating since I wasn't accustomed to being nurtured, especially by someone my own age, but it wasn't and that wink made something feel strange in my stomach. Strange but not in a bad way.

"Do you live here alone?" I asked so that we didn't dip into a silence that I would be unable to get out of again.

"My dad lives here too but he's away on business," she said as she stirred eggs around in a frying pan.

"What about your mom?"

"She died when I was seven."

"I'm sorry about that." We had something in common after all, "both of my parents died."

"Do you miss them?" she asked as she sprinkled some green herbs over the eggs then transferred them from the pan to a dish and put the dish on the table.

"No." I really didn't want to talk about me, I wanted to talk about her but when she looked surprised by my response I felt the need to clarify, "I was eight weeks old when they died in a car crash so I don't have any memory of them. I know I'm supposed to miss them because they're my parents but how do I miss something I can't even remember?"

She sat down across from me with two plates, two forks, and a plate of toasted bread, "I understand that, it makes sense."

"Do you miss your mother?" This was not a question on my list but then again, when I mentally formulated the list I hadn't known about her parents.

"Yeah, everyday," she sighed and looked away. I thought I saw a tear coming to the surface of her eye. For the smallest second I thought I felt painfully sad but then it was gone before it could really register, did I feel sad for her? "Sometimes I miss her so much that it's hard to breathe. I let myself feel sad for a few minutes but then I try to focus on other things. I can't allow myself to get really sad, it wouldn't be good for anyone." She looked at me like she was self-conscious awaiting my response while pulling at one of her curls.

"Yeah." What an idiot. I probably should've said something comforting but I didn't have the words. Kids where I came from didn't talk so openly, at least not when I was watching them, so I was out of my element.

I shifted my weight in the chair and took an aggressive spoonful of eggs, burning my mouth in the process. I coughed, my eyes watered, she giggled and poured juice from a pitcher into my cup.

"Thanks," I choked out. "So where do you go to high school?" I changed the subject to get back to my mental list.

"I don't go to high school actually." Now it was her turn to shove a piece of toast into her mouth to clearly avoid elaborating on that.

But I wasn't falling for it, I could wait until her mouth was empty, "Did you graduate?"

Chew, chew, chew, swallow.

"No, I'm sort of home schooled." Forkful of eggs in the mouth.

I looked at her, she wasn't looking at me, which meant she was hiding some kind of information, "Sort of home schooled or actually home schooled? And who home schools you when your dad is away on business? Do you have a teacher come to your house?"

She put her fork down and took a deep breath, "Aurelious, there's something that I should tell you about me, about us and how we live."

I knew it. I knew there was something that wasn't normal here. I put my fork down too, wiped my mouth on my sleeve and readied myself for her revelation.

Chapter Six

Anira was literally one breath away from saying something important when she was stopped by a quick knock at the door followed straightaway by Brekwyn coming in without waiting to be invited. His smile immediately annoyed me, was he always happy? I mean even his knock was cheerful.

"Good afternoon you two, I wasn't sure you were ever going to wake up." It's possible that I may have been snarling because he clearly just interrupted something important and, from the way Anira instantly clammed up, it was obvious that whatever she was about to tell me just got put back on the shelf. He laughed at my expression and rumpled my hair, a gesture that I quickly shrugged off, swatting his hand away. He didn't seem to notice my reaction or if he did it didn't appear to dampen his stupid, jovial mood.

"What do you mean by *afternoon*?" I spat out while attempting to smooth out the fresh knots in my hair.

"I mean it's the afternoon," he said with his absurdly perfect, white-toothed, smiley mouth, "as in it's no longer morning."

That seemed impossible, I hadn't slept past six in the morning in years and now all of a sudden on my first day here I sleep until the afternoon. I was doing a really crappy job of protecting myself from these quacks.

"You were tired, it's good that you got the sleep you needed," Anira said but was quick to add, "not that I know what you need." Smirk.

I looked around. This whole place was strange and everything that was going on here was just a little off and now, it appeared, so was I. This realization frustrated me, which didn't help my attitude.

"Are you seriously always this happy?" I asked Brekwyn, he seemed as good a target for my spite as anyone.

He thought about what he was going to say, "No, certainly not when bad things happen. But I do what I can to avoid bad things and you make me happy today, Aurelious. I'm happy that you're here and you're safe." Weirdo.

"I was safe where I was," I grumbled. Psh, who was I kidding.

"Really?" He smirked with his head cocked to the side.

I didn't respond, obviously, I wasn't.

"So, how about some time outside, maybe explore the area a little bit, see how you like it here," he said changing the subject.

A light bulb went on in my head, "That sounds like a good idea, Anira why don't you come with me and show me around?" I stood up right away and headed toward the door before either of them could object. If I could get Anira away from Brekwyn then maybe she would finish what she was going to say before.

"Okay," she said pensively from behind me but I was already out the door and headed down the steps. I turned to see if she was coming alone. That's when I noticed her house. It wasn't a house. It was actually a trailer, a shiny metal trailer. I looked around me. This was not the only trailer, there had to have been thirty of them and surrounding all of them for as far as I could see, was nothing but trees.

No wonder she was home schooled. There's no school here. No wonder they wouldn't tell me the name of the town they lived in. They didn't live in a town. They lived in a freaking forest. And as of last night, so did I.

"Umm," I said out loud, with a *what the hell is this place* expression on my face.

"Mother Nature has blessed us with perfect weather for your

first day here," Brekwyn said taking a deep breath with his head back, soaking in the sun, totally disregarding my obvious puzzlement. Wait, did he just say *Mother Nature*?

"What?" That question was literally about everything, not just the *Mother Nature* comment. Oh, crap, were these people crazy environmentalists living in the woods? I thought someone established that the environment was just fine and that Global Warming was a hoax. Guess nobody clued these hippies in, maybe if they had a t.v. then they would've gotten the update.

Brekwyn flinched so slightly that it was almost imperceptible. If I didn't spend my life watching people I would have missed it, just like I would have missed the definite worry that revealed itself in a miniscule line in his forehead. Was this a moment when Brekwyn wasn't happy and, if so, what changed his mood? But in a flash whatever that was disappeared.

"Beauties," he said looking past me, the smile returning. Another interruption.

I turned around to see what he was talking about. Two children, a boy and a girl, were walking towards us. Great, Hansel and Gretel just strolled out of the woods to make this place even weirder.

They looked like twins and must have been around nine or ten years old. Their skin was tanned, their eyes were brown, and their hair was wavy and dark. There was a similar look to all four of the people around me right now. Even the style of their clothes was the same, loose and colorful like it could've been homemade.

At some point they came to a stop and just stood there as I examined them from head to toe. At the same time that I realized they were just staring at me with expressions of awe on their angelic little dirt smudged faces, I realized that I was just staring at them too, taking in every detail of their physical appearance. I'm not sure what happened to me or how long we were standing there like that and I'm not entirely sure that I would've stopped staring at them if it didn't suddenly and quite unnaturally, completely out of nowhere, get perilously cold.

I could've tried to disregard the cold as something that I felt inside my body, like a reaction to the Children of the Corn who were now smiling and nudging at each other with their dirty little fingers. But I knew it wasn't inside me when I saw the vapor of my breath as I exhaled. I turned toward Anira and saw her breath too, her arms had goose bumps, her lips started to quiver. This made no sense, it was a sunny afternoon in the end of June, it was supposed to be hot and two seconds ago it was hot. But now my fingers and toes were going numb and my ears started to hurt.

"What's up with the weather here?" I asked to anyone as I huddled in on myself to try to get warmer.

Brekwyn, who's breath I mysteriously couldn't see, was walking over to the children when he said, "Sometimes we do have sharp drops or spikes in temperature and occasionally some other weather phenomena here in these woods." He stood behind them and rested a hand on each one's shoulder, "But it doesn't usually last long." And as soon as he said that, as quickly as the coldness came, it was gone.

"What are we in a valley or something?" I asked straightening up taller than I was before because I didn't want to seem like such a delicate flower, I mean these two little kids looked completely unaffected and totally unconcerned. I had to be more macho than nine-year-olds right?

"Actually this piece of land is situated in a valley," Brekwyn responded, also standing straighter but he looked like he was proud of my clever geographical knowledge. Interesting, it was really just a guess on my part but I pretended that I knew what I was talking about with a know-it-all kind of nod.

"So this is Tanent," Brekwyn said gesturing toward the boy, "and this is Seylane," the girl. "They're going berry picking and thought you might like to join them."

Berry picking? Was that a joke, did people actually do that? So no private chat with Anira then? I looked at her, she smiled and shrugged, "I have to get food ready for the festival tonight anyway so it's better that you go with them. We'll talk when you get back," she added quickly and then ran back up the steps into her house, I mean trailer.

"Alright, I'll go with you I guess," I said to the children, after all, in terms of getting information, who better to ask then kids. They usually knew a lot but were too naïve to keep it to themselves.

"Great," Brekwyn said, walking past me and then said to the children "be back in time for the festival."

"Wait, what festival?" I asked.

"Tanent and Seylane can explain that," he said without turning back around.

So, Brekwyn was gone and Anira was gone, it's just me and Tweedle Dee and Tweedle Dumb. Now what?

"Um, I'm Aurelious. Aurelious Forty," I said shoving my hands in my pockets.

"We know who you are Aurelious," these were the first words spoken by Seylane.

"Let's go!" and these were from Tanent who took off toward the woods. So I did what any overly curious teenager would do, I followed the shirtless, shoeless boy with twigs and pine needles in his hair. Totally normal. Totally normal.

Chapter Seven

"Did you pick berries where you're from?" Seylane asked, grabbing my hand. Her hand was colder than it should be.

"No." The question was almost laughable considering where I was from, but I didn't laugh and I resisted the urge to yank my hand away. The urge was strong but she was so little and I wasn't a total dick.

"Do you know your last name's a number?" Tanent yelled from twenty yards ahead. He impatiently paced back and forth waiting for us to catch up.

"Yeah, but to me it's just a last name. What's your last name?"

"Ha! We don't have them!" Tanent literally laughed at the absurdity of my question until Seylane shot him a look to shut him up.

"We don't have last names because no one has the same first name," Seylane explained calmly, sounding far older than her twin brother and older than her nine years. Yeah they told me.

"But how does everyone know who you're related to?"

She shrugged, "Everyone just knows."

I couldn't go further with this particular line of questioning because the handholding was getting distracting and I had no idea how to get out of it.

"Uh, so Brekwyn, what can you tell me about him?" I muttered.

"He's the leader," Tanent said picking up a pinecone from the ground and throwing it at a tree.

"The leader of what?"

"Everyone in the village," he said as if it should be obvious.

"Not the leader really," Seylane chimed in, "but he's in charge and he helps everyone and makes us feel better and fixes things."

"Like what things?"

They thought about it, "Anything, Brekwyn can do everything!" Tanent said.

"Huh," that was thought provoking. "And where's the village?"

"Well it's where we came from," Seylane said. Tanent ran ahead again and was quickly out of sight.

The path we were walking on was clearly well traveled and defined; any leaves had been flattened or otherwise pushed aside. It was mainly dirt with the occasional rock or tree root. It would be easy to find my way back if I needed to, if these two turned out to be really creepy. The canopy of trees overhead kept the hot summer sun from beating down on us but reminded us that it was there in occasional bright white patches on the uneven ground. We came to a fork in the path and Seylane guided me toward the right.

"What happens if we go that way?" I pointed to the other direction.

"There's three trailers at the end of that path, that's where we have our lessons when the weather says we shouldn't have them outside," she said absently, paying more attention to where we were going. I was straining to see if I could catch a glimpse of the trailers. I couldn't.

The trees started to thin out, exposing us to more and more of the sun. I should've been getting warmer but instead I started getting colder. And colder. And colder. I heard a shriek from up ahead, it was Tanent. Instinct kicked in and I ran toward his direction, remembering to break free of Seylane's grasp so I wouldn't pull her along.

"Aurelious what's wrong?" Seylane called from behind me, running as fast as she could to keep up.

I didn't answer, I just ran. My breath came out in puffs of smoke faster and faster as I ran toward the sound of Tanent shrieking again. I could feel sweat forming on my head but it wasn't from the heat since I was freezing, it was from fear, I was concerned, I was worried about Tanent. I was worried about someone other than myself.

"Tanent!" I yelled when I emerged from the forest into a small open field. The sun was so bright without the protection of the trees that I stumbled at first and had to shield my eyes. I scanned the field, it was all high grass, I couldn't see him. Seylane caught up to me and tried to grab my hand again but I pulled it away, cupped both hands around my mouth and called out again louder, "Tanent!"

Another shriek came from the far edge of the field, the tall grass moved aggressively in one spot. I ran toward the movement, small dead braches with thorns tore at my legs, but I didn't stop. I saw something, something black, black fur, an animal. Oh God, is that a bear? I had no plan; I just kept running, pounding through the brush. The animal must have heard me because it stopped, I could only see part of it's back standing completely still before it turned and ran toward me. And then, out of nowhere, it was blazingly hot again and before I could register anything the animal jumped at me, slamming me down onto my back.

I put my hands up to protect myself from what would likely be a brutal attack. I felt its mouth, its wet salivating mouth. But I didn't feel its teeth. What the hell? I opened my eyes just in time to see the black dog standing on my chest swipe its big, sloppy, pink tongue all over my face. You have got to be kidding me. And as if it heard someone call its name, its ears perked up and it ran away. What. The. Hell.

"Ha!" Tanent laughed as he came to a skid beside me kicking up dirt onto my saliva-filled face.

"Are you okay?" Seylane asked standing over me.

"Yes," I grumbled as I sat up, unsuccessfully brushing the dog prints off my shirt. I looked around; the dog was nowhere to be seen. "Are you okay?" I asked Tanent, annoyed at myself for panicking about this kid.

"Oh yeah, we were just playing," he said and offered a hand to help me up which I did not take, enough of this hand holding crap. He didn't seem to notice.

"I thought you were getting attacked," I said to him, my annoyance on full display.

"By an animal? Ha!" Again with the laugh, did this kid laugh at everything? "That would never happen."

"It could happen," I was trying to damper his good mood which was a total dick move on my part but really why was everyone here so freakin' happy? And, by the way, before you go getting mad at me for not being nice to this kid, he didn't even notice that I was being obnoxious.

"No, it couldn't," he said confidently.

You would think living in the woods would've made this kid more knowledgeable about wild animals. Maybe his parents were doing a bad job of raising him.

"Whatever," I said and we all started walking again, "you guys were gonna tell me about a festival or something?"

"Oh, we love festivals!" Seylane said brightly, plucking a lone purple flower from the high grass and tucking it behind her ear.

"Why do you have them?" I looked around to find that path we were on before, it was somewhere behind us.

"To celebrate things," Tanent said. He pointed to the edge of the field, the spots of red on the bushes suggested we found the berries.

"What are you celebrating tonight?" I wiped the sweat from my forehead and plucked a thorn from the sleeve of my filthy t-shirt.

"You, of course!" Seylane said and put her arm around my

waist for a hug. Ugh.

"Why me?" I asked and stooped to tie my shoe, aka unlatch this child from my body.

"Because we've been waiting for you and everyone is so glad you're here!" She smiled, plucked a red raspberry from the bush in front of us and popped it in her mouth. The red smears around Tanent's lips already suggested he went for the handful rather than the single pluck.

I looked up from my crouched position on the ground, this was weird, "Who's everyone and why have you all been waiting for me?" I stood up slowly, really looking around at where I was, a small field in the middle of the woods, miles from anywhere. Uh oh.

"The whole tribe," Tanent said with his mouth full, "we've been waiting cause we knew you'd come."

"Tribe? What? Why did you know that I'd come?" So this was an elaborate plan of Brekwyn's then? Maybe he was a serial killer after all, maybe this festival was where they were going to sacrifice me to their weirdo, trailer living, no t.v. watching, no shoe wearing, kids running around in the woods, stupid happy, way too touchy god.

Tanent looked at me seriously for a second, literally one second, shrugged and picked some more berries, "That's just what we know."

So that's the end of that conversation I guess. Okay, let me assess what I now know. They have no last names, their *'tribe's'* village is really just a bunch of trailers in the woods, Brekwyn's their leader-ish, and they're home schooled, and have a weird fondness for Mother Nature. Oh crap, it's a cult. I went from a life of abusers, neglectors, just general assholes who I cared nothing about to a cult? I mean, which one was worse? Really which one?

Was this what Anira was going to tell me? I thought back to our breakfast. She was reluctant to say anything but she was about to when Brekwyn interrupted us and then she stopped.

Was she also drawn in by him? Was she here against her will? Did she need me to save her?

"You know what, we should probably start to head back." The sun was starting to get lower in the sky, the heat subsiding just a little bit.

Seylane pulled up the bottom of her shirt to make a pouch that was now filled with raspberries and blueberries. Tanent, in my absent-minded theorizing, had filled a small bucket.

"Where'd you get the bucket?" I asked him as we all turned to walk back across the field.

"The growers leave it here for us," he said.

"Farmers?" I sort of corrected.

"Nope, growers," he actually corrected.

"Whatever."

Anira's trailer was at the entrance to the path when we emerged from the woods. I looked at the two kids for some sign that I should make a run for it, but they were just happy and normal, and oblivious, completely carefree. So I shrugged and headed toward her steps silently praying that she was alone so I could find out what she was going to tell me. She opened the door just as I was about to knock.

Anira stood there, dressed in her outfit for the festival looking like no person I had ever seen before. Her hair was wavy and loose and she had a scarf around her forehead that had little gold coins on it. In her ears she wore large gold hoops. Her shirt was red with purple stitching around the neck, which was rounded but wide so one shoulder was exposed. One smooth, bare, perfect shoulder. The bottom of the shirt was pulled in around her ribs and tied there with a purple ribbon. She had a chain around her stomach that was made of twisted silver and gold. Her thin, wispy skirt hung low on her hips and was made of different patches of color. She had anklets made of coins and bells on both of her ankles and her feet were bare.

My mouth went dry at the sight of her. If I died in that moment

I wouldn't have even noticed because I was so consumed with looking at her. I wanted to touch her. Her naked stomach was beckoning me to put my hands on it, to feel its warmth, its softness.

The edges of my field of vision started to blur, all I could do was picture touching her. I could almost feel what it would feel like. I could see my hands on her hips, my lips grazing her soft skin. I could feel her hands in my hair. She wanted me to touch her. It felt so real. My heart was pounding. I started to reach out.

"Aurelious." Brekwyn's voice brought me back to reality. Suddenly reality felt very harsh. I looked at him and for the first time he wasn't smiling. He wasn't frowning or angry, he just looked serious and focused as he came toward me from around the front of the trailer.

When he had my attention his smile returned, but if I looked really closely, I could see something else in his eyes. Concern maybe?

"Why don't you head inside and get cleaned up for the festival, our friends and family are anxious to meet you."

"Yeah, okay." I felt like I was coming out of a fog and was too confused to even consider my sacrifice, cult theory. I walked up the steps and past Anira, completely avoiding looking at any part of her.

"There's a towel in the bathroom for you if you'd like to shower Aurelious," she said, but her voice was pensive. Did she know what just went through my mind? Had it gone through hers too?

I heard Brekwyn say one thing before I closed the bathroom door behind me, "Maintain your self control Anira, always be aware of what you can do."

Chapter Eight

"I put an outfit for you on the bed in that room." Anira pointed to the room I was supposed to sleep in the night before. She turned away from me standing there with a towel wrapped around my waist, trying not to look. She was awkward and maybe a little uncomfortable, as if the sight of my body made her feel the same way that her body made me feel. I liked this, whatever this was, it was new and exhilarating.

I closed the door behind me and looked around the room. It was tiny, just enough space for one single bed with a small table and lamp next to it. The bed looked like it was carved directly from a tree. The quilt that I used the night before was carefully folded at the foot of the thick mattress. I wondered if she thought I was planning to sleep there tonight. I wondered the same thing myself. Three tambourines hung on the wall. I would have thought they were just a clever decoration but upon closer inspection they looked well used. Who played the tambourine anymore?

The room was actually really warm and inviting, the outfit she laid out, on the other hand, was absurd. Purple pants and a billowy light blue shirt, you have got to be kidding me. Well I don't know if billowy was the right word, but the sleeves were long and a little bigger at the wrist than the rest of the arm, the body was sort of straight, there was no collar but a v-neck and around the neck was three rows of stitching in red, orange and yellow.

I held the purple pants with the drawstring waist up to me and saw that they only came to the middle of my shins like Tanent's did. They looked fine on Tanent because he was a little barefooted boy with twigs stuck in his hair. Maybe they were for someone that was six inches shorter than I was. I looked over my shoulder to see if anyone was standing behind me silently laughing and getting ready to tell me they were just kidding. No one was there. I could choose to put my regular clothes back on but they were dirtier than usual thanks to the dog incident. Crap. I'm going to look like such an idiot.

"Perfect," Anira said, as I appeared in my new outfit, and she laughed at my '*are you kidding me*' face.

"I'm looking at us both right now Anira, is this a costume party?"

"No, just a regular festival." She was still smiling although the smile was starting to waiver.

"So what's with the costumes?"

"Aurelious," she said, suddenly serious, "there was something that I wanted to talk to you about."

Here it is. This was what she was going to say earlier. I straightened up and crossed my arms over my chest to prepare. Would she ask me to help her escape from this cult of oddly dressed extremists? Would she warn me that if I stayed I would be sacrificed to their alien god of ludicrous fashion?

"These clothes," she started to say as she tugged on one of her curls, which I now realized was what happened when she felt insecure, "they aren't a costume actually. We don't wear them every day, well some of the older people do but most of us don't. Mainly we wear them now for festivals or special occasions. They represent part of our tradition."

"What tradition has people dressing up like gypsies?"

She must have looked at me for a full minute before she said, "Our tradition Aurelious, we are Gypsies."

Oh shit.

I went from one world of crazy people to another world of crazy people. Is this really my fate, that I should be surrounded by lunatics my whole life? I mean I'm not crazy am I? If you were me you would think this was a little odd wouldn't you?

"Aurelious please say something." She was tugging her curl and pleading with her eyes, presumably in response to my mouth hanging open but emitting no words.

"Anira, I am going to ask you this once," I took a deep breath, tucked my hands even further under my arms and tried to stay rational, "are you in danger? Are you being held here against your will? Do you need me to help you escape?"

It was all she could do to hold in her laughter, "No!" Then she looked like she was offended, "Why would you think that?"

"Because you're wearing a ridiculous costume," that she happened to look amazing in and made me feel weird in all kinds of places, "and I am wearing a ridiculous costume and you just told me that you're a Gypsy."

"I believe I said 'we' are Gypsies and these clothes are not ridiculous costumes, they're traditional Gypsy clothes." No longer tugging at her hair, her hands went to her hips, yup I was offending her.

"Except that you do realize that Gypsies aren't real right? You do realize that they're fictional characters made up for books and movies right?"

"Actually we're quite real, thank you very much. You just don't know about us because you've been living with Gadje your whole life."

"What the hell is Gadje?" I asked, my voice slightly higher and louder than usual.

"The people you've been living with, it's everyone that isn't a Gypsy." She was starting to raise her voice too.

I put my hands on my head, took a few deep-cleansing breaths, and walked around in a circle. She couldn't be serious, could she?

"What exactly do you mean when you say 'Gypsy', like what makes you a Gypsy?" I attempted to calm down, and search for some clarification.

"Well, we live together in this community but our community is the people in it not the place that the people are in because we move from one place to another. We're pretty sustainable so we don't have a lot of interaction with the outside world, the world you came from," she followed my lead and spoke more softly. "I don't mean to make it sound like we're from another planet, because we're definitely not, but we're different from the Gadje. Just like you knew you were different from them, we know that too. And we may have a different opinion about this planet. For example, we're very fond of her so we try not to cause too much damage and we offer our thanksgiving for her at all of our festivals."

"Who's her?" Who's her, did I miss something.

"The Earth." Okay now she just might have taken it to a different level. I rolled my eyes aggressively. "It's not freaky," she said when I cocked my head to the side and looked at her like she was a wacko, "we don't sacrifice a goat or anything like that. We just appreciate what the Earth has given us and we're a little more in tuned to the Earth then Gadje are."

Okay, so no sacrifices, that's a good sign. I guess I can cross that one off my list entitled '*What is wrong with this place*'. Actually I guess I can mentally cross everything off and just write the word *Gypsy*. I have to tell you, this was not at all where I thought this conversation was going to go. This didn't sound scary or threatening though, it just kind of sounded like they were Earth loving hippies. As far as I've ever heard, hippies were peaceful people, which explains the whole 'nice' thing, so maybe Gypsies were the same.

The thing that was throwing me off the most wasn't the revelation or the bizarre outfits. It was that she was so sincere. She really believed all of this. She was proud to be a Gypsy, her pride revealed by her annoyance to my exasperation and slight ridicule. I knew how it felt to be ridiculed and I didn't actually want her to feel that way and that was throwing me off too. She was just standing there, vulnerable, waiting for me to respond.

"So you want to stay here, you're a Gypsy and you want to stay with these Gypsies?"

"Yes of course."

"And you think I should stay with you too."

"I would like that very much."

"I'm not making any promises," I folded my arms across my chest again wishing for my laptop now more than ever, my head was ready to explode with all of this new information and no outlet for it, "but I'll go with you to the festival."

She smiled and her whole beautiful face lit up, "You won't regret it, it'll be fun. When was the last time you had fun?"

I'm not sure if I'd ever actually had fun, "Anira, I'll go to the festival but that doesn't mean I'm gonna stay here."

"You're free to leave whenever you want." Clever girl. "But we should get going. The festival must be in full swing by now. I'll get this pot of food," she grabbed a yellow ceramic pot off the stove, "could you just grab the tambourines off the wall in your room?"

"Tambourines? Anira, that's a little cliché isn't it?"

"Where do you think they got the ideas for the movies from?" I think she was trying to be funny. "And you have to take off your sneakers. They look ridiculous with that outfit."

"I don't think this outfit needed any help from the sneakers to look ridiculous."

Oh, Aurelious, what are you doing?

Chapter Nine

With tambourines jingling in my hands we left our shiny little sanctuary and headed off to the woodland Gypsy festival. Yeah, you read that right. But I had no idea what that meant. I could hear music playing and with each step we took closer to our destination, the music got louder and I could hear people talking and laughing.

"When we get to the festival, Brekwyn will introduce you to everyone," she explained as we walked through the maze of trailers. I noticed they were set up in rows so there was some order to how they were placed. "You might feel a little over-whelmed because the whole tribe will be there."

Tribe again? Oh right, cause that's what you call a freaking set-tlement of Gypsies.

"I know when you met Tanent and Seylane and even when you met Brekwyn and I that you felt a little consumed by looking at us right?"

"I'll be fine." I wasn't about to reveal anything that could be seen as a weakness even though she was totally accurate.

"Yes, you will be but if you felt like that before you might feel like it again only because there are so many of us and we're all new to you." She looked at me, waiting for me to acknowledge that strange feeling that I had when I saw them, I didn't give in, I just continued to look straight ahead. I know that I zoned out before and in having that knowledge now, I was sure I wouldn't do it again. But I shouldn't have been so confident because a minute later we were at the festival and with all of its dancing, laughter, music, colorful clothes, and glowing firelight,

I was completely lost.

The next thing I knew, Brekwyn was in my head pulling me back from wherever my mind was going. I could see his face with a look of peace, smiling at me but not with a big, toothy smile, just a gentle one that made me want to follow him out of where I was. "Welcome, Aurelious," he was saying and now I realized that he was just there standing in front of me, "your family is waiting to meet you."

My family? Is that what he said? I focused on Brekwyn to bring myself back to reality but I was still dazed like I was when I saw Anira dressed in her Gypsy outfit earlier. My head felt so strange. If I didn't know better I would think I was drugged but since I didn't eat or drink anything that someone else didn't eat or drink before me, I knew that wasn't it. This was just something that was happening inside my head and they all seemed to be prepared for it.

I looked at Anira. She smiled and grabbed my hand quickly but I immediately pulled it away when I felt that familiar tingle again. What was that?

"Aurelious, are you well?" Brekwyn asked softly so those new people around us couldn't hear.

"Yeah, I'm fine," I lied, but I was not about to admit my vulnerability. Being vulnerable was the kiss of death where I came from.

"I'm going to introduce you to the members of our family, if you get overwhelmed we can stop."

"Don't worry about it." Real tough Aurelious, real tough.

I was introduced to so many people and I forgot most of their names shortly after the introduction. As much as I wanted to, I couldn't concentrate on everyone individually, there was just too many of them. And they all wanted to touch me in some way. Not in a creepy sexual way but in an affectionate and friendly way. They patted me on the back or gave me a hug or shook my hand.

I didn't like it, all this touching made me uncomfortable, I wasn't used to it. The only touching I remember was the kind that stung or ached or made my mouth or nose bleed. I didn't understand this display and what was worse was that each person that touched me didn't make me feel bad. I know that sounds weird but I understood how to feel bad, I didn't understand how to feel, what was this? Welcomed? Why were they so happy to see me?

We made our way through the crowd and I was able to stay present, sort of, but when Brekwyn said, "Aurelious, this is Megana and this is Telera," I was lost once again.

The edges of my vision blurred, everything seemed to slow down around me. The air felt thicker, it took more of an effort to breathe. Megana was older than Telera. Her hair was so white that it was almost glaring in the light of the fire or maybe it was a reflection of the moon. Her skin was dark and full of deep lines. She had three large gold hoops in each ear. She was sitting, so her brightly colored dress was pooled around her feet, I couldn't tell how tall she was but she seemed very frail.

I looked over to Telera, her hair was mostly white to frame her face but it gradually got darker toward the back. Her skin was lighter than Megana's but still very tanned and she was showing the signs of age, or deep thought, in more superficial lines. She had one gold hoop earring in each ear. Her shirt was green with red trim and her long, flowing skirt was striped in red, orange, and green. Both of the women had several charm bracelets on each wrist.

I felt like I wasn't at the festival anymore, everything around us seemed to fade away or was blurry in the background. The sounds around me became muffled but as they started to speak to each other I could understand every word.

"You found him Brekwyn," said Telera, "your mother would be so proud of you, as we all are."

"Thank you, Telera," Brekwyn replied, I felt like I was moving in slow motion as I looked from one to the other when they were speaking. "He has so many conflicting thoughts and little trust in anyone but he has already started to develop, I know that he will have a great ability."

I wanted to speak, to interrupt them and say that I heard them, I heard them talking about me. But I couldn't, it's like I was just watching this scene play out in front of me and I wasn't really there.

"When will you start your training?" Telera asked. Megana was silent but looking at me.

"I will start tomorrow, first thing," said Brekwyn, "it's developing sooner than I expected, he'll have no choice but to understand what's happening to him. He'll have to learn to trust or we will not succeed."

"Anira will help him understand," Telera added.

"Yes, they are forming a deep connection already just as we suspected they would," Brekwyn said.

Now Megana spoke, "He will have a lesson sooner than you plan, Brekwyn." She was looking away from all of us. "The Inglore sends his messengers tonight."

"Aurelious." Brekwyn's face was all I could see at first, and then my field of vision expanded bringing me back to reality. The sounds and smells of the festival came rushing in so quickly that I almost felt sick. It was like some kind of carnival ride or bad 3-D movie. Suddenly there was no more time for introductions.

Brekwyn took me by the arm and led me off so quickly that we were practically running. This was not the peaceful, calm man that I had only seen up until this point. There was another side of him and although he was certainly not frantic, he was definitely determined. He was looking at Anira as we went toward her and her at him. The cup she was holding dropped to the ground, sending shards of the shattered painted glass and its liquid contents everywhere. She didn't even acknowledge that she dropped it. Instead she stepped right over the mess and ran to us. Something was seriously wrong, that was a look of fear in her eyes.

"Inglore's messengers come tonight, they know he's here, or at the very least they suspect it." She knew what he was talking about. I had no idea. "Get to the digger, go underground. I will come for you tomorrow when all is clear and we will start our training. It cannot start soon enough." He was quiet as he spoke to her his voice was almost imperceptible.

"What should I tell him when he asks?" She was talking about me.

"As much as he can handle, Anira, you are the one who will know how much he can bear." Brekwyn kissed her forehead, Anira took my hand, and we ran.

Chapter Ten

"Anira stop!" I said after we were away from the festival. I pulled my hand from hers, "You don't need to hold my hand." I was agitated enough not knowing what was happening, all of which seemed to be related to clueless little me, but holding her hand was only making the situation with my nerves worse.

She looked at me frenzied and, as if she didn't care what I had to say, she grabbed my hand again and started to move. I yanked my hand away, "I'm not a child! I said you don't need to hold my hand!"

"But I need you to hold my hand Aurelious! I'm not holding your hand because I think you're a child I'm holding your hand because I'm afraid. I need to feel you, to know you're with me." She was gasping for breath and tears started to form in her eyes.

I felt an overwhelming sadness and soon, I felt her fear, "Why are you afraid?"

"Because I promised you would be safe and right now, you aren't. You won't be safe until I get you out of here. Aurelious please, we don't have time for explanations now. I'll explain everything later. We have to go."

I can't say why I believed her. I only know that I felt something. Something ominous in the air started to reek of danger. I had no choice but to follow her and no time to ask more questions. So I reluctantly gave her my hand and again we ran.

We wove our way through the maze of trailers and were in the woods before I knew it. My bare feet stung as they landed on small rocks and pinecones but I kept moving. Sweat began to form on my forehead. I started breathing harder, my heart raced. What the hell was this thing we were running from?

The moon lit our way but it could have been pitch black and it wouldn't have mattered, we were running too quickly for me to notice where I was or where we were going. I was following her. She knew exactly what she was doing. But when we stopped I recognized our destination, three trailers at the end of the path. Anira walked up to the middle one, knocked on the door, and waited. The door opened, slowly at first, and then with more confidence when whoever was inside saw Anira.

"The Inglore sends his messengers tonight," it was all that she said and I guess it needed no more explanation.

"Take the boy in the back," this was a man's voice and as we went into the trailer I was able to see him. He was dirty, that was the first thing I noticed because he was really dirty. Literally brown, dry dirt in his hair, dried dirt in streak marks where it clung to sweat earlier in the day trailing down his face to his neck, under his finger nails and all ground into his clothes, and covering his bare feet. I looked from his feet back up to his face. He smiled and patted me on the shoulder as Anira led me to the back of the trailer.

Once inside the last room, the man closed the door behind us and opened the door to the closet. He bent down and grabbed a rope from the floor. The rope was actually a handle that pulled up the section of the floor itself, clearly a passageway to somewhere else. I looked in and could see a wooden ladder. Quickly, Anira climbed down. I looked at the man and he gestured for me to follow her. We said nothing to each other.

Once I got to the bottom of the ladder, the man closed the floor above us. We were in complete darkness for a mere second before Anira lit a match which then lit a torch. We were in a small space beneath the trailer. I guess this would be our hiding spot, hiding from whatever we were running from. It was really small but it would be fine, it could fit the two of us standing up comfortably and when we needed to sit down we would be able to with our legs bent. And if I wanted to leave all I had to do was climb the ladder.

"Ready?" Anira asked.

"For what?" To have a huge conversation about what the hell was happening, to spend the night in a hole with you? I could probably do that. She just smiled at me, turned and banged on the wall. Jeez. And then the wall opened. Of course it did.

Chapter Eleven

"What the?" I was rendered speechless from what I saw. There was a warm glow of candlelight beckoning for us to move past the woman that opened the door, wall, whatever. She looked similar to the Gypsies at the festival, but her skin was paler, much paler. Her hair and her eyes were brown but her skin was so pale.

Curiosity trumped every other feeling that exploded through my body at this point. I had to see what this was. So after a very brief hesitation but no discussion I followed Anira down a hallway. The walls and floor were dirt, we were under the woods, and I could see what appeared to be tree roots in the ceiling. Our path was lit by Anira's torch and candles placed into small holes carved into the dirt walls.

We walked about thirty feet and then the hallway opened into a great hole in the ground. It had to be fifty yards across, but I'm not great with eyeballing measurements like that. Around the hole was a walkway, like a continuation of this hall that went in a circle around the hole and back here to the entrance again. There was a railing that went along the outside of the walkway so you didn't fall into the hole. This was a good thing because when I looked over the railing, I couldn't see a bottom.

What I could see was a series of railings like this one that suggested there were floors below us. There seemed to be about ten to fifteen floors. Judging from the roots and dirt ceiling above us I'd say we were on the top floor. As I looked around the walkway I could see doors all around, some open, some closed, some with light coming out from them, some dark. There were other hallways leading off the great circle like the one we came in on, maybe the trailer we came through was not the only entrance.

"Anira, what is this?" I whispered as I followed her. It was so quiet that anything above a whisper would have been deafening.

"This is where the Anglasic Gypsies live. They live below the surface of the Earth, essentially living within it. The Angalsic's have chosen to live below the Earth because that is where they feel they have been called. For generations they've been living below you and others without any of you knowing. Almost all of them have never been to the surface, which is why their skin is so pale. They've never seen the sun. They're very happy and at peace underground."

"So there's more than one kind of Gypsy?"

"There are many different tribes of Gypsies that are like us."

"What's the name of your tribe?"

"We're the Baliel Gypsies, one of the surface tribes," she was also whispering as she explained. I couldn't help but look in some of the open doors and what I saw amazed and confused me.

They looked like little apartments. I saw living rooms and small kitchens, chairs and rugs, lit by candlelight or small torches or lanterns. I saw people, Gypsies, pale, pale Gypsies reading and cooking and playing with their children. We passed what appeared to be a common room or a meeting room that was big enough to hold many people and had some large tables and chairs, all of which appeared to be made of carved wood. The floors, walls, and ceilings were all dirt, even in the homes.

We came to a closed door. Anira opened it and walked in.

"This is where we'll stay tonight." She closed the door behind us. "There are several extra rooms down here just in case we need to come down in an emergency."

"What was this emergency?" I asked.

"Our hope is that we prevented one, or many. For now." She

was very serious and deliberate when she spoke as she began lighting the candles and lanterns with her torch.

"But what were we trying to avoid? Obviously it had to do with me and whatever an Inglore's messenger is, so what exactly is going on?"

She took a deep breath and sat down on a couch. She gestured for me to sit next to her, an offer I declined with the brush of a hand. Standing near the door was, as usual, my preference.

"Aurelious, there is something that you need to understand about Gypsies. It was our intention to ease you into all of this because it will seem a bit unbelievable at first, but we don't have the luxury of that kind of time. There are people who call themselves gypsies but live with and among Gadje. You may see them on television or working Gadje jobs, that is not the kind of Gypsies that we are." She looked at me as if to determine how close I was to running out the door, when she saw I wasn't moving, yet, she continued.

"We're the kind of Gypsies that the characters in Gadje stories are modeled after, which was something that our ancestors orchestrated to keep us safe. But it's only our physical appearance and traditions like festivals and music that the stories know. Who we really are and what we really do is known only to us and Gypsies like us. You will not find our Gypsies living among the Gadje but discreetly tucked away, just a figment of someone's imagination."

"Why did your ancestors orchestrate these stories?"

"Mainly to keep our people safe. The simple answer is that if anyone ever saw us, they would assume that we were in costume, not that we were actually Gypsies. It was dangerous to be so different in many parts of the world during the time when they came up with this idea, so it was a precaution."

"How was it done?"

"It was simple. With little more than a tale, a Gypsy planted the seed of the idea of us, revealing only what we would allow them to know and that tale grew and grew into grand fictitious stories," she smirked. "Unfortunately, for them, it's far too easy to influence the Gadje which is part of this whole bigger story."

"Yeah, so let's get back to the bigger story."

"Okay, so I told you before that we are more in tuned to the Earth then Gadje are. There's a reason for that. Gypsies believe that we're here to protect the Earth and her inhabitants to the best of our ability. So basically, we take care of her, and it has always been that way for us. But there are so many more Gadje then there are Gypsies so in order to do what we are charged with doing, we've been given gifts." She fiddled with her skirt as she looked at me again to judge my level of belief. It wasn't that high.

"What kind of gifts?"

"Well, we can kind of do things that Gadje can't do. Each Gypsy has one gift, but there are often more than one with the same gift and gifts can vary in magnitude, so some can be stronger than others."

"Yeah, yeah, what kind of gifts?" I repeated.

She took a deep breath, "Remember when Tanent and Seylane came over to the trailer and it got cold right before you left?" So she did notice that, I responded only by squinting my eyes. "Their gift is that they can conduct the cold."

"Is this a joke?" I folded my arms across my chest.

"No." She pulled at a curl.

"What does that mean that they can conduct the cold?"

"Simply, they can change temperature and make it colder. But they're young and haven't been trained because their gift is just manifesting itself. Usually we get trained around ten years old. So they don't have control over it yet, it's kind of dictated by their emotions right now and it's more intense when they're together."

I can't believe I am going to say this, but it made sense based on what I had experienced with them today. It explained why it got colder when they were excited. But, come on, this is ridiculous right?

"What other gifts are there?" I asked with a highly exaggerated exhale.

"There are those who can conduct heat the same way the twins can conduct cold, others can expedite the growth of organic matter like plants, some can manipulate metals or control other elements of weather, some can communicate with animals, some can move rock others can move dirt. Like this place down here, Donheil, the digger, created the whole structure. He was the man who let us in the trailer."

"One man did all of this?" I looked at her with an expression that exuded disbelief. "One man couldn't do all this in a lifetime."

"But it would only take him a matter of hours," she said softly, her eyes pleading for me to believe her. "His gift is so strong that with his mind he can do anything with or to dirt."

This made no sense. I walked around the room trying to process it. I thought about the hole and the hallway we came through, I thought about the walls and the ceiling. It was such an unbelievable structure that her explanation was the only one that made sense. And there was no logic in that at all.

She must have mistaken my silence for acceptance because she continued on, "Our gifts are mainly based in Nature. We aren't magic, we can't cast spells, we can't do any gift that we don't have not even if we try hard or read a book about it or wish for it. We can do what we, as individuals, were born to do."

Then it dawned on me, I turned quickly to face her, "What's your gift Anira?"

She tugged at a curl again, "I can influence emotion."

"But emotion isn't Nature."

"Actually, it is. It's the most natural part of all human beings. Emotion is affected by all elements of Nature and is Nature at her most intricate. For me, if I am not careful, others can feel my emotions. But I can also feel theirs and if I choose to, I can change them."

I thought about that misplaced feeling of peace that I felt around them, was that her? "Have you changed my emotions?"

"Only to try to help you." She stood up when she saw my face change from disbelief to anger, "But you have to understand that I didn't want you to be sad." She came to me and grabbed the front of my shirt. She had tears in her eyes, "Please don't be so angry."

"How do you know I'm angry?" I pulled away from her. "Is it the expression on my face or are you feeling it?"

She didn't respond, "Anira, how do you know I'm angry?" The volume of my voice rose with each level of panic that I was feeling. How could someone change my emotions, or more importantly how vulnerable was I when someone knew how I was actually feeling, not how I was pretending to feel?

"I can feel it," she knew it wasn't what I wanted to hear because she would have also been able to feel my panic, "but I wouldn't use what I know to hurt you or anyone else. It isn't what we're supposed to do, I only use it to help and that's what I've tried to do. If I didn't have to feel you then I wouldn't, but I can't help it!

"It made me feel like I was dying that night that you came with us. What those terrible Gadje put you through your whole life made you so sad, so broken, and those feelings are inside you and they hurt so bad, I feel that pain and I hate it. I hate them for what they did to you because I can't stand to see you so damaged. It isn't right. It shouldn't have been that way. You shouldn't have been with them for so long." She was crying, tears were streaming down her face and all I wanted to do was cry too. I couldn't feel my anger anymore. All I could feel was her sadness.

"Why are you saying that?" I yelled at her. It was easier to yell then to give in and cry, "Why do you care so much? Why do you care how I feel? You don't even know me."

"But I do know you. I know who you are, I know what you are, we all do." She slumped back onto the couch and put her face in her hands.

I stared at her, processing nothing because it was simply impossible to process. Finally, I said softly, unsure if I wanted to know the answer, "So what am I?"

She looked at me with tear stained cheeks and red swollen eyes and said, "You're the one we've been told about for generations. You're the Gypsy raised by Gadje. You're a prophet."

Chapter Twelve

"You have that wrong. You must have been looking for someone else." I was no one's prophet. I wasn't even someone's son.

"No, Aurelious, we aren't wrong," she sounded exhausted like if she wanted to fight she wouldn't be able to. Like if she wanted to lie and create an entire fantastical world of gifted Gypsies, she wouldn't be able to. "Brekwyn was searching for you, he knew it was you. He can hear it."

I walked back toward the door, "What does that mean, he can hear it?"

"You, he can hear inside your head and he can only hear inside a Gypsy's head."

Now I started to get angry again only this time I walked away from the door and toward her, "What do you mean he can hear inside my head?"

She looked at me with a blank expression, "He can hear your thoughts."

"Are you kidding me?" I yelled, she stood back up her expression went from blank to angry, her feelings reflecting mine.

"No, I'm not kidding you," she said back forcefully but without yelling, "I know it's horrible for you. I can feel your emotions and he can hear your thoughts and yet, we haven't taken advantage of you in any way like the Gadje would have if they could have known what was going on inside you."

"Do you even comprehend the kind of violation that this is? Do you even understand how messed up this is?" Forget it, I had enough I started toward the door.

She ran ahead of me and stood in front of it, "Yes, I understand but it is what it is, this is just what we can do but Brekwyn and I couldn't do this if you weren't a Gypsy, gifts like ours that involve a person's mind and emotions don't work on Gadje."

"Please get out of my way Anira, I'm serious, I'm not dealing with this crazy shit anymore!" I yelled, my arms still tight across my chest.

"Stop yelling, these people down here have done nothing to you. Your yelling is going to disrupt their peaceful lives and they're only trying to help us."

"Great, thanks for reminding me. What the hell are we doing down here? All you've done is tell me these ridiculous stories about your gifts and try to convince me that I'm just like you."

She pushed her anger, my anger, aside I could feel her calming me down and although it was working I knew it wasn't real. But I didn't tell her that, I just backed away, it would've been better for me to leave with a rational mind anyway. I ran my hands through my hair and walked around in a circle taking deep breaths to help clear my head.

"Yeah, that's the thing, you aren't just like us. You aren't just like anyone."

"Why not?"

"Because of your gift."

"I don't have a gift."

"You do though. You have one of the greatest gifts and only one Gypsy alive at a time has the gift you have."

Again I looked at her in disbelief but thought I would indulge her by asking, "So what am I?"

"Aurelious, you're the Reader."

"What does that mean?" I shook my head and tossed my hands in the air. Everything she said was more ludicrous then the last thing that came out of her mouth.

"The Reader has the ability to know what a person is going to do before that person does it. You can see what a person's choices are in any situation, and then you can see the decision that the person makes as well as the impact of their decision. You can also see the impact of the decision that a person did not make in that same situation. You advance in time to see all of this before the person you are focusing on even knows that this choice and action they will make will be in their future. You can see someone's choices and the decisions they make and, ultimately if you choose to, you can alter their decisions."

"That makes no sense. I know I can't do that."

"Not yet, because you haven't been trained to use your gift. But think about it. Think about how observant you are. You know that you are far more observant that any normal person, you notice things others don't and you feel them. You are called a Reader because you can do exactly that, you can read but what you read is people. And you can advance, read ahead, and know what they're going to do."

"So you think I can see the future?"

"Not the way you're thinking. Our fortunetellers can do that, but only in small glimpses and it's random. Fortunately Megana foresaw what was going to happen tonight. You can see just what will happen with one person, the person you're focusing on and what you see is based on the decisions they make."

"What's the big deal about this gift then? What's so great about it?" I still knew that she had the wrong person but I was curious to see what kind of story she could come up with.

"The big deal is that when you can see a person's decisions before they make them then you can intervene and change them. If a person was going to turn left you could make them turn right, if a person was going to open a window you could convince them to open a door instead."

"This gift sounds like it has no purpose, why do I care if someone turns left or right?"

"Those are just simple examples, the point is, that when you can change what a person intends to do then you take away their free will and what's a person who can't exercise their free will?"

I thought about it for a minute, "A slave?"

"Exactly."

"So you think I want Gypsies to be my slaves?"

"No, not Gypsies and we don't think you want that."

"If not Gypsies then who? I thought you said gifts don't work on Gadje."

"For all other Gypsies that can do things related to the mind and emotion like Brekwyn and I can, but not for you. That's what the prophecy states. *'The Gypsy raised by Gadje will be the greatest Reader of all generations, the one who will read both Gypsy and Gadje alike.'* That's you."

"It's not me Anira," I folded my arms across my chest again and wished for my laptop to help me make sense of all of this. I hated having to talk about it but talking was my only option without my computer.

"It is you Aurelious. Brekwyn knows it's you."

"Because he can read my mind? I'm pretty sure there is no place in my mind that has any knowledge of this crap."

Now she took a deep breath, "Brekwyn has among the greatest abilities of all. His coming was also foretold by the fortunetellers, generations before his birth. His gift would be so all encompassing that it was thought of as more of a power than a gift. Shortly after he was conceived, the tribe knew that this child would be the one they were waiting for.

"He has all of the gifts that we have individually but to a much greater extent, some say that his abilities can rival those of Nature herself. He can manipulate the weather and bodies of water, he can move rocks, he can extract, find and alter metals and precious stones, he can communicate with animals, he can make plants grow or die, he can move waves of sound and

67

light, and so much more.

"Hearing thoughts is believed to be a special power, which other Gypsies do not have, and is a way for him to help the young to understand what's happening within themselves. It can be very confusing when you start to develop your gift. Many Gypsies in our history didn't survive the process of the realization of their gifts because as children it's almost impossible to verbalize what's going on inside you when it's about something like this. We believe that Nature gave Brekwyn this extra gift so he can ease the process, he knows what a child's gift is before they know it so he can explain what's happening to their bodies and in their minds. But as they grow in their acceptance of and ability to use their gift, eventually their thoughts become softer until he can no longer hear them. He only hears the thoughts of those whose gifts are still developing." She tugged on a curl again, revealing her insecurity. She had to know that the more she spoke, the more unbelievable this all became. But she continued.

"Brekwyn uses his power only for good and he hasn't unleashed the full magnitude of it yet. He keeps himself very restrained so he feeds off of his positive feelings only. His power can be so strong that he has the potential to be very dangerous in the quest for good and he knows this. Sometimes it's the possibility of what he can do that tortures him so he's always careful with his emotions. He doesn't allow himself to feel darkness or negative feelings for fear that he will unleash himself fully. He's always known this, his entire life, even as boy he was a boy of peace. We'll all change in some way if Brekwyn does." She was so sad when she said this last sentence.

I just looked at her with confusion that I knew she could feel, or I would know she could feel it if I actually believed any of this.

"He found you, Aurelious, and he'll train you to use your gift for the good of the world. He'll help you to help others not hurt them, just like he's done for us."

"So if he's this all powerful Gypsy who can protect everyone and do everything then why are you worried that I'll make the

Gadje my slaves? Can't he just stop me?"

"It's not you that we worry about. It's not you that we know wants to enslave them. There are Gypsies whose intentions are not good, who hate the Gadje for what they've done to the Earth. There are Gypsies who want revenge on the Gadje and would use the Reader to get their revenge."

But if Brekwyn had such extreme abilities, shouldn't he be able to defeat these other Gypsies? As soon as I asked myself that question, another one dawned on me, "Is Brekwyn the only Gypsy that's this powerful?"

"No, there's one other."

And suddenly I knew why we ran.

Chapter Thirteen

"The Inglore that you were all talking about, he's the one who's looking for me and he's the other one with all of the powers isn't he?"

She nodded. "Aurelious, I can't say anymore." She looked completely exhausted. "You have to process what you've heard. You have to understand it and start to believe it."

"That's not likely something that'll happen anytime soon." I was exhausted too but my mind wouldn't stop screaming that this was all completely illogical.

"I think it would be best to get some sleep and start fresh in the morning." She stood up slowly like her muscles ached. "There are two bedrooms in the back where we can sleep."

"I'm not going to sleep."

She sighed, "Aurelious, I've said that you're welcome to leave whenever you want but it's not a good idea tonight. Will you stay 'til morning at least?"

"I don't know."

"If you leave, he'll find you. It may not be tonight or tomorrow but he won't stop until he does."

"And what happens if he finds me?"

"I have no idea." She slumped looking totally dejected and sad and walked into the darkness that engulfed the back of this strange underground apartment.

I was alone again. Even though she was there and I knew there were other people down here, I felt completely alone just as I did when I realized that my laptop was gone. I paced back and forth, my arms folded over my chest, my fists clenched under my arms and I thought about everything that she had told me tonight. Then it dawned on me. Maybe she was making all of this up. Was she making fun of me? Was this an elaborate prank? It would be easier to believe that she was lying because it was just too unbelievable otherwise. And if she was lying then was she worse than the people in my old life?

Yeah, I get it, those people were abusive but I knew that that's what they were. They didn't pretend to be anything else. But her and Brekwyn, they acted like I was important, like they wanted me around. And now she tells me all of this? It's cruel isn't it? Isn't it cruel to try to make someone comfortable, to try to break them down and then tell them these outrageous stories? Did she think I was stupid, that I would just fall for all of this nonsense? I mean you wouldn't fall for any of this would you?

I wasn't going to let it happen again, whatever game she was playing I was not going to be the pawn anymore. There was no Inglore. There were no messengers. This had to be just some bizarre practical joke and me the pathetic victim once again. Screw these people and their ridiculous lies and screw the people in my old life too, I didn't need any of them and if I was meant to wander the Earth on my own then so be it. They wouldn't make a fool out of me anymore, no one would. I made up my mind and did what I always do. I left.

This time I would leave without anyone knowing, if no one knew then no one would follow me and try to humiliate me anymore. It was easy to be quiet, the dirt cushioned my footsteps, and the only sound I could hear was my own heartbeat. I stood outside our door for a second to get my bearings. It was dark, darker than it was when we came in. All the doors that were once open and offering some light from the inside were now closed. Presumably its occupants all sleeping peacefully now that the ruckus we were making was over.

The candles that lit the walls were dimmer, having burned down a bit since we passed them before. I used the railing around the hole as my guide and made my way, slowly, quietly, back toward the way we came. It felt like it took longer than it should have but that could've been because I was moving so slowly or it could've been that I had the nagging feeling that I should've just stayed. But I pushed that feeling aside like I did with most of my feelings and was grateful that no one was around to know how apprehensive I actually was, if I were to believe that sort of thing could happen.

The opening to the hallway that led to the ladder appeared on my left, so I walked down it only to find that it came to a dead end. There had to be some kind of handle here, some way for me to open this thing. I felt around, my hands digging in the dirt for something that would get me out. I found nothing. I started to panic. I couldn't be trapped here. I couldn't be trapped underground. I started breathing harder. My heart started pounding. How was I going to get out?

I pounded on the wall of dirt with the sides of my fists, sweat dripped into my eyes. I coughed because of my inability to take a real breath. I was trapped. There had to be another way out so I whipped my body around to find that other way and came face to face with a tiny, pale, Gypsy woman.

"Peace child, I can help you," she said barely above a whisper.

"I need to get out," I gasped.

"Then out you shall get." With that she made a sweeping motion through the air with her arm and opened the wall.

I ran into the space with the ladder but before I went up I looked back, "Is this a trick?"

"There is no trickery here."

"You're just gonna let me out?"

"If it is your wish to leave then I cannot keep you." She had the slightest smile and her head cocked to one side. I couldn't tell if she was creepy or whimsical. The dim light didn't help.

Suddenly I was unsure of myself, of my decision to leave. So I asked this strange woman, "Do you think I should go?"

"You are not an infant in need of guidance nor can I presume to advise you in a situation that I know not. You must do your will. You must take your journey." She slowly walked away, vanishing into obscurity, and the wall closed.

I was in complete and total darkness. I could almost feel the oxygen evaporating as I took each breath far deeper than I should have. I didn't think about that woman or what she just did with the wall. I didn't think about that place under the ground that I was just in because if I thought about any of these things then I would have to believe what Anira told me and I was determined not to believe any of it.

I slowly crept up the ladder, each rung creaking in protest. I bumped my head on the ceiling, which I knew to be the floor of the closet in the trailer. With excruciating slowness I pushed up on the floor. I looked through the crack I'd made. No one was there so I pushed it up further. When there was enough space to get my body through, I climbed out and into the closet. The closet door was closed so again, I opened the door slowly, searching for signs of life with each inch. No one was in this room either.

I couldn't risk going through the rest of the trailer. For all I knew Donheil the digger was in the kitchen making a sandwich so I did what I thought was logical and went to the nearest window. It was already open by some small miracle and was just big enough for me to squeeze my body through.

The metal frame scraped against my sides, I could feel the top layers of my skin being scratched off but I didn't care. I had to keep moving. I landed awkwardly on the ground below the window and ran toward the path, grateful that I knew that it ended at Anira's trailer.

The moon was high in the black night sky and gracious enough to light my way through the trees if just barely. My intention was to sneak into Anira's trailer, I knew she wouldn't be there, and change back into my clothes and shoes like a normal person. I ran as quickly as I could but I didn't know this path like Anira did. Numbing pain shot through my toes each time they met with a tree root or rock hidden in the shadows trying to slow me down. My knees and palms of my hands burned more and more each time I fell. I was scared, this whole thing was scary and I felt like a fool for falling for any of this. But I was determined to find my way back and leave all of this behind so I persevered. My perseverance paid off when Anira's trailer appeared in front of me.

I waited for a minute in the obscurity of the tree line to catch my breath and to make sure no one was around. There was no one here, which felt even weirder. I went right into her trailer and directly into the room where I left my clothes. I changed as quickly as I could throwing the Gypsy costume on the floor where I felt it belonged as one of the props of my degradation. My feet ached when I put my shoes back on, the soles raw and sore from running through the woods. When I had everything I came with which is just what I had on, I went back out the door.

I looked around the back of the trailer for another path, the one that got us here from the road that led us away from my other life. My confidence in my decision to leave grew with each passing second that left me undiscovered by my cruel pranksters. But then something happened that changed the course of my intention. I heard a noise that stopped me in my tracks.

Chapter Fourteen

I couldn't be sure what I heard at first. It wasn't near me but off in the distance, it sounded like commotion. I listened harder. Then it registered in my brain that it must've been the festival. While I was running for my life like an idiot, the rest of these people continued to party with me being the joke of their night. I had to see what they were doing. I wouldn't let them see me, but I had to see them, I had to confirm that I was right.

I crept through the maze of trailers back toward the direction of the sound, the direction of the festival that we fled from only a short time before. I had that ominous feeling that I felt when we left, a dangerous heaviness in the air. It made a lump in my throat. Everything in my body told me to turn back but I disregarded all of it. My curiosity overruled everything else, it always did, a down side of being so consumed by observing the world around me. I listened for the music to guide my way but I didn't hear any. As I got closer I heard voices but not conversations like one would expect at a party, then again, I hadn't actually been to any parties. Instead it was just one voice at a time. It was a man's voice. Maybe Brekwyn was telling them the story of how he made me his sucker.

The fire was still burning because I could see the glow getting brighter as I got closer. I hid behind trailers, one at a time, each taking me that much closer to the festival. I was close. I could hear them better. If I stopped walking and listened I could've heard their words but I wanted to see them too, I had to get closer. My heart was pounding.

"Hey," someone whispered from behind me out of nowhere. I jumped, my heart in my throat, and whipped around.

He stood in a shadow so I couldn't make out his face but I knew it was a boy, around my height. I could see the outline of crazy messy hair in the glow of the fire, "Shhh," he said. "You shouldn't be here," his whisper was barely audible.

"Who are you?" I couldn't think of what else to say.

"I'm Danyon," he said, "and you're not safe here."

"Why not?" I was whispering but I wasn't about to fall for this again.

"They aren't supposed to know you're here."

"Who?" How many different plans did they have for this prank? Did they rehearse every scenario?

"Come here I'll show you." He climbed up a ladder attached to the back of the trailer we were standing next to. My curiosity and I followed him.

On our stomachs we inched toward the front of the trailer until all of the participants of the festival were in full view. Everyone was standing around, there was no dancing, no laughter, and they were focusing on two men who were circling Brekwyn like lions sizing up their prey.

"That's who," the kid said, he was still in too much of a shadow for me to see what he looked like.

"Where is he Brekwyn?" one of the men asked. He had an accent.

"Where is who?" Brekwyn had a smirk on his face, his thumbs hooked into the waistband of his pants. They were trying to intimidate him. It wasn't working.

"You know who," the other said. "Where's the Reader?"

"There's no Reader here."

"Inglore knows you have him, he'll pay your price, just hand him over to us."

"I do not trade in human life like your fearless leader," he laughed out, mocking them when I thought he would be mocking me. "But even if I did there still wouldn't be a Reader here."

"Nonsense, let's not make this more difficult than it has to be."

I was looking at Brekwyn waiting for his response. I was thinking about who these men were, who the kid was that brought me up here, who any of these people were. I was thinking about Brekwyn and how he looked confident and both bored and humored at the same time, but then his expression changed. He was concentrating on something like he was listening, but no one noticed. Only I noticed and I knew what he was concentrating on, I knew what he was listening to when from across the space between us, in one quick movement, he looked right at me.

Crap, he heard my thoughts. Crap, she was telling me the truth.

I didn't know what to do. I panicked again. I turned to ask that kid what I should do but he was gone. What the hell?

Brekwyn didn't wait for my feeble brain to figure it out.

"Enough of this nonsense, look around you," he was finished toying with these men now that I was so close, "you know what you're looking for and you don't see it here so be gone with you. We have a festival to enjoy without your continued disruption."

"Inglore will have what he wants."

"You are wasting your time and mine," the wind started to pick up, "and you're disturbing my family." It started to rain. But I could only see the rain, I couldn't feel it because it wasn't raining on me, it was only raining on those two men. And the wind, I could hear it and I could see the clothing and hair on the men moving but not on anyone else, not anywhere near me.

"Name your price," they were persistent, too persistent, and now it was Brekwyn's turn to stalk them like they tried to stalk him so their persistence was futile. The men started shifting from one foot to another and sending each other sideward glances attempting to see when the other would raise the flag of surrender. The fire blazed angrily behind them catching the back of one of their shirts. On fire, the messenger whirled around, screeching as the other pounded out the flames that the rain, conveniently, didn't hit. The wind only aggravated them before they were beaten out. He wasn't hurt but they were sufficiently scared.

"I suggest you take your leave and don't come back here. You won't like what happens to you if you do." I heard a low rumble and saw their legs wobbling as they tried to keep their balance. The ground below their feet shook and started to crack and they needed no more encouragement to leave. They were off running like little cowards. As soon as they cleared the area the rain and wind stopped and the fire went back to its normal size. Brekwyn was doing all of that.

Everyone started talking about what just happened, but not the wind, rain, and fire, no they were talking about the two men as if they were a bigger deal then whatever all that other stuff was. They weren't even acknowledging it, like they were used to it. Brekwyn was the only one not engaging with anyone around him, he stayed where he was, the only movement he made was to put his finger to his lips and, looking directly at me, signaled that I stay quiet and hidden right where I was. And that is exactly what I did.

Chapter Fifteen

The festival was over. The mood was clearly dampened by the unwelcomed visitors. I didn't move from my perch because I knew, as Brekwyn did, that they could still be in the woods. At some point he left. I didn't see him leave I only know that when I looked for him I couldn't find him. But I did see all of the people cleaning up, putting out the fire by some force of Nature that they created, and heading back to their homes.

It was quiet when everyone was inside. Not as quiet as it was underground because here there were crickets and other nocturnal creatures' disrupting the silence but it was quiet none-the-less. I noticed the stars. There were so many of them, I never saw this many stars in any of the places I used to live. But the peacefulness made me anxious. Peace was not something I knew how to do.

I started to fidget. I must have tied and untied my shoelaces six times. I needed to move from this spot, I didn't know where I needed to go but I didn't feel like I should be here anymore. Surely by now those two men were gone and I wasn't in any imminent danger. Besides, how would they know they were looking for me anyway? Only Brekwyn and the Inglore could hear my thoughts, allegedly, so to those others I could just be a regular kid wandering around.

I decided to take my chances. I was far more used to taking my chances than I was with sitting quietly waiting for whatever happens next. I crawled across the top of the trailer and back down the ladder. By now my eyes were well adjusted to the light, or lack of it, so I could see pretty clearly. As I walked through the maze of trailers I tried to figure out where I should go, but I was so preoccupied with my thoughts that I didn't pay attention to where I actually was going until I looked up and found myself in the middle of the woods. Uh oh, how did I get here? And if I wanted to go back to the Gypsy village, how do I get there?

I turned around and started walking toward the direction I thought I came from. Before I knew it though, the path that I thought I was on was no longer. I found myself climbing over fallen trees and stumbling down ditches that could only be described as a collective graveyard for slippery leaves. The moon that lit my way began to torment me by casting evil shadows all around. I felt my heart starting to beat faster again, my throat going dry before it started to close, my lips turning cold. Sweat dripped down my back, where was I?

I turned again, trying another direction. I started to run with my hands out in front of me, low hanging branches smacking at my already aching palms. But everywhere I turned more menacing looking shadows appeared, playing tricks on my weary mind. I wanted to cry out, I wanted to scream for help but I didn't know how, I was never allowed to cry for help.

I stopped, out of breath, drenched in sweat, mentally frantic and fell to my knees. I couldn't go anywhere, not by myself, not anymore.

"You lost?"

I looked around me and saw no one.

"Or are you running away?"

The voice came from above me. I looked up but I couldn't see anything as the shadows engulfed the trees around me.

"Who's saying that?" I asked, was this a trick?

He giggled, "It's me, Danyon."

"Where are you?"

"Right above you, can't you see me?"

I focused harder, giving my eyes time to adjust to this more intense darkness. And then it appeared, a foot attached to a dangling leg hanging over a large thick branch.

"What are you doing up there?"

"Just visiting. What are you doing down there?"

"I don't know."

"So you're lost then?"

"Yeah, I think so." I felt dejected, I didn't have the energy to put up a fight with this kid or to pretend like I was in control.

"Don't worry, Brekwyn will take you back."

"Is he up there?" I sat up, were there other people in the trees?

"No," he laughed, "but he's on his way to come get you."

"Get me?" I stood up, achingly, but attempting to act like I still had some strength left. "How does he know where to find me?"

"I sent a message to him."

"Why'd you do that?" I started getting panicky.

"So he can take you back."

"Well, I don't want him to take me back. And I don't want him to know where I am," I said feeling that familiar obstinacy again. Brekwyn told me to stay on top of the trailer but I left. When kids were caught disobeying in my old life, we were seriously, um let's call it, reprimanded. I had no idea what was going to happen here but I didn't feel like finding out.

He laughed again, "Why would anyone not want to see Brekwyn? That makes no sense." He laughed even harder.

Was he serious? I didn't get the chance to ask him. Because from behind me I heard, "Why thank you Danyon, that is very kind of you."

"Narc," I said under my breath to Danyon. When he didn't respond I looked up, the foot and dangling leg were gone, of course, but I was still caught.

"Aurelious, it's a relief that you're safe, perhaps I wasn't clear in my suggestion that you stay where you were on top of that trailer. These woods may not be safe for you to travel alone."

"You're worried about my safety? What about the kid in the tree?" If I was going down, I was taking him with me.

Brekwyn smiled, "No, I'm not so worried about Danyon in these woods, he'll be just fine."

"Right, because it's totally normal to be sitting in a tree in the middle of the woods by yourself at night."

"Well he isn't by himself but yes, for him it is totally normal. Normal here and normal from where you grew up are not the same thing."

"Yeah, I'm starting to see that."

"You've seen a lot so far, more than I'd intended for so early in your stay here." Somehow we were walking back through the woods as we spoke although neither of us said anything about leaving the area.

I didn't respond, I just took a deep breath and kept following him. I did notice that he didn't seem too angry at me for leaving. Maybe he wanted to catch me off guard when I was more vulnerable like one or two of my foster parents used to do.

"Does Anira know you left?"

Again I didn't respond but I thought about our conversation and how I tried to convince myself that she was lying.

"She doesn't lie," he said responding to my thoughts.

I stopped in my tracks, "Were you just listening to what I was thinking?"

"Yes."

"So, basically I have no kind of privacy around you people then, is that true?" I didn't wait for an answer, "If you can hear my thoughts and Anira can feel my emotions then how am I supposed to act like none of this is completely off the wall crazy? How am I supposed to protect myself with the two of you invading the one space that no one is supposed to be able invade, which is my head?"

"Well, that's the point, isn't it Aurelious?" he said softly, "You don't need to protect yourself here because we aren't going to hurt you."

"That's bullshit Brekwyn and you know it."

"On the contrary, what's bullshit is you assuming that everyone you meet will treat you in the same manner as the people you once knew. I understand that it'll take time for you let your guard down, I can't blame you for that. You had a very difficult and unnatural childhood for someone like you. But I can promise you that if you let your guard down then the abuses that you suffered will no longer impact your life. It may be hard for you to believe but the impression left by those offenses doesn't run as deeply on you as they would a Gadje child." He was walking beside me, looking at me, "You never tried as hard to find human connection as a Gadje child would have because you were never meant to be there. Your connections are here and now that you are where you belong, you don't need to spend the rest of your life assuming that everyone is out to harm you. You're valued here, we're your people, not the Gadje, and someday soon, when you stop fighting so hard, you'll see that it's true."

But fighting was what I understood, how would I ever learn something else? The task seemed daunting, too daunting. It would be easier to just keep fighting. I was good at that.

"Soon you'll be better at something else, you'll see."

But what I saw at that moment was that somehow, we were standing in front of Anira's trailer.

"Get some sleep, you've had a very challenging day," he said. I didn't protest, instead I approached the door but before I went in he said, "Aurelious, tonight Anira took you underground for your safety but also for the safety of the rest of this tribe. You have a lot to learn. Not just about your gift and being a Gypsy, but you have a lot to learn about being part of a family. Your first lesson is that you don't put the safety of your family in jeopardy for your own selfish will. You're entitled to have errors in judgment just like every other human being, as long as you learn from them and as long as they do no harm especially to this family. I'm not here to punish you for your faults but please don't mistake my good nature for weakness, I assure you that mistake is one that no one is entitled to."

It was almost impossible to swallow past the lump in my throat created by that last sentence. I think it's safe to say he made his point.

Chapter Sixteen

I woke up with a jolt, pain and panic shooting through my body. I lurched off the couch, gripping my hands to my chest, coughing as a reflex to the nausea in my stomach. What was happening? I staggered to the door, gasping for breath. I fumbled for the handle and practically fell down the three steps and onto the ground as I opened it. The blaze of morning sunlight burned my eyes and forced them shut.

I groaned and doubled over, the pain in my chest ached. I wanted to scream and cry at the same time. The feelings forced me to my knees, I needed help, something was desperately wrong. Through clouded eyes, I saw Brekwyn running toward me. I reached my hand out to him but he passed by me, leaving me on the ground to die, or so I thought.

"You'll be better in a moment Aurelious," he said as he leapt over my writhing body. Then I heard it, crying, coming toward me.

"Brekwyn," it was Anira, "he's gone!"

From my knees I looked behind me, I could see her but she didn't see me yet.

"He's gone Brekwyn! I woke up this morning and he wasn't there!" She was crying and practically breathless. "We have to find him!"

"He's here Anira, peace girl, he's here. He's fine." He stood in front of her with one hand on her shoulder and the other on her face like he really wanted her to focus. Her cheeks were stained with tears, her eyes red.

The pain started to subside, the panic evaporated, I could breathe again. Cough. Cough. Okay, now I could breathe again. The coughing got her attention.

"Why did you leave without me?" Instantly enraged, she stomped over toward me, the orange in her eyes flaming up in anger, I started to get angry.

"Did I need your permission?" I stood up, shakily. Cough.

"Well, it would have been courteous," she yelled.

Brekwyn took a deep breath and we both started to calm down.

"You scared me half to death you know. I thought for sure the Inglore captured you and was doing something horrible to you already." A tear spilled over the rim of her eye. I felt sorry for her. I didn't want her to be upset like this, not because of me.

"I'm sorry," I said, and for the first time in my life, I actually meant it.

"Why did you leave?"

"Because I didn't believe you." There was no point in hiding the truth around these two.

"And now?"

"I've seen some things," I rubbed my hand across my chest where the pain seared through it only moments before, "and felt some things that suggest you were being honest."

"Only suggest?" She cocked her head to the side and put her hands on her hips.

"Baby steps Anira, baby steps."

She walked toward her trailer, "I'll make breakfast," she said but then turned and asked, "Why were you on the ground gasping for breath?"

"You tell me." I folded my arms across my chest knowing full well that it was because of the intensity of her emotions.

"Never mind," she said with a wave of her hand and went inside.

I turned to Brekwyn who was smirking at us for some reason only he knew, I guess. "She's pretty emotional, huh?" I didn't have experience with girls but this didn't seem typical.

"Every gift has a downside, sometimes several. It's not all easy or magical. Anira is an empath, so she feels the emotions of others and as part of her gift can project her feelings on those around her. She can also mask emotions of others as well, becoming sort of a buffer but with great effort still. As she continues to develop it'll get much easier.

"Hers is a wonderful gift and can be truly helpful. But as a consequence, her emotional depth runs far deeper than any other person so the feelings she feels are typically much more intense and they can also change in the blink of an eye. It was hard for her in the beginning, as it is with most young Gypsies, but she is acutely aware of her gift and what it means and how it can affect those around her. She's usually able to keep her emotions on a fairly even level."

"Was that an example of a fairly even level?"

"Not exactly, you're challenging her Aurelious, you're making her work to keep herself in control."

"Why?"

"That's a bigger story."

"Let me guess, you're not gonna to tell me?"

"It's not for me to tell. Anira will tell you when she's ready."

"Is she always gonna be like this?"

"No, we all eventually level off. We manage to even out the gift and its consequence. With time it all becomes second nature."

But between you and me, she wasn't so bad. I know that to you it probably seems like she is way too emotional but that's not how it seems when you're with her. If I had to describe her in that moment I probably would have said she was passionate. And passionate is not a bad thing to be. I would also probably say that she was interesting and trust me, coming from someone who watches the world and the people in it like I have my whole life, being interesting is a very high compliment. But what do I know about compliments.

Chapter Seventeen

I've never been one to start up a conversation but, like the day before, breakfast seemed like a reasonable time to get some answers. We were sitting at a table outside of Anira's trailer eating fresh fruit and pancakes. The air was warm. The sun was shining. All in all, it was the picture of a beautiful summer day that any normal person would be enjoying. But I think we've established by now that I'm not exactly normal.

"Last night I heard you say to those men that they knew what they were looking for," I jumped right in. "So if I was going to assume for the sake of this conversation that I'm the person you think I am, which let's be clear, I'm pretty sure I'm not."

"You are," Brekwyn said with a wink before eating a piece of juicy melon.

"Whatever," I brushed him off and continued. "So do they know what I look like?"

"Probably not."

"Then how would they know I was the one they're looking for?"

"There's something that a Reader has that no other Gypsy has."

"What?" Was it some invisible mark, some sweet fragrance, a glow about me?

"You read too much fiction," he laughed, "no Aurelious, you have blue eyes."

I stopped with a forkful of pancakes half way to my mouth and thought about the people that I met here. I certainly couldn't remember everyone but those that I could and who I was now picturing in my mind all have brown eyes, well at least not blue eyes, Anira's were brown flecked with orange, Brekwyn's were basically black. "There are plenty of people in this world with blue eyes," I said.

"Not Gypsies," Brekwyn said.

"There isn't one Gypsy with blue eyes?" I needed to be sure I understood this.

"Well, there is one," he said and pointed to me.

"Besides me," I rolled my eyes like a brat. "There are no Gypsies with blue eyes."

"No."

"That's weird."

"It's the Reader's mark, Readers are the only marked Gypsies, we don't know why," he explained as Anira and I listened on although I'm assuming she already knew this. "And the color of a Reader's eyes is more unique then just the fact that they're blue. Your eyes will change. They'll get lighter as your gift gets stronger."

"Right, well I'll believe that when I see it," I said in my best snarky '*I still don't think I'm your Reader*' voice.

"You'll see," he smiled that peaceful smile.

"So all Readers have blue eyes and only one Reader can be alive at a time," I wondered then if there was some kind of death curse that Reader's had, like did we all suffer the same kind of dramatic death?

I looked up at Brekwyn about to ask about it, but he already heard what I wanted to know and I couldn't be sure, but it looked like he was a little sad.

"There's no fate regarding death for the Reader's. Their life span is individual to them as it is to every other person."

That was a relief, "Did you know who the last Reader was?"

"Yes." Anira looked at Brekwyn when he answered and, with a slight smile on her face that could have resembled pity, she put her hand over his.

"So how did he die?"

"The last Reader was a woman," he took a deep breath and crumbled little pieces of biscuit between his fingers, "she died giving birth to me."

Oh no. I suddenly felt really awful for him. "I'm sorry for you Brekwyn."

"This is something that will always sadden me simply because I know that she loved me enough to give her life for mine. Although she gave all of her love to me when she carried me and it courses through my soul even now, I still sometimes wish that I could know someone that selfless and pure at this point in my life."

He put down the biscuit pieces, folded his hands and talked to me, directly to me, "When I was born, as was foretold, there were forces from nature and the Earth that combined to make me what I am. These forces were so extreme that no woman would survive the birth, she would have to give all that she was in order for me to be born healthy, in order for me to survive the birth. Those who were with my mother at the time have spoken of her strength and courage in the process of my birth and they spoke of the calm she had even though she knew that the advent of my life meant the end of hers.

"I don't know why it was me, Aurelious, why I was chosen, just like you don't know why you were chosen to be the Reader. But it's imperative of us to honor those who sacrificed for us by being all that we're supposed to be and by finding ways to use our gifts for the benefit of others." He smiled slightly now, as though he was reminded that there is a bigger picture and that the tragedy that surrounded his birth was for some greater good.

You know, I was just thinking, if this was all true, it might not be so bad.

Chapter Eighteen

I was anxious to prove Brekwyn and Anira wrong, I was sure that I wasn't this Reader that they'd been looking for. So when Brekwyn suggested some preliminary, training I was quick to oblige. As usual, my curiosity overruled everything including my skepticism, so I was interested to see what he thought we would accomplish here.

"So if my eyes get lighter as I get better at whatever I'm supposed to be doing, how light will they get?"

"I can't be sure, I've never heard of a Reader whose eyes got white but they will become a lighter blue and they will always keep a darker blue rim around the light blue of the iris. You can sort of tell the ability of the Reader by the lightness of their eyes." Brekwyn was pretty matter of fact about everything, even though this was totally bonkers.

We followed another path as we walked into the woods just east of where the festival took place the night before. We were the only ones here that I could see but it didn't feel as terrifying as it did the night before. The monstrous shadows from last night were just shadows today.

"So about this Inglore, why does he want me and what will he do with me if he finds me?" Not sure I want to know the answer to this one.

"This is what we know about Inglore, we know for sure that he detests the Gadje. It borders on an obsession with them in a hateful way. We believe that if Inglore had the chance to control the Gadje, a chance to take away their free will, he would do it. It would be like a game to him. We cannot be sure what he'll choose to do with them once he has control but there is the possibility that he will find a way to enslave them.

"You see we don't understand where his bitterness toward the Gadje comes from but we know it's there and we know that he's unstable in many ways. It's the unstable part that makes him particularly threatening because it's that part that can make this plan of his into something big and deadly or something less impactful that he finds amusing. Now that you're a reality, he actually believes that his plan could work, and he's right it could. If he used you and your gift in the right way, you could help him to control the Gadje, their actions, their decisions, it could be extraordinary."

"But not extraordinary in a good way?"

"No, not in a good way, not for them and in turn, not for any of us either. There's a balance of power in the world as we know it now, there won't be if Inglore gets his way and whenever the balance of power is shifted too far in one direction, bad things happen. It won't end well not for him, not for the Gadje, not for any other Gypsies."

"Can't I just tell him that I won't do what he wants?"

"Inglore has great strength, you're not as strong as he is and you never will be simply because of the sheer force of his power. It can be deadly. As a matter of fact it can be deadly very easily for him. But when you understand where you're vulnerable and where you're strong then anything is possible. However, there is one more thing that you have to understand. If Inglore manages to exact his plan, we will fight him. We'll do everything in our power to prevent it from happening. He knows that you'll be useful to him if this happens too. As a Reader you're one step ahead of everyone that you focus on so if it came down to a battle, the one who employs the gift of the Reader will be almost impossible to defeat."

So, the Inglore wants to use me to control the Gadje. That didn't sound like such a bad idea actually, at least not with the Gadje that I knew. What would be so bad about revenge? What would be so bad about making them pay for what they did to me?

"Be careful Aurelious, revenge is a dangerous path to go down. It's hard to get off that path and when you live in such a bitter frame of mind, your life becomes miserable."

Damn mind reader. "If I didn't say that out loud Brekwyn then assume it wasn't for you to hear," I said kind of pissed off at the reminder that I couldn't even think without intrusion.

"It won't be forever," he laughed off my outburst like I was being overly dramatic, but the mind reading was annoying. "When you get to a place where I can no longer be of service to you in your training then your internal voice is silenced for me."

"Forever?"

"Forever."

"Then let's start training."

Chapter Nineteen

"You have to start your training by learning to refocus your mind," Brekwyn said as he sat down on a fallen tree. He gestured for me to sit next to him. "What your mind is capable of is something that most of the world cannot understand, including you at this point. Your own mind can be a hurdle in your process if you don't take the time to retrain it to accept this other reality. At first you'll hear things differently, much more intensely, you'll be able to hear even the smallest movements that are not audible to anyone else. Then as you master that you'll push your consciousness to a different level and be able to see the choices that a person has to make, you'll go further and see what they decide and what happens as an immediate result. I cannot tell you what this feels like because it's an experience that I've never had and there's little written about the journey that a Reader takes. It's believed that the less anyone knows about it, the safer the Reader will be."

"How do you know any of this then?" I wondered aloud to him.

"When my mother realized her fate as she carried me in her womb, she created a journal of insights to help me as I grew older. She wrote a few things about what a Reader goes through but not enough to endanger the Reader should the journal fall into the hands of someone else. As a result I have a bit of insight but most of this you'll learn on your own."

"Why would I be in danger?"

"You'll be in a different kind of state, a meditation of sorts, almost like a trance. You're body is here but your mind is not.

That makes you vulnerable. You'll learn how to protect yourself eventually but for now, it's very risky and you can't do it on your own." Great, more vulnerability.

He picked up a twig and casually broke it into small pieces, throwing each piece to nowhere in particular.

"So what am I looking for when I start a reading, is there some kind of sign like some signal or something?"

"It'll be a way that you see things. You'll recognize a change in your own consciousness, I think you've already started to experience it like when you were looking at Anira before the festival yesterday." He looked at me and I remembered what I thought about when I looked at her and then remembered that he knew what I was thinking.

"Uh," I stumbled. Was I supposed to apologize for that?

He waved his hand and shook his head like he was trying to get the image, my image, out of his it, I think he may have gagged a little bit. We moved on without any further acknowledgement, "You'll be able to see that a person will choose to help someone cross the street. You'll see that a person will fall off the last step. You'll see that a person will betray their fellow man. But in order to do that, you have to look deeper than what's on the surface." Ugh, this seems impossible.

"Listen to the sounds of the woods Aurelious, what do you hear?" Brekwyn closed his eyes and listened as if to signal I should do the same.

"I hear the birds," I said quickly, eyes staying open.

"What else?" he asked.

"Just really the birds." I took a deep breath kind of bored with this already.

"Sit for a moment and hear those birds then block out the sounds they're making and see if you hear anything else."

Alright I'll throw him a bone. I listened. All I could hear were the birds. They seemed so loud. Were they getting louder? I closed my eyes and listened harder. I started to picture myself pushing through the birds, parting them like a curtain. Behind the curtain of the noisy birds there was a bright white background. It was peaceful there. I felt the warmth of the sun on my face and I could hear something else, what was it? It was like the trickling of water, not a river or a lake just a tiny stream making little tinkling sounds as it flowed over the rocks. And there were trees, and the leaves, I could hear them brushing against each other just slightly when the wind blew, it was a soft wind, I could hear it. Where were the birds? Were they gone?

"Aurelious," Brekwyn's voice was soft. I opened my eyes and looked over to him but said nothing. "That's how you challenge your own mind."

I felt like I was sleeping, like I was dreaming. I was actually drowsy. You know how you feel when your alarm goes off in the morning way earlier than you think it should? That's how I felt.

"It was like a dream because it's not something that's on the surface or what we can really see. You have to engage your subconscious, you have to get away from what you believe that you see and hear to what is actually there. When you focus with your subconscious mind, all of your preconceived notions, your judgments, and your prejudices are gone, just like they are when you're actually dreaming when you're asleep. You let your guard down and everything else came in. You're also tired because you were there for a while." He smiled a soft, knowing smile.

"What's a while?" I wondered sleepily.

"About an hour and a half." He started to get up.

"What, are you kidding?" That woke me up.

"I'm not kidding."

"There is no way it was that long!" I argued getting to my feet and feeling lightheaded.

"Come on, let's head back and get some lunch and our supplies for the next few days. You have a lot of work to do, you're going to have to get a lot quicker with your meditations." He patted me on the back.

"I'm gonna need a watch."

If all of this stuff about me was true then I, well, I have no idea what I would do. But it couldn't be true, could it? Then my stomach growled which it wouldn't have done unless significant time had actually passed since breakfast. Oh no, please don't let this be true. This was just way too big to be true.

Chapter Twenty

I felt more awake by the time we got back to Anira's, and hungrier, so the table full of food outside her trailer made my mouth water. She must've been anticipating our return and was out the door and down the steps within a second of us getting back.

"How'd it go?" she asked. I felt little prickles of excitement on my neck. I can't be sure if it was her excitement to see how the training went or my excitement to see her, which surprised me. And by the way, she looked amazing.

She was wearing another skirt that hung low on her hips and a top that went just to her ribs so pretty much her entire stomach was bare and enticing. Her skin was smooth and the curve of her body called out for me to touch it, to run the tip of my finger from her waist over the smooth line of her hip. There was nothing sharp or angled about her body, every part just curved and flowed perfectly into the next part. The edges of my vision started to blur, my mouth started to water. I wanted to..

"Aurelious," Brekwyn called to me. He was shaking my image out of his head again. Damn mind reader. "Let's have some lunch shall we?"

I merely grunted in annoyance when I sat down, Anira looked at me as if to say *"What's your problem?"* but she was good enough to keep that comment to herself. Obviously she knew that I was aggravated because it was a feeling and therefore she could feel it and by now it's pretty obvious that Brekwyn would know why I was annoyed since he could hear my thoughts which only made me more annoyed!

I took a deep breath and filled my plate with some kind of grain salad with fruit and vegetables, cheeses, nuts, and biscuits. This was a feast, all it was missing was the side of beef.

"You're not likely to see a side of beef here anytime soon." Brekwyn smiled at me as he ate a piece of cheese.

'Stop listening to me Brekwyn!' I shouted in my head fully aware that he could hear me. He rolled his eyes in response, which was kind of surprising and normal.

"We don't really eat too much meat here," Anira said after looking at both of us probably wondering what the silent exchange was all about.

"Why not?" I asked with a mouth full of delicious savory biscuit.

"We tend to eat what we grow," she explained. "And to be honest, when you have friends and family members that can communicate with animals, eating them becomes less appetizing."

I nodded. It made sense. I mean it made sense if you believe that there are people that can communicate with animals and I'm not saying that I believe that. Yet.

"So, back to my question, how did the training go?"

I looked at Brekwyn unaware of how to answer that.

"It went really well, he progressed through the first phase with much more intensity than I'm accustomed to when I train the children," Brekwyn said. "It may have something to do with the fact that he's older and that he's going to be quite powerful."

"Whatever you say," I replied obnoxiously. I still wasn't buying that whole hour and a half business. "By the way, do either of you have a watch I can borrow?" Who am I kidding? These people probably use sundials.

"Sure, I do," Anira said popping right out of her seat and into the trailer to get it. I stand corrected on the sundial thing.

"Why do you resist accepting that you are who we say you are?" Brekwyn asked while Anira was getting the watch.

I thought about it, "Why do you resist accepting that I am not who you say I am?" Ha, clever me.

"Because I know who you are." Okay maybe not so clever me.

"Look Brekwyn," I started to say, "I think I'm being pretty open-minded just by virtue of the fact that I'm still here. I'm interested in what you have to say and what you all seem to think about me but I can't be convinced until I actually see things happening."

"You mean like the things you saw last night?" Anira asked having re-joined us, watch in hand.

"Yeah, like last night, but more of that kind of stuff."

"So you want Brekwyn to just make things happen to prove to you that we are who we say we are?"

"No, I saw what Brekwyn can do."

"That wasn't even a fraction of it," Anira smirked.

"Whatever, I saw something," I huffed, "but I want to see what you think I can do."

No one said anything for a few minutes. I imagine that they were wondering how they could show me that but the truth is, if any of this was real, I was the one who had to prove it to myself. The only way to do that, I assume, is to let Brekwyn train me.

Brekwyn and Anira started talking to each other about Tanent and Seylane and how they would need to start their own training soon. I had nothing to add to the conversation so I just watched them. It was interesting to see how two people that obviously had a close relationship to each other interacted. I'd seen this from a distance all my life when I observed people from my self-imposed isolation, but I'd never seen it up close before. They didn't act like they had a romantic relationship. They were more like relatives or friends who knew each other forever.

I found myself drawn in deeper then I had been before, quicker too. The edges of my field of vision were fully blurred before I even had the chance to notice it. I found myself concentrating on Anira, everything else faded away. I didn't hear what they were saying anymore. All I could do was see her. At times her image appeared to be moving in slow motion, other times it seemed to be moving in real time. When she laughed her nose crinkled which made me feel like smiling. Almost without knowing it she would push her hair back from her shoulder and the sunlight would glint off of her tanned skin.

I didn't wonder what they were talking about, all I cared about what watching her actions. She picked up her knife and started to cut an apple. She cut out one wedge and ate it. I saw the muscles in her jaw as she chewed and the muscles in her throat when she swallowed. She picked up the knife again but it slipped out of her hand, she reacted by grabbing at it but she grabbed the blade instead of the handle. She flinched and looked at her hand, it started to bleed.

I wanted to jump up and help her but I couldn't. I was stuck where I was, I tried to reach out but my arms didn't move. I started to struggle, struggle to move, struggle to breathe, and struggle to ask for help from Brekwyn. But where was Brekwyn? All I could see was Anira.

"Aurelious," I heard Brekwyn but where was he? "Aurelious."

His image started to appear, and then suddenly he was in my face calling my name, "Aurelious." The rest of the world came back in violent clarity. I had that uncomfortable feeling of being on a roller coaster like I did at the festival. It was awful, I felt sick. The sounds and the smells around me were overwhelming. I looked at Anira's hand, it was fine, she hadn't cut it.

"Aurelious," I felt his arm on my shoulder and I pushed it off. With great effort I stood up, dizzy as soon as I reached my full height and braced myself on the table.

"What the hell?" I said rubbing my face in my hands.

"Aurelious let me help you," Brekwyn said supporting my arm

with his hand.

"Stop touching me!" I yelled at him, "Leave me alone!" I ran off toward the line of the trees, what the hell was happening to me?

"Aurelious!" Anira called behind me, "Let us help you."

I felt myself calming down. They were doing it they were making me calmer. Maybe I didn't have to run away but I had to be by myself, I had to rationalize this in some way. I didn't want to say anything to them but the image of Anira and the knife kept popping up in my brain. The thought of her in pain made me start to sweat, why did I care so much about this girl?

I took a deep breath and turned around, "I just need to be by myself for a few minutes," I said, reassuring her that I wasn't running away for good, yet. "And Anira, don't cut that apple with that knife."

As I was turning back, I saw Anira and Brekwyn look at each other and smile. They knew what I was reluctantly figuring out, that they were right about me.

Chapter Twenty-One

They gave me time to myself like I asked. I don't know how much time since I forgot to take the watch when I staggered away from the table and ran like a baby. I was embarrassed by my behavior. I should've just told them what happened although, let's be real, they probably already knew. But I didn't know what happened, nothing like that ever happened to me before. It felt weird. It felt bad. And all I know is that I saw her cut her hand, I saw it bleeding but then a minute later when all of those images of the rest of the world came flooding back in, her hand was fine. But I saw it bleed I know I saw it.

I was sitting on the ground with my head in my hands grasping for any reasonable explanation, desperate to come up with something when I felt her touch the top of my head. I knew it was her because her touch made my head tingle. Which only added to my distress, why did her touch make me tingle?

I stood up and took a step away from them, she looked concerned at the sight of me, and so did Brekwyn. "Why do you all always feel the need to touch me?"

"What's wrong with touching?" she asked, she really didn't know.

"I don't like it," I said emphatically, "I don't like all of the damn touching!" I rolled my shoulders and shook my head like I was trying to shake off the feeling of the contact.

"Who doesn't like to be touched?" She was perplexed.

"I don't!"

"But why not?"

I ran my hands through my hair and then crossed my arms, protectively over my chest and took another step back, "Because I don't!"

Anira looked at Brekwyn as if she wanted him to explain this weird thing, not everyone likes to be touched, it isn't that weird is it? "He's had bad experiences with touch in his childhood. His experience with touch is violent, not affectionate."

Immediately her expression went from confused to sad and she came toward me with her arms outstretched as if it was her own reflex to my pain. I backed up again. She stopped, "Aurelious, please," she begged, "I won't hurt you. I touch you because I care about you, touch is not harmful here."

"But I don't like it, Anira!" I yelled at her. I shouldn't have yelled, but I didn't know how to communicate this. "It confuses me, I don't know how I'm supposed to feel about it. Am I supposed to like it or not, am I supposed to run from it or not, am I supposed to fear it or not? I can't figure it out."

"Does it feel bad when I touch you?" she asked with a tear in her eye.

"I can't explain how it feels," I was still yelling. "People hit me or pinched me or poked at me or pushed me, that's what I know about touching. So it's always bothered me because it's always been a source of pain or humiliation." I was spilling everything out. Without my laptop to hold my thoughts I had no other choice but to speak. "But then I'm here and people are like patting me on the back and shaking my hand and putting their arm around me and it doesn't feel bad. But I don't know how to not feel bad about it! Can you understand that? It's always been bad and now it isn't, how am I supposed to make sense of that?"

"Don't try to rationalize it!" she yelled back in response to me, and I suspect she didn't really want to be yelling either.

Brekwyn put his hand up, "Aurelious, you're confused because your issue is not really with the physical pain, that's only what's on the surface. The tragedy of your childhood is that you were where you didn't belong. You never formed relationships with

105

the people you met because you shouldn't have been with them. It isn't a natural habitat for people like us. So you thought all along that you were burdened by the physical or emotional abuse that you suffered at that hands of those Gadje but in reality your greater burden was not being with us, where you belong, not being able to form your human connections. You're confused because you assume that you shouldn't like to be touched or cared for based on how you grew up, but here you do like it. And you wonder why you can so easily move on from what you've always known. You're not betraying your past or the person that you've always been by accepting your new feelings, you are becoming the person you were always meant to be."

I walked around in circles running my hands through my hair and then crossing my arms back over my chest. Is it really that simple, could I just let my past go because it's irrelevant compared to my present and my future? Was my past really just an accident, some unfortunate mistake?

"Please Aurelious, please stop thinking of us as those Gadje, we aren't them and you aren't them." Anira had her hands clasped together like she was praying that I would finally understand, "We touch here because we care about each other. They hurt you and that sickens me, I am so desperately sorry for the pain you suffered as a child but that isn't what happens here. Haven't we proven to you by now that we are not the same people? Haven't we proven to you by now that we aren't here to hurt you?"

"Anira," I wanted to say that they hadn't proven it but it dawned on me that in reality they had proved that they didn't want to hurt me.

As much as I tried to pretend that I had to protect myself from these people the truth is, they had already protected me. No they'd done more than protect me, they saved me. They saved me from the Inglore's men and they saved me from the life I knew before. The life I never belonged in. They saved me from the hands of my foster parents, my foster siblings, and the derelicts that lurked around the darkened corners of the dangerous places I lived.

I'd known Brekwyn for many weeks now. And in all that time, he's been nothing less than kind to me. Even when I pushed him away, even when I treated him badly, he was still nice. He noticed me, when I tried so hard to go unnoticed, he pushed through everyone and everything and he found me. I lived better in the few days that I'd been here with them then I had in my entire life.

I dropped my hands to my sides and I looked at them. They weren't here to hurt me. They wouldn't hurt me. I knew it from the minute I met them but I tried to fight the urge to trust them, to trust my own instincts. But I didn't need to fight here. Finally, finally I didn't need to fight. Do you know what happens when you realize that for the first time in your life you aren't in danger and there are actually people that want to protect you from it? You let yourself cry.

Every feeling I had ever felt seemed to rush through my body and soul, overwhelming me. Every fear that I desperately tried to suppress, every hope that I dared not have, ran through my veins. Every time that I wished for more and cursed what I had, flooded my brain.

I fell to my knees. And with my face in my hands, I cried. I have no memory of the last time I cried because it wasn't safe to express emotion that way. But here, I am safe.

Anira knelt down next to me and hugged me to her and it didn't feel bad anymore. It felt safe. I heard her crying with me and I didn't feel worse. I felt safe.

Brekwyn knelt down on the other side of me and put his hand on my back and I didn't pull away. I felt safe.

And as it has done every day since I met these people, my life changed.

Chapter Twenty-Two

Eventually, I didn't feel the need to cry anymore and a sort of numbness set in. Everything that I knew about the world meant nothing in that moment. I needed to learn it all, all over again. It was time to see my world differently. That was a big realization to have but first I had to understand what happened at lunch.

"When we were at the table I saw Anira slip when she was cutting an apple and cut her hand instead," I said to Brekwyn when I was ready to start talking again. "I tried to help her but I couldn't move and then you were calling my name and I felt sick from the sounds and smells and sights around me which didn't seem to be there when I saw her cut her hand. But her hand was fine. I know I saw it bleeding, but when you were calling my name it wasn't. Was that a reading?"

"Well, it was the beginning of a reading," he said softly, knowing that I was going to try to look at all of this from a less defiant prospective.

"If that was just the beginning then I don't think I want to do this because I'm helpless when I'm in it and I feel like I was on a bad roller coaster ride when I come out. It's not great."

"It won't always be that way," he explained. "When our gifts are developing it can be exhausting both emotionally and physically but with hard work, they become second nature. You won't always feel like that."

"You're sure I won't always feel like that?"

"You're the only one who knows what it's like to be a Reader, this is the one gift I don't have, so I can't be positive. But if it's like the other gifts then, yes, you won't always feel like that," he assured me. "Aurelious, how and when you use your gift is up to you. So if it doesn't become a part of you then you don't have to use it. Nature gives us the gift but the choice to use it is always up to the Gypsy."

It was time to start my training for real. I was ready. I was ready to find out what I could really do. I was ready to find out who I really was supposed to be. I think.

They brought packs with them into the woods filled with food, a few extra clothes, some other supplies and a tent. Brekwyn and I put on the packs and said goodbye to Anira. We would be gone for a few days.

"Train hard Aurelious," she said softly with her hand on my cheek. The touching part was something she needed to do, it was part of her tradition, I would make an effort to understand it. "The harder you train, the faster you'll develop, and the easier it will all become. Trust me I know this from firsthand experience," she smiled.

"I will," I said softly, and you know what I did? I smiled back. Okay, it was just a little one but it didn't hurt and my face didn't crack and I didn't hate it. Neither did she.

"Be well cousin," Brekwyn said to Anira and kissed her on the forehead, so they're cousins? Interesting. "Take care of our people. Danyon can find us if you need us."

"Okay," she smiled.

And off we walked into the woods, destiny awaiting us.

Chapter Twenty-Three

The sun was setting by the time we came to our destination, a small clearing by a lake. The shore was not sandy here rather it was just the end of the tree line. You could actually see some of the tree roots going into the lake while their branches hung like a canopy above the water.

"This is where we'll make camp," Brekwyn said putting down his pack. I could tell it was heavy and although it was getting cooler, it was still really warm but Brekwyn hardly broke a sweat. I on the other hand looked like I just ran a marathon.

"Have you ever set up a tent before?" Brekwyn asked.

"Uh, no. None of my foster parents were big on camping," I said looking at the tent that he was taking out of the bag. Well, it was more like a tarp and some poles.

"I'll explain to you how to do it, it's easy once you get the hang of it," Brekwyn smiled. He started giving me directions, take this pole and put it through this loop, then bend this thing and... Oh please, I was no Boy Scout.

"Dude, if I bend this anymore it's gonna break," I said, wiping the sweat from my eyes with my shoulder.

"It won't break, it's got more to give." He was so calm about this.

I could feel my face getting redder in the effort to fit pole A into freaking loop B, it was so annoying. My sweaty hand only made the job more difficult and pole A slipped out of my hand and whipped back and forth practically smacking Brekwyn in the head. It would have if he wasn't so damn agile.

Brekwyn started laughing.

"I don't see what's so funny about this," I panted when I retrieved the wildly flailing pole A.

"I apologize," he said while still snickering. "You're doing a great job."

"Yeah, really great." Imagine the sarcasm oozing out of that sentence. "I thought you were supposed to be such an awesome teacher, if this is how it's going to go with my training then we may as well quit now."

"You're right I shouldn't laugh." He was literally still laughing. I was grumbling like an angry ninety-year-old man.

"Now what?" I said really aggressively when that stupid pole A was finally in its place.

"Now take a step back and look at what you've accomplished." He wasn't laughing anymore, just smiling now and maybe gloating a little.

Huh, I actually set up a tent. Me, I did that. With barely any help from *He Who Finds My Misery So Funny*.

I turned around, wiped the dripping sweat off my forehead and smiled. But I didn't let him see it.

I set up the two sleeping bags inside and he handed me the rest of our stuff to put in. Everything we brought was stored in the tent before we set off to collect firewood from the branches and twigs on the ground around us while we still had a little light.

Brekwyn set up a circle of rocks that would be a barrier for the fire, keeping it contained to where we wanted it. I was waiting for him to bring out a lighter but, of course, he actually started rubbing two sticks together. I was instructed to watch this one. Fortunately I didn't have to participate like I did with the stupid tent.

There was a whole process with timber and gently blowing on things and smoke and blah, blah, blah, poof we had a fire. It looked easier than setting up the tent, I was pretty sure I could do that without a problem.

As the sun set we ate sandwiches that Anira packed us. I watched as the sky went from grey streaked with pink and orange to navy blue to black littered with the tiny white lights of the stars. I was peaceful. I was comfortable.

"Why don't you just fight the Inglore?" I asked out of nowhere, poking the fire with a stick.

"I'm a peaceful person Aurelious," he explained as he sat back against a log, hands linked behind his head. "If I can avoid a fight, I will."

"Are you afraid of him?"

He snorted, "No. Inglore wears his emotions on his sleeve. He's an open book. Conflicted, maybe one of the most conflicted people I've ever encountered, but easily figured out. At least he always was on the few occasions that we've run across each other. So, he doesn't frighten me."

"But isn't he more powerful than you?"

"Yes, for now."

"What do you have to do to be as powerful as him?"

"I have to tap into the darker side of myself, but I have no interest in doing that."

"Why not?"

"It's a hard place to come back from. Inglore is an example of that. I believe he lives far more in his darkness then his light. If you do that long enough, eventually the dark side takes over, and that's not a person I want to be. It's not who I want to be for myself and it's not who I want to be for my tribe. They deserve better, they deserve to live in peace and happiness."

I'm pretty sure that I lived more in my dark side than in my light. As a matter of a fact, I'm only just now seeing what light could maybe be like. Would I come back from it, would I become lighter? Or was I really destined to be more like the Inglore?

I knew he heard what I was thinking but he didn't say anything he just stared into the fire. I was the only one who could determine if I would stay like this, maybe even get worse, or if I would see a different side of things. One path would be easier than the other. I had to decide how much effort I wanted to put in. I had to decide which side felt better.

Sleep was going to be a welcome distraction. I was so tired that as soon as my head hit the pillow, I was unconscious. But my peace was short lived.

"Aurelious." I heard my name. Someone whispered it.

I opened my eyes and sat up, I was alone in the tent. Brekwyn's sleeping bag was untouched.

"Aurelious." This time it came from outside, it sounded far away.

I unzipped tent and slowly crawled out. The moon was bright and high in the sky.

"Brekwyn," I called softly.

No answer.

The embers in the fire were still glowing orange. I couldn't have been asleep that long. I made my way toward the lake, "Brekwyn," I called again.

"Aurelious." This time I heard the voice more clearly, it was a man, but it was still far away, it must be Brekwyn.

I turned and walked toward the direction of the sound.

"Brekwyn, is that you?" I said in a loud whisper.

"No." The 'no' was loud and right in my ear, so close I could feel his breath when he said it.

With my heart in my throat, I whipped around. No one was there.

"Who is that?" I yelled.

"You know." The voice said again in my other ear.

I whipped back around. No one was there.

Then I heard sickening, maniacal laughter coming from behind me. The air was heavy with a feeling of dread so I did the only thing I could think of. I ran. But the laughing didn't stop, it followed me, laughing and breathing down my neck.

"I'm gonna get you," he laughed.

I panted, running as fast as I could, stumbling over things I was too afraid to see.

"Brekwyn, help!" I yelled as I ran.

"Ha, ha, ha, what can Brekwyn do?" The voice seemed further away. I was outrunning him.

I caught a glimpse of something shining in the moonlight and I ran toward it. It was a door handle. There was a building in middle of these woods. I went inside and quickly closed the door behind me.

I slumped against the wall and desperately tried to catch my breath. There was no lock on the door, I had to move further inside and find a place to hide.

I was in a hallway; there was a light in the distance. I made no sound as I moved toward it, wiping away the dripping hair that clung to my forehead. The light blinked on and off and on again. I kept going, hugging the wall, too petrified to look back.

"Aurelious." Oh God.

I started running again. His voice came from behind me so I could only go forward. A light bulb hanging by a cord from the ceiling was casting the light I had seen when I came in. On its own it started to swing back and forth as I approached but as terrifying as that one thing was, I couldn't stop and I couldn't turn back. I flinched as I ran under it, but nothing happened except that I now could see the end of the hallway, just the end, no turns, no doors, the end.

"Uh oh, what now?" he mocked. I heard his footsteps matching mine.

I ran as hard as I could to the end of the hall, slamming myself into the wall. Maybe it would open; maybe I could break through it. But I couldn't. I pounded on it. I looked for a lever or a handle or a hinge. But there was nothing. I was trapped.

"Tsk, tsk, tsk," his footsteps stopped, "why are you so afraid?"

I could feel his breath on the back of my neck. All of the blood drained from my face, I was cold, I could feel my heart pounding in every vein in my body. I wanted to cry. I wanted to scream. I wanted to die. But I didn't, that would've been too merciful.

A cold, bony hand rested gently on my shoulder and I think my heart stopped.

"Come on," he whispered in my ear, "you know you're curious to see who I am. You can't fight your own curiosity, it's so much stronger than your will."

"I know who you are," I choked out.

"Yes, of course you do," he said. I could feel him smiling.

I straightened myself up. Inglore was determined to find me. He would stop at nothing. And now, it appears, he has succeeded. A fleeting thought ran through my head. I wondered if Brekwyn was dead. I wondered if he had to kill him in order to get to me. He laughed at my thought.

Slowly I turned around. Shock raged through my body when I looked up and stared into the fat, sweaty, smug face of my foster mother.

"Aurelious," she said. But it wasn't her voice.

"Aurelious." It was Brekwyn's voice.

"Aurelious, wake up."

Chapter Twenty-Four

I was drenched in sweat from my palpable fear and unconscious, imaginary physical exertion.

"It's not going to happen," Brekwyn said with his hand on my shoulder, having heard my dream. "Inglore is not going to get you and neither is your foster mother." He was gentle but emphatic.

He sat back on his heels to give me room to sit up, "That was a dream?" I asked, the sleep was heavy in my voice.

"Just a dream," he assured me softly.

"That was the realest dream I've ever had." I rubbed my face and head to wake up.

"That's because your subconscious mind has been activated, it'll level off," he said confidently then patted me on the knee and exited the tent, "Let's get to work!" All freakin' happy again, great.

Create a mental picture of what the next half hour is like. He is in a pair of shorts, that's it, he's strong and tanned and soaking wet from apparently swimming in the lake while I was running from my foster mother Inglore. He has prepared breakfast for both of us and is energetic and happy. I, on the other hand, can hardly straighten up when I get out of the tent because I'm so stiff from sleeping on the stupid ground, I'm pretty sure there was rock under my sleeping bag. I can actually feel my hair standing on its ends all over the place and can probably scrape the line of dry drool from the side of my mouth. And of course I'm grunting and groaning because I'm a cranky old man with brittle bones. Not great for me, not great.

Then let's add this little gem that happens while I'm eating my breakfast hunched over like a cave man. He walked away when he heard a tiny crunching sound of some creature foraging through the dead, dried leaves on the ground. I'm watching him as he and a squirrel stood facing each other just looking at each other. It was like one of the weirdest things I had ever seen. When was the last time you saw a squirrel engaging in a staring contest with a human man? Exactly. Never.

"Brekwyn, what is going on with the squirrel?" I practically shouted when their actions were freaking me out enough to want to interrupt. If I didn't covet food the way I did I would've thrown my bread on the ground in exacerbation. The creepy little squirrel looked at me and then back at Brekwyn before running away.

"He's keeping an eye on the woods for us. Letting me know if anyone's around," he said like that was a normal thing to do. He ran his fingers through his hair to shake off some of the excess water.

"He just told you that?"

"Not in words so much as pictures I guess you could say."

"That little squirrel is our lookout," I said it out loud to try to make it seem reasonable to my brain. "What's he on the look-out for? The Inglore or his people?"

"He's just keeping me informed about anything that's going on around us that I can't see." Right.

He sat down across from me, "Each Reader has their own in-dividual process for what they do, that information is theirs alone for their safety." Oh, so we're just forgetting that whole squirrel thing and jumping right into the training? Great. I guess that's the way things work in Crazy Town. He laughed at my thoughts and kept talking, I rolled my eyes because he in-vaded my own private sarcasm. "What they can see, how far ahead they can travel, all of these details are Reader specific. You will keep that knowledge to yourself so it cannot be manipulated by anyone whose intentions are less than admirable.

"But before you go any further in your training you must promise me that you will go at the pace I tell you to go at and never, until you are extremely well practiced which is a long time from now, never use your gift when you're in the Gadje world."

"Why not?"

"That's where you're most vulnerable. Here we can protect you, but out there, who knows who's lurking out there." He looked off into the distance and I understood what he meant.

"Alright, I won't use it there." At least not for now.

"When you're in a reading, you have a few minutes of sight, as far as anyone knows, not hours or days so it's not like predicting the future. You know that you can change a course of a person's actions but you don't do that until you're out of your reading, like you did with Anira and the knife. Do you understand this?" he asked as we stood up and started wandering aimlessly.

"Like if I saw someone cross the street and get hit by a car I could tell them to wait on the sidewalk for a minute until that car passes them safely." Kind of a morbid example but it was the best I could come up with on such short notice.

"Yes, that's exactly what it's like. Although it is an amazing thing to be able to do, preventing accidents is not the sole purpose of your gift simply because a person couldn't live like that and it doesn't help people like you think it would. Just using it for that purpose changes not only you but also the people around you.

"Think about it. If someone knew that you could tell them when they were going to fall or drop a dish or get hit by a car then they would become so dependent on you, on being around you. They would stop living freely like they do now and look to you for validation for their every move. Should they light this candle, should they walk this path, should they say this thing, should they eat this spoonful of food? It would become a prison for everyone who knows you."

"So what's the purpose of this gift then?" I asked stubbing my toe on a tree root I didn't see, for the thousandth time.

"You'll still help people Aurelious, but with bigger issues, ones that face mankind and the planet."

"So now I'm Superman?" I mumbled.

He smiled, "Contrary to what you may believe, the Earth is suffering terribly and that suffering is at the hands of the Gadje. Not all Gadje of course, some are quite conscious of their care for the Earth but they unfortunately are in the minority. Gadje are busy keeping up or trying to get ahead, they're surviving and sometimes they do what's easy and quick, though bad for the Earth, just because they're otherwise occupied with living the life they created. We don't believe they're consciously destroying the world we live in but rather the destruction is a consequence of their need for convenience. Life is fleeting and if things don't get significantly worse in their lifetime then it isn't theirs to worry about. There appears to be little consideration for who comes next, who inherits the Earth after we're gone."

"Instant gratification."

"Yes," he smiled at me, "but there's one thing that the Gadje don't seem to realize. It seems that most of them are taking the Earth for granted. You see, as people, we need the Earth to survive but the Earth doesn't need us for her survival as a matter of fact she'd probably be healthier without people. We take and take and take, and the Earth gives and gives and gives. At some point we do have to give a little back."

"The Gadje need to be educated."

"Maybe you'll be the one to educate them."

Maybe, I thought. But how am I supposed to educate you all about this? Do you have any ideas?

"That's where your gift comes into play. You will help us plant the seeds of ideas in their minds that will change the way they use this planet and all of her resources."

"That seems like a huge task."

"It is," he smiled, "baby steps, Aurelious, baby steps."

"And Inglore doesn't want the same thing?"

"Well, certainly he wants the Gadje to stop destroying the Earth for sure. He just wants to go about it in a different way." Right the slavery thing.

As we walked I noticed that he never stumbled or stubbed his bare feet on anything then I looked a little closer and saw that the small rocks in his path rolled away as he approached. Fallen pinecones rolled away. Sticks rolled away. Never did he step on anything that could hurt his foot.

"Uh, are you moving all of those things out of your path with your mind?" I asked, so distracted by this phenomena that I couldn't possibly concentrate on any more of the environment conversation.

"Of course," he said like it was no big deal.

Oh, oh ok. Yeah sure. Totally. Of course. Normal, normal, normal.

Chapter Twenty-Five

We sat under some trees to begin a "listening exercise" as Brekwyn called it. This was going to be like yesterday when I listened to sound of the birds. The purpose of this, as he explained it, was to learn what it feels like to get into a reading and, once in there, to let my mind get deeper and deeper, to read more and more. This wasn't about seeing what would happen before it happens, it was just about continuing to change my state of mind.

"I want you to listen to the lake, go deep inside and let your mind see what your eyes cannot. Close your eyes and just relax."

At first I couldn't really pick out the sound of the lake from the other sounds around me. It wasn't a particularly windy day so the lake was relatively calm. I listened and I listened but couldn't find it.

"Clear your mind Aurelious. Your goal is to listen to the lake so push all of the other sounds aside."

I listened again. I could hear the sound of an animal rummaging through the dead leaves on the forest floor so I pictured that image and then saw myself putting that image somewhere else, moving it aside. I could hear a few leaves rustling above my head so I pictured the movement of those leaves and put that image aside. Things were getting quieter. I heard Brekwyn's breathing so I moved it aside. I heard my own breathing so I moved it aside. Now I could dimly hear the sound of water. It was a faint lapping sound. I could tell that it was the subtle movement of the water as it rolled against the shoreline. In a different place I could hear it hitting the large, curling roots of tree. I could hear movement in the water. It was some kind of water animal, gently paddling its little arms and legs kind of lazily going nowhere in particular. A turtle maybe? I could hear bubbles popping on the surface of the lake, there were fish just below, the gulps of water through their gills sending up bubbles to the surface, their darting movements making subtle changes in the current.

"Aurelious," Brekwyn was saying gently, I don't know if it was the first time he said it or if he had been saying it for five minutes. I opened my eyes and looked at him. He was smiling at me, I was exhausted. "You did really well my friend. Take some time to rest here now, we can continue with more work when you have gotten some sleep."

I didn't argue with that, I didn't say anything at all. I just closed my eyes again, and I slept and dreamt of nothing.

When I woke up about an hour later, Brekwyn and I resumed our walk until we came to a clearing where there was an opening in the canopy of trees, a small opening where you could clearly see the bright blue sky. We sat again and this time Brekwyn had me listen to the sky above us. It was easier to clear my mind now that I discovered how to take away the other noises. It's a peaceful place to be, this place of listening, it felt like I was kind of floating around the world, not really being a part of it, just an observer. A more efficient version of the person I had always been.

When I came out of it I was tired again.

"Why am I so tired?" I asked Brekwyn when he called me out of wherever I was.

"You're using a strength and ability that you have never used before. It's an activity in your mind but it is still just like the most intense physical workout you could do. Like physical strength, you need to continue your training to get in shape, eventually it will become easier and this tiredness will be but a distant memory," he explained.

Instead of sleeping again, we had some lunch that we brought with us and I felt refreshed and more awake when we finished. We were pretty far from our camp now so we started to walk back. When we got there, I was instructed to listen again. This time I was to listen to a small chipmunk that was digging just outside of our campsite. I wasn't listening to its thoughts just its sounds and the sounds that it created with its actions.

This made for three listening experiences in one day. You would think that just sitting down listening would be easy, kind of a lazy experience. But that intense concentration had taken so much out of me and left me totally exhausted. I could not stay awake for dinner or conversation, as much as I wanted to talk to Brekwyn and learn more about the world I was in. Sleep was just banging on my head. When Brekwyn called me out he could see that I was at my limit, he only said that I had done well, better than he could have thought, as I crawled into the tent and fell asleep.

By the way, I used the watch. Each time I went in it felt like only minutes but each time was at least an hour, sometimes more. You can't imagine how disturbing that is.

Chapter Twenty-Six

I woke up in the middle of the night and looked over to Brekwyn's sleeping bag, he wasn't there. I thought I heard him talking outside of the tent. I fell back to sleep. Did I dream that?

I felt different in the morning. My head hurt, my brain hurt. I felt like I was in a fog. Something wasn't right.

When I unzipped the tent I felt even stranger. There was a thick fog rolling off the lake and rising into the air like smoke as it crept along the forest floor. I could see the lake and the forest around me but not nearly as far as I could yesterday. It was as if the weather was a reflection of what it felt like in my head. Where was Brekwyn?

I stood in front of the tent I just came out of. I didn't move my body, just my head and my eyes looking for Brekwyn. Then I started to feel it. It was a feeling I had before, when did I feel like this? Oh, right, the night when the Inglore's messengers came. It was that ominous feeling. There was danger here.

I wanted to move, go somewhere else, but I couldn't think. I couldn't think about where to go. I felt like my brain and my body were barely awake. Every part of me felt like it was moving through thick mud. The danger in the air was getting heavier, just as the fog was. I had to get out of here, but how do I do that?

I saw some movement off to my right. I turned my head slowly because it just wouldn't move any faster. I wasn't sure what the movement was because the fog seemed to be getting thicker. As the movement grew closer I saw the shape of a person.

Closer, I could see the black hair. Closer, it was Brekwyn. He was running.

I went to open my mouth to speak but he put his finger to his lips, silently telling me to say nothing as he ran toward me. I could hardly hear any noise from him. I focused and realized that it was very silent in the forest. Not a sound from any animal or leaf, no breeze, no movement on the lake.

Brekwyn was by my side. He leaned over to whisper in my ear, "Follow me."

I did. We ran, being near him made my body work but not my brain. I couldn't think I could only follow.

We ran as fast as we could through the angry terrain of the woods. Low hanging branches desperately swatted at my head as we ran by, trying to knock me off course. Rocks and fallen limbs rose up from the ground daring me to trip over them and slow our pace. Ditches filled with decades of season changes tried to trick us into being swallowed up. But we persevered we ran and ran.

I was out of breath and sweating. Every muscle screamed and burned in my effort to keep up with Brekwyn. My heart raced faster than my feet could. The only thing that stayed dormant was my brain. I couldn't even ask what was happening because I simply couldn't think.

We stopped, finally, and Brekwyn pulled me over to a grouping of huge rocks. They seemed to come up out of the lake. We went behind them and between them. The rocks started to feel like walls. They were closing in around us as we went further in, they weren't physically moving but the formation was getting steeper, tighter, and higher around us. Then I noticed the wind. It started as a breeze but quickly escalated. It whipped through the walls of the rocks. I looked up to see leaves flying above us at a great speed. I could see the fog moving like someone from the direction that we came from was blowing it away. I felt Brekwyn pull my arm and we started to run again. I still couldn't think but I could feel. The danger was getting closer.

Brekwyn, ahead of me, turned to the left and disappeared. I

didn't panic I just followed. I turned left and I disappeared. There was an opening to a cave within the rocks. We went in further, we were walking again. We stopped deeper inside the cave, far enough that we couldn't see the opening anymore.

"Don't move," Brekwyn whispered so softly I could hardly hear him. It was so dark that I could barely see my own hand until my eyes adjusted. Even then it was difficult to see Brekwyn who was standing right next to me.

But I could see the fog. It was still all around us and it was still quiet, except for the wind. The wind got louder. I could hear it whistling through the halls of rock that we came through. I could hear it roaring up above. That threat in the air was crushing, it felt hot, it felt heavy, and it felt familiar. I dreamt of this danger the other night. Only now I wasn't dreaming, now I was being chased in real life. Now, if I wanted to, I could give in to my curiosity and find out who it was that was taunting my subconscious. My curiosity always won.

Chapter Twenty-Seven

Without thinking I moved past Brekwyn toward the opening of the cave. He was out there, just beyond the walls of rock. My movement was silent and quick. The wind grew even stronger as I got closer to the entrance. It was getting lighter I was getting close. I could feel the wind and the danger. He was right out there.

Then, a hand grabbed my elbow and pulled me, hard, back toward the darkness. I tried to struggle but my brain forgot how and gave in. We didn't move once back deep inside the cave, didn't make a sound. I don't know how much time passed. The sound of the wind became almost deafening I could feel the rock trembling above, below and around me. And then it grew quieter, calmer. Slowly the wind died down. Then there was nothing but silence again.

I looked over to Brekwyn. He was standing so still with his head up. His eyes were closed. I just watched him and waited. I looked down at my arm and noticed that he was still holding onto me. I looked back up at his face again. His eyes were open now.

The fog around us started to disappear. My head started to clear, slowly. We walked out of the cave and I could see the sun shining above the rocks. We went back in the direction that we came from through the rock until we were in the forest once again. I could hear the sounds of nature around us that were missing before. I could hear the birds and the movement of the lake. I could hear the sound of animals going about their normal routine of hunting for food and shelter.

The longer we walked, the clearer my brain became. I was able to start to think, with each step I was able to think more. And the more I was able to think, the more my heart rate increased, the redder my cheeks got, the more nauseous my stomach became.

When my brain was finally clear, I stopped dead in my tracks, "Brekwyn," I said, practically yelling. "What the hell was that?"

He took a deep breath and looked at me, he didn't look like his normal happy self, instead he looked worried, "That was Inglore."

Oh shit.

He started pacing back and forth. It looked like he was fighting his own anger. He clenched and unclenched his fists. He pointed at me as if he was going to say something but then put his finger down and kept pacing. This wasn't good. He took another deep breath, then another. Then he stopped pacing and took another deep breath. He turned to me and with what appeared to be great self-restraint he calmly and quietly said, "Aurelious, when I ask you to stay where you are it is for your own safety. In the future, if I were to ask you to stay where you are another time, please do so."

Oh, right, I started to walk out of the cave. Oh right I left the roof of the trailer the night the messengers came. Oh right I left the safety of the underground world that same night. Oh, right.

I raised my eyebrows and cocked my head to the side, then crouched down to untie and tie my shoelaces, "Sorry," I said without looking at him, I would have to remember to try to do that next time.

"It's okay," he sighed and was genuinely calmer. "Fortunately you're safe. Let's move on."

"Wait a minute, if he was so close to me, why didn't he find me?" He should have been able to hear me, right? Though, after experiencing the intensity of that wind, I'll be honest, I was glad he didn't find me.

"The fog," he said as he picked up a stick and started to break it into small pieces. "The foggy feeling that you had in your head was me blocking all the noise that your thoughts make. I tried to slow your thought processes and put a kind of barrier in there so that he couldn't hear you. It worked. The fog out here just slowed them down since they don't know these woods. It left us some time to get a bit of a head start." He threw the last piece of stick into the lake.

I should've been mad. Up until that minute, every time he was rooting around in my head and Anira was rooting around in my feelings, I was seriously annoyed by the violation. But today, just today, I was glad for it.

Before this morning, I wondered if maybe I was more like the Inglore. Before this morning, I wondered if maybe it was him that I belonged with not Brekwyn. But what I felt in that wind, the power, that peril, it was scary. Scarier than any foster family I had been with, scarier than wondering when my next meal would come, scarier than going to a new school again and being bullied for being the weird foster kid with the ridiculous name before being forgotten, again. This was a kind of scary that I just wasn't brave enough for, no matter how much I pretended I was and no matter what my curiosity thought.

That was the moment that I made up my mind to stay here, to learn this new way of life from these people. To allow myself to take part in happiness, glimpses of it at first but maybe real happiness in the future. The kind of bad that I felt that morning was not the kind of bad I wanted to live. Not anymore.

Chapter Twenty-Eight

We got back to what was left of our campsite and surveyed the damage. The tent had been ripped to shreds and our clothes and sleeping bags were strewn everywhere. The food was trampled. It looked like a tornado or a herd of wild horses had just run through there.

We gathered our belongings putting what had become garbage in one pile and what was still salvageable in another. While we cleaned up, Brekwyn set about explaining what I had missed while I slept.

"During the night someone from our family came to me to tell me that Telera and Megana foresaw the coming of the Inglore, that he would come today himself to look for you. Regardless of what I told his messengers the other night, he knows that you're here. He is not a stupid man. It's dangerous when he's this close to you because just as I can hear your thoughts right now, so can he. Which is why I had to do the fog." Brekwyn's thoughts were deep, he was even frowning just slightly, I could see it in the tightness of his forehead.

"Anira?" I sat up straight, panic ripping through my chest at the thought of her being hurt by that psychopath, followed immediately by panic about why I was panicking over her in the first place.

Brekwyn put his hand up to calm me, "They're safe, they went underground."

"All of them? Like the whole tribe?"

"Everyone is safe, they have all gone underground. When I

found out about Inglore during the night, I went back to our village. Everyone was already preparing to leave by the time I got there. I went with them to make sure they all got to safety before getting back here. Good fortune got me back here in time, before Inglore and his people."

That was what had concerned him. That was the tension I saw for the first time in his face. He was afraid he wouldn't be here in time to protect me. But he had gotten back. He saved me again.

I frowned, looking out over the lake. I crossed my arms over my chest, thought for a moment, then took a deep breath and did something completely unnatural for me. I put my hand on his shoulder and said, "Thank you Brekwyn."

He looked at me, I saw some of the tension release from his forehead, and he smiled again that calm, peaceful smile.

We sat for a minute in silence, allowing our bodies to decompress. But we could only have a minute because our mission for me to understand who I was and whatever the hell I was supposed to do just got way more important.

"Aurelious, it's imperative to continue on with your training. Inglore will be back at some point," he stood up, stretched his arms and took a deep breath. He smiled down at me.

"Our family is staying underground today. Tomorrow we'll meet them back at the village. I imagine we'll have a lot of cleaning up to do." He laughed a small laugh, an attempt to make light of the situation so I stayed focused more on my training then what may have happened at the village.

Our food supplies were destroyed but when you're with Brekwyn that doesn't really matter. As my greedy stomach growled, not caring at all about the events of the morning, Brekwyn took a seed from his pocket. Crouching over an area that he cleared of debris, he waved his hand over the dirt creating a small hole into which he dropped the seed then with a similar wave, covered the dirt back over it. He kept his hand hovered over the area and right in front of my eyes a tiny green stem poked out of the ground. He kept his hand in the same position but raised it up higher and higher as the stem grew into a vine, sprouting leaves and yellow flowers. Then as I watched just below one of the flowers, the vine started to swell and swell until, within a minute of planting the seed from his pocket, he stood in front of me with a fully ripened cantaloupe.

It's good to know Brewkyn.

"So, you have a really great understanding of how to listen, now let's practice getting out on your own, without someone calling you out," he said after we finished the juiciest, sweetest melon I had ever tasted. "Close your eyes and choose what you'll focus on." I chose a bird in a nest to the right of us.

"Listen to my voice and start to focus on your target."

I pushed aside the sounds of the lake and the breeze, I pushed aside the squirrels chasing each other up a tree but I kept the bird and I kept his voice. He kept talking and I could hear him but I couldn't really understand his words. I could just hear his voice. The sound of the bird got stronger, louder. His voice was getting softer. I could hear the creaking of the twigs in the nest as the bird shifted its position. Now something was missing, I couldn't hear Brekwyn anymore. I looked up at the bird in my mind and then let it fade, I had to go and find his voice again. The bird faded and faded and I heard him again, softly then louder, I could almost not hear the bird it was so faint. I could hear the lake again and the breeze. I could hear Brekwyn loud and clear, I was back. I opened my eyes. He was smiling at me.

"You did it. How do you feel?" he asked.

"Good. I don't feel tired like I did yesterday. Maybe a little disoriented like waking up from a power nap or something. But I feel okay."

We didn't waste any time with resting today, instead we moved right along. I focused on the bird once more, my goal was not to lose Brekwyn at all. I had to find the line between getting fully immersed, cut off from my physical surroundings, and being in far enough to listen to the bird while still being a part of everything else around me.

I got in quickly. Pushing away the other sounds was easy now as I pictured myself actually moving the sounds away with my hands like they were an object I could touch. The bird was where I left it but its breathing was different now and there was no creaking of the nest, no movement. It had fallen asleep. I could hear Brekwyn but still could not understand what he was saying. His voice was like a murmur but if I focused too much on not understanding his words, then his voice would get louder and the sound of the bird would get quieter. I went back a little further to the bird, checking in with the murmur of Brekwyn's voice with each mental step that I took toward it. The steady breathing of the bird grew louder and louder and for a moment I lost Brekwyn's voice. I stepped back and found it again, it was faint but it was there. It was calm and even like the bird. This was the line that I could not cross. I had one foot in reality and one foot in my mind.

I stayed there, memorizing the feeling. The bird moved. A muscle twitch maybe? It moved again, this time it seemed more startled. It stood up in its nest. I could hear the twigs and leaves move ever so slightly with the birds change in position. I could hear it ruffle its feathers. I could still hear Brekwyn. It stretched its wings and crouched before pushing out of the nest and into the air. The bird was gone but I could still focus on where it was. The nest settled back into place. I went back to Brekwyn.

Opening my eyes, I had to blink from the brightness of the sun. It had gotten so much brighter than it was before. My eyes watered a little bit at the sting of the light.

"I found it, I found my place, the line that I can't cross on my own," I'll admit, I was proud of what I had accomplished. I knew that when I was alone I could not cross that line because I wouldn't be able to get back, I'd be lost inside my head. With Brekwyn I would always be safe, he would get me out, but I couldn't put that burden on him, I couldn't rely on him forever, I had to be able use my gift on my own.

He patted me on the back and put his arm around my shoulder, "Soon you'll know more about being a Reader than I do. You're going to be extraordinary."

I smiled at the uniqueness of receiving and accepting a compliment. It was kind of awesome. "You didn't sleep at all last night," I pointed out, thinking all of sudden that he must be pretty tired.

"No, there were more important things than sleep." He ran his fingers through his hair and then scratched the back of his neck.

"You can get some rest for a little while if you want, I can just practice." I was anxious to get back to that line that I found.

"It's better if you don't go into a reading on your own right now," he said stretching his arms. I knew he was tired. "You've only tested your line once. You need more practice then that before I can let you go on your own."

"Yeah, I get it," I said making a conscious effort to think only of Brekwyn taking a nap. "I'll just hang out here then, you go ahead and sleep."

"Maybe just an hour," he said looking around for a place to lie down. "You sure you feel comfortable?"

"Yeah, no problem. I haven't been alone in a while so it's a good time for me to think. Especially since you'll be sleeping and not listening to my thoughts," I said, half joking. Look at me, thinking of other people and making polite conversation.

"Well then, if you need me, just wake me up, I don't need too much sleep." He headed over to a sunny spot where he could lay in the leaves and moss. I sat on the bank of the lake and tried not to think about doing a reading.

Until I looked over and saw Brekwyn's breathing, it was even and slow. His face was relaxed. He was asleep and mentally I was out of there.

Chapter Twenty-Nine

I knew about the line I couldn't cross. I knew how it felt. He would never know that I was in a reading if he was sleeping. I just had to make sure I got out before he woke up. I looked around for my target.

There was a lazy reed sticking out of the water, gently dancing back and forth with the current. I decided to focus on that in my mind. Now I needed to find something on the outside to focus on. I wouldn't be listening to Brekwyn's voice, so what was my reality going to be? I looked around. There was nothing in nature that was constant like his voice was. A breeze blew but it stopped. A squirrel jumped from one tree branch to another but then continued on and went away. I came to the conclusion that the only constant thing was me. What part of myself could I focus on?

It didn't make sense for me to talk or hum or make noise. If I was really going to be great at this, I should be able to do it without anyone knowing that I was doing anything at all. Maybe they would know if they really concentrated on me or if they knew me really well and saw a change in behavior. But everyone shouldn't know and seeing some kid staring into space mumbling constantly would probably be pretty obvious.

Breathing. Everyone did it so it wouldn't make me stand out. I could hear it if I really listened. I had to block out my breathing yesterday so that I could concentrate on listening to the lake. This was the only possibility, the only thing that made sense. My breath would have to keep me in reality.

I inhaled really deeply. The air was so clean here. I could practically smell the sunlight. I could feel the oxygen coursing through every cell in my body. I breathed deeply again. I felt myself getting lighter and the sound of my breath getting louder in my ears. I started to look for the reed. I pushed aside the birds and lapping of the water. Breathe. I could even hear the sounds of Brekwyn's breathing so I pushed it aside. My own breath was the one I had to hear. I went toward the reed in my mind. Breathe. The reed twisted back and forth, its thin green leaves vibrating in the air around it. Breathe. A click, something landed on the reed and made a new noise, a dragonfly. Breathe. The reed bent down from the weight of the insect. It got closer to the water. Breathe. Plink, the tip of it touched the water and then sprung back up as the dragonfly flew away. I could hear the drip of water tossed off the end of the reed as it sprung back and forth, regaining its height now that its brief tenant was gone. Breathe. Silence, the reed was still, it was calm, waiting for the next breeze to make it dance. My breathing got louder, the reed more distant. But I wasn't done with this yet, I wanted to hear more than the reed.

Brekwyn, the perfect unsuspecting subject. I found his breath, it was easily recognizable since I had just put it away. It was even and smooth, he was still sleeping. I imagined his head in my mind. Breathe. What was he dreaming about? Breathe. But I didn't know how to get inside his head. I stayed there mentally staring at him, listening for something. But there was nothing, no sound other than the sound of his breath. This was pointless.

I decided to let other sounds back in. The first one was a small creature, a chipmunk maybe. I could tell it was small by the sound of its movements. They were jerky and quick. What if I tried to listen to that creature? Did I have some more time? Brekwyn's slow, even breathing suggested I did so I filed it away and focused only on the chipmunk. How far could I follow it?

Its direction was a little erratic. I could hear its tiny feet hitting the earth. Breathe Aurelious. It was bounding away from or toward something. It stopped, I could hear its heart beating, it was so fast. Off it went again. I knew I was getting further and further away from where we were. I felt like I could see this creature in my mind as well as its surroundings just from listening to it.

Should I stay with it?

It was running faster, anxious to get to its destination. It stopped again. I could hear the fur on its neck move as it turned its head from side to side. It was looking for something, or listening. Breathe. It started to run again and then changed its direction to head more toward the lake. It stopped again, its heart racing.

I wondered where it was and how far we had gone from where my body was. I decided to let in some of the sounds around it to see if I could figure out where we were. One by one. Breathe. I expanded my range of understanding from just the animal to the area around it. Breathe. Leaves. Breathe. Lake. Breathe. But there was something else too. Breathe. What was it? I moved toward that something else in my mind. Breathe. I got closer. That something else got louder. Breathe. And then I understood what that other sound was. Breathe. It was the murmur of a voice. Breathe. Someone else was here.

Chapter Thirty

I freaked out and lost my focus. My reality came screaming back to me. It was not a gentle progression out. I felt like I was slammed in the stomach. It took my breath away. I staggered to my feet but I couldn't see, the sunlight was so bright. Water flooded my eyes. I steadied myself on a tree, blinking and squinting to let my eyes adjust. Brekwyn was coming toward me. He felt my reaction in his sleep.

"What's the matter Aurelious?" By now he was by my side.

"Someone's here Brekwyn. I heard them. I was following a chipmunk or something to see how far away from myself I could hear and when it stopped I listened around it and I heard a male voice." My eyes had adjusted and I frantically looked around us.

"What do you mean you were following a chipmunk?" He looked confused and annoyed.

I was busted. There was no way around it, I wasn't supposed to do this and I did, as soon as he was asleep I defied him.

He didn't wait for me to answer, "Aurelious, do you not understand the danger you're in?" He ran his hands through his hair and started pacing again, this was twice in one day. "I was asleep, someone could have been here and you wouldn't have even noticed, you were completely defenseless." Then it dawned on him and again on me, the reason I woke us both up was that someone was here.

I saw it register on his face. He'd have to deal with my inability to follow instructions and my apparent need to put myself in danger another time. For now we had to find out who was in these woods with us.

"Did you hear what he was saying?" Brekwyn wasn't in a panic but he was taking me very seriously.

"No, I couldn't make out any words or hear who he was talking to."

"Do you know where he is?"

I pointed in the direction that I knew the chipmunk had traveled. "He's that way, closer to the lake."

"Well, let's not just stay here. Let's go find out who our neighbor is?" Was that a sparkle in his eye, like he was excited for an adventure?

"What if it's the Inglore or his men?" I asked.

"We have to find out what we're up against, if anything." He started to jog in the direction that I pointed to. Here we go. "Okay Aurelious, you followed the sound so you lead the way."

I wasn't a tracker but it wasn't too hard. I knew which direction we had to go in and that he was somewhere closer to the lake rather than deeper into the middle of the woods. We jogged for a few minutes until I felt we might be close to where I heard the chipmunk stop. We slowed to a walk to keep ourselves quiet. I heard something so I stopped.

I put my finger over my mouth to signal to Brekwyn that we shouldn't talk but listen instead. I heard noises though I couldn't figure out from here what the noises were. We moved closer, slower. There was a clearing up ahead. I turned to Brekwyn who was just behind me, I pointed to indicate that whoever was here was right ahead in that clearing. Was that a smirk on his face?

We moved up behind a large tree, now I was starting to worry. What if this was a mistake? We didn't have any weapons or anything to defend ourselves. I certainly couldn't *listen* anyone to death there was no fighting skill in that. Brekwyn would probably have a few tricks up his sleeve. This was it, the moment of truth. It was time to face whatever was there. For a second I thought about turning back but I couldn't, not now that my curiosity was engaged and basically slamming its fists on the inside of my head to keep going forward. So I moved my head around the tree and looked.

Chapter Thirty-One

It was a boy about my age, obviously a Gypsy. He was wearing orange pants that were wide in the leg and came just below his knees. They had a drawstring waist, like pants that I wore to the festival and like Tanent wore the day I met him. He wasn't wearing a shirt or shoes. He wore a gold coin on a cord for a necklace and he had anklets on each ankle made of the same cord. He had some around his wrist too, mixed with other bracelets mostly made of thin metals. The reflection of the sunlight revealed a coin that was woven into his hair on the side of his head facing us, behind and below his ear. He was lying in the grass with his eyes closed resting his head on a black dog that was staring straight at us.

As I stood there looking at him, he started to laugh.

"You can come here," he said. "You don't have to hide behind the tree." He still had his eyes closed.

I recognized the voice.

Brekwyn laughed, patted me on the shoulder and walked past me toward the boy. "Your friends make it impossible to sneak up on you," he said to him.

He stood up to meet us. "That and because you aren't exactly quiet when you're running through the forest. You sounded like two horses." He and Brekwyn laughed and hugged each other, ugh more laughing and hugging.

"This is a very hard person for us to take by surprise, especially in a forest. Aurelious this is Danyon."

The Narc.

"Yeah, I recognized the voice," I said, not really interested in hanging out with this kid.

He smiled and laughed, "I recognized your face." Was he making a joke?

"I had no idea what your face looked like since I never actually saw it." I crossed my arms over my chest.

"But I met you twice already."

"In the pitch black. I wasn't wearing night vision goggles." I looked away from him.

"I have no idea what night vision goggles are," he replied turning toward Brekwyn with a shrug.

"They help you see at night, Gadje wear them sometimes when they're doing surveillance in the dark," Brekwyn explained.

"Hmm, weird." He seemed like he could care less but I only know this because I was looking at his reaction to my sarcasm out of the corner of my eye. I was curious to see if I was getting to him while trying to seem like I wasn't.

"So where are your friends that told you we were coming?" I asked looking around and not seeing anyone else around us. Which of course meant nothing. They could've been hiding in some Gypsy camouflage.

He looked around, "Um, there's one." He pointed to a bird flying overhead.

"Are you serious?" I asked in a way that exuded disbelief.

"Yes," he said again assuming that this was normal and something that actually happened in the real world.

"So you can communicate with animals?"

"I can." He squinted when he looked at me, trying to understand why I was being such an asshole.

"Well it must be like a regular Narnia around here for you then." I smirked at my own sarcasm which I was sure was going to go right over his head.

He laughed, "Pretty much."

I guess I was wrong about that going over his head, "You know what I'm talking about?"

"Of course, I do know how to read," he said, making an effort to throw some sarcasm back at me.

I looked at Brekwyn who didn't look too pleased with the way I was treating Danyon but stayed silent for the moment, "So you're allowed to read things that aren't written by Gypsies?"

He nodded his head before Danyon jumped in and said, "Who said C.S. Lewis wasn't a Gypsy?"

Then it was his turn to smirk, and walk away with his dog before I got the chance to respond. Damn it with this kid. Who did he think he was always walking away? That's what I was supposed to do.

Frustration boiled under my skin. Brekwyn took a deep breath, again, probably thinking at this point that he should have left me back with the Gadje. I wondered if he liked Danyon better than me.

I would have to figure out what to do about Danyon.

Chapter Thirty-Two

Danyon's dog, who I now recognized as the one who attacked me my first day here, walked beside him toward the lake. He rested his finger tips on her head as they walked but neither of them seemed to notice that he was doing it. I heard him call her Poppy and then have what looked like a silent conversation with her. This animal communication thing was really weird. I mean, yeah, everything was really weird but this was really, really weird.

"Maybe while you're here Danyon, you can help Aurelious with his training," Brekwyn called behind him.

"Sure, what would I do, I've never even met a Reader?" He was excited and started bouncing. Not really bouncing, maybe that's an exaggeration, but moving around for sure. Enough that Poppy started wagging her tail hard enough to move her whole body.

"Go about your normal business, Aurelious just needs someone to focus on." Brekwyn turned to me, "You're getting into your mind so much faster but you need to practice getting out quicker without getting hurt like you did before. And it's time to take the next step. You know how to be in a different reality, based on your listening exercises, but it's time to push yourself and go further. It's time to start to see, it's time to start to read. Are you ready for that?"

I smirked, "Yeah, I'm ready." And I was, I mean, if Danyon was going to do something cool like talk to animals then I was going to do something even cooler like, well, whatever it is I'm supposed to be able to do. But it better be better than what

Danyon can do.

"Aurelious, most of what you do from this point forward is up to you. You'll have to figure out how your gift works, I can't tell you exactly how it feels or what to do." My gift was definitely better than Danyon's if I was the only one who could do it, I snorted, and then refocused when I remembered that Brekwyn could hear my thoughts, as evidenced by his deep sigh and shoulder slump. "All I know for sure is that you have to push yourself and it will literally be like a physical push, somehow when you're in your listening phase, force yourself to move forward. Then we'll take it from there." He looked away, thinking, and then looked back at me and said, "I remember something that my mother wrote down about the Reader. She said that the Reader must open his eyes. Maybe that'll help you."

I guess it was good to be the only one who could do this, but the downside is that no one could really tell me what to do. Of course, I've been taking care of myself in some way my whole life so maybe all of that prepared me for this. I wasn't afraid to go at it alone, as long as I knew I could get back. I looked at Brekwyn when I thought that.

He smiled softly, cocked his head to the side, and said, "I won't leave you in there. I'll make sure you get back out." I believed him.

Danyon was off playing with Poppy and I found a tree to sit under. It was time to do this thing.

Chapter Thirty-Three

I pretty much thought I was a genius at the listening by now. It didn't matter that I'd been doing it for only a couple of days, I was pretty confident in my ability to do that. But the thing is, technically that wasn't my gift. I had to push myself further if I wanted to access the actual, alleged, gift. And, motivated by wanting to be better than Danyon, I was all hyped up and ready to push myself.

I watched Danyon for a while. I noticed the way he interacted with Poppy. They had a bond that would be evident to anyone, even someone that wasn't as observant as I was. If he wasn't so annoying, I think he would probably be kind of fun to be around. He was energetic and seemed to be a happy person. Maybe that's what made him annoying. Oh, forget it. Let's see what this kid was going to do before he does it. Or, whatever.

I was totally in the zone and listening only to him within maybe ten seconds of starting my process. I mentally patted myself on the back about my ability. So here we were, just me and Danyon. I heard him throw a stick into the water, the air around him moving as he did. I heard the bracelets on his wrist jingle as his arm moved. Breathe. I listened harder. I could hear his feet sink into the sandy mud just below the surface of the water, I could hear a spray of water as it hit his back, was this Poppy shaking the excess off her fur onto him? Breathe. I listened harder. He laughed and I could hear his lungs contract and expand as he did. He was throwing the stick again, I knew this not only because of the sound of his bracelets but because I could hear the muscles in his back and stomach and arms changing with each millimeter of movement. I could hear inside his body. But I needed to go further. I needed to go forward. I pushed. I concentrated. I willed myself to go further.

Then, there was a rush around me. There was a blur. It was fast like I was being pushed from somewhere. I could not hear my breath anymore and I didn't want to go find it, I wanted to find out what just happened. Then I remembered what Brewkyn's mother wrote and, in my mind, I opened my eyes. There was a haze around the edges of my field of vision but I could see clearly. There was no sting from the sunlight, no need to take time to adjust, I could just see. But when I listened I heard nothing and it didn't matter.

Poppy was rolling in the grass, she got there so quickly because just a second ago, Danyon was throwing the stick into the water for her to fetch it. Where was Danyon? He wasn't at the water's edge where I saw him before I started all of this. I looked around and saw him over by a tree looking up into it. How did he get there so quickly? He didn't, I realized. He wasn't there yet, I was. That rush I had felt was time flying by.

I focused on him. He was talking to a squirrel in the tree. I didn't know what he was saying I just knew that he was talking to it. He turned and looked off to his right. I followed his gaze. He was looking at Brekwyn. Brekwyn was looking at me. His hands were on his hips and he looked worried.

"Breathe Aurelious," Brekwyn was saying to me, he wanted me to go back. "Breathe," he said again. But I thought I couldn't here in this state of mind. Could I? "Breathe." I was looking at him, he started to come toward me and I was no longer focusing on anything but Brekwyn. Was I reading him? I was so confused. I felt his hands on my shoulders and still heard him telling me to breathe but I blinked and I couldn't see him anymore, I couldn't see anything. Were my eyes closed?

"Breathe Aurelious," I heard him again, his voice was louder. I couldn't get back to Danyon, I wanted to see what was happening but I couldn't, I could only hear Brekwyn and those annoying birds. They were so loud.

"Aurelious."

The wind sounded like a tornado and the gentle waves on the lake sounded like the pounding surf of the ocean. I could hear myself. I could hear my breath. I started to cough. I put my hands up to my ears to muffle the sounds. I could feel Brekwyn's hands on my shoulders. It was all so loud. I pushed my hands into my ears even harder and put my head in between my knees. I could hear myself groaning.

"Deep breaths Aurelious," Brekwyn's voice was soothing and although I could hear it over the deafening sounds of nature, his voice itself didn't hurt. I took deep breaths like he said, one after the other after the other.

Slowly I took my hands down from my ears, I was almost afraid to, afraid that everything would be so loud. It wasn't, it was normal now, the birds were singing. The pounding waves were just gentle ripples and the wind was just a lazy breeze. I realized that my eyes were squeezed shut but opening them only made me shut them again, the sunlight stung my eyes like needles and tears ran down my cheeks.

"You're okay," Brekwyn was holding me against him, "you're okay." He soothed me like I saw parents do to their children as I watched from a distance.

It took a few minutes of blinking a lot before I could see and my eyes didn't hurt. By this point, Brekwyn was sitting on one side of me and Danyon was sitting on the other, Poppy was over by a tree sniffing around.

"Are you okay?" Danyon had a look of concern on his face. He should've been making fun of me. Any kid in my old life would have been making fun of me if they saw me curled up in a ball with my hands over my ears and tears streaming down my face. Although let's be clear here, I wasn't actually crying, my eyes were just watering from the sting of the sunlight. Just to be clear. But back to my point, why wasn't Danyon making fun of me?

"Yeah, I'm alright." Maybe he wasn't terrible. "I couldn't get out, I didn't want to. It was peaceful then it was just confusing." I looked over to Brekwyn, "I think I was reading you but

I could hear you and I didn't think I was supposed to be able to hear."

"No, I was attempting to project my image into your mind as best I could which I can only do as long as I can hear your thoughts. You lost your hold on reality and you needed to get out. You were in so deeply that trying to get in your head was the safest way to get to you. It was more gradual," he said. "That's why you need to always keep your place, don't cross that line you found before." It made sense now. Everything made so much more sense.

We sat in silence for a second but then reality set in. I looked at Brekwyn and smiled, knowing that I had just done my first reading, I think.

He smiled back, "So, how did it go?"

"Good," I said trying to be casual. "I mean I think I did it, I definitely saw stuff happening."

Poppy started barking, she was looking at something in the branches of the tree she was sniffing around. Then she looked over at Danyon.

"I'll be right back," Danyon said and he jogged over to Poppy. He was looking at her and she at him, then she looked up into the tree, so he did too, then she looked back at him and he back at her. This must have been some conversation about something in the tree. Then she walked away like she didn't really care about whatever was bothering her anymore but Danyon stayed.

He was looking up into the tree still. I moved my head a little to see what he was looking at. He was looking at a squirrel.

"This was what I saw," I said to Brekwyn without taking my eyes off Danyon. Brekwyn perked up. "I know what happens next, Danyon turns to his right to look at something else. This is when I thought he was looking at you but he wasn't because you just told me that you weren't really there."

Together we sat, silently, waiting to see if Danyon would turn and look at something like I said he would. We waited to confirm if I had done it.

And then Danyon turned to his right and looked at something. Exactly like I said. Exactly like I saw.

Brekwyn and I looked at each other. I couldn't contain my excitement and I smiled the biggest smile I had ever smiled maybe in my whole life! I did it! And Brekwyn was smiling too, he was proud of me, I could see it in his eyes, I could feel his pride for me in my own heart. We high fived each other and then he put his arm around my shoulder in sort of a half hug and rubbed my head which did not aggravate me at all.

He was about to say something when Danyon came over looking serious. Brekwyn's smile faded when he saw Danyon's face, and my triumphant moment ended when he said, "There are spies in these woods Brekwyn. And they know what he just did."

Chapter Thirty-Four

"Speak Danyon," Brekwyn was on his feet in a second looking around. "How many are there?"

"Not many," Danyon said still looking into the woods, rather then at us, "Two, maybe three." He looked back up in the tree to talk more to his informant. "The Inglore sent spies after he couldn't find you this morning."

Brekwyn was frowning, his brow furrowed and he started pacing back and forth tapping his finger on his lips, "Well, we need to intercept them, there's no other option. It's one thing for Inglore to suspect that he's here, it's another thing for him to know that he's both here and actively training."

"I know who we're looking for and in which direction they fled," Danyon said, he was bouncing on his toes, all energized and ready for whatever was going to happen next.

"Then let's go," Brekwyn's frown turned into a look of intensity and purpose, "Aurelious, follow us and don't interact with these spies, let us handle it."

"Whatever you say," I said under my breath, but in truth if these people were after me, I couldn't promise that I would stay in the background and just let them handle it.

Danyon led the way and we started running. I was able to keep their pace but with great effort. Clearly these two were in much better shape than I was but I wouldn't let them know that. Danyon wasn't even wearing shoes, how is it possible that he was able to fly through these woods so easily? He was annoying me again.

My lungs were screaming by the time we slowed. With my hands on my hips taking slow, deep but deliberately quiet breaths, I acted like I was totally fine. Though I also had to hide the limp I suddenly acquired as the muscles in my legs started to seize up from the exertion. Some things I was adapting to really quickly, all of the running through the woods was not one of them.

We were close so we all started looking around. In my mind I would spot them first and take care of business at least before Danyon. But I'll be honest I didn't see a trace of anyone, I didn't catch a glimpse of a scrap of fabric from someone's torn shirt, I didn't see a footprint, I couldn't hear the sound of panting, other than mine, or footsteps ahead. I don't know what told Brekwyn and Danyon that we were close because as far as I was concerned, there was no one here but us.

We stopped, "There they are," Danyon said but he wasn't looking ahead where I was looking, instead he was looking up. Of course he was.

"Good work Danyon," Brekwyn patted him on the shoulder, damn it.

"Where are they?" I shoved my way past them like I was going to climb these trees and start a battle. Who did I think I was?

"And there they go," Danyon said shooting me a look like I just messed things up.

We started running again. Now please understand that I cannot see anyone in these trees. Granted I couldn't run and look up like Brekwyn and Danyon could but you would think that I would see someone.

We stopped again. I tried to push myself toward the tree that they were looking in but Brekwyn put a hand on my chest, reminding me to let them handle it. Reluctantly and like a sulking child with shoulders slumped, I stayed in the background.

But I was curious, as you know, so I couldn't help but look up and try to see the faces of these hidden emissaries. I had to search for a minute because the people I thought I was searching for were not actually people. This I realized when I saw two raccoons peering over a branch and staring at Danyon and Brekwyn. Of course this is what was happening right now, of course the spies are animals.

"Are you kidding me?" I asked and was quickly silenced by Brekwyn. I tossed my hands in the air and walked away. There was nothing I could do here but wait until Tarzan and the Raccoon Whisperer stopped talking to those raccoons. I mean, I feel kind of foolish for even writing this part of the story because it seems so unbelievable but if I'm going to tell you this whole story I have to tell you these ridiculous parts as well, I guess.

Chapter Thirty-Five

Their conversation, if that's what we're going to call this, didn't take long. I was brooding under a tree when Brekwyn and Danyon came over to tell me what had happened.

"We've taken care of the matter," Brekwyn assured me. "At least for now."

"And how did we do that?" I asked, picking up a rock and throwing it because I was still annoyed that I was helpless in this matter and Danyon wasn't.

"For some reason, raccoons are easily deterred on missions like this," Danyon said with a perky, irritating smile on his face. He was either oblivious to the fact that he annoyed me or he just didn't care. Either one of those two options just pissed me off even more. "Especially when they're young like those two are and when it's during the day. They're supposed to be sleeping right now, they're much more reliable at night."

This is not normal. This is not normal.

We were walking back toward the remnants of our campsite now, they continued to explain, "Essentially we persuaded the raccoons to go back to sleep and informed them that Inglore did not have their best interest at heart when sending them on this mission," Brekwyn said.

"So why do you still look worried?" I asked seeing a tiny muscle twitch in his forehead. His forehead is what gave away the concerns he tried not to show. But I only know this because I've been studying him.

He smiled, giving in to the fact that I couldn't be fooled this time, "Because this won't stop and as long as he perseveres like this, our family is in danger."

I thought about it, he was right. I saw what happened to our campsite and I felt the intensity of the wind. He haunted my dreams and now he even hired animals to haunt my reality. It was me he was after and as long as I was here, these people who had been nothing but nice to me, were in the path of his destruction.

I thought about leaving before I could make myself not think about it, because I didn't want Brekwyn to hear me. But it was too late.

"Nonsense," Brekwyn said in response to literally nothing said out loud.

Danyon looked at him and was about to ask what he was talking about when it occurred to him that Brekwyn was responding to something I thought. He looked away again completely unfazed, not a care in the world. He looked around, I noticed that he looked around a lot and sometimes smiled out of nowhere or for no reason that was readily obvious to me.

"But if it's me that he's after then I shouldn't be here."

"I explained before that you are a part of this family now, and what happens to you happens to all of us," he had his hand on my shoulder as we continued to walk. "There is strength in numbers, we'll all protect each other. Inglore cannot beat us, he will not beat us."

He was so confident and sure of himself, that line of worry vanished from his face. I believed him. I believed we could do this. Inglore wouldn't find me and everyone here would stay safe. But I should have been more cautious, and if I knew then what I know now, I would have been.

"In your reading, you saw what Danyon was doing," he smiled at me, "this was a great accomplishment but you can do more than that. We'll assess the remnants of our campsite and devise a way to transport all of our materials. While we do that I want you to focus again on Danyon and do a reading. But this time I want you to go even further and look for him to make a decision. That's what your gift really is."

"Okay." I shrugged because I had no clue how to progress further, but then again I never really had a clue about this gift and it seemed to be working out so far.

We were at the campsite so I found a place to sit while they went about figuring out how we were going to transport all of our stuff now that our packs were relegated to the garbage pile.

I was into my reading almost immediately and was entirely focused on Danyon.

I felt the push and knew when I opened my eyes that I would be in a time beyond where they were in their reality, the same reality that you live in, but not the one that I was currently in. He was already spreading out a large piece of the tent on the ground, breathe, and he started to pile things on it. Breathe, I had to remember not to loose my place this time, breathe. I had done this once already, this time I had to go further. Breathe. I focused. Breathe. I wanted to go further. Breathe. But everything stayed as it was. Breathe. My eyes were open and I could see but I needed to see differently. Breathe. I focused my mind and looked for what I couldn't see and then I felt it.

This was a push again, but this push was stronger than the other one. This one almost knocked me over, mentally. Breathe. And I felt like I needed to open my eyes again. Like I had a second set of eyelids and when I opened these the world looked totally different.

Everything around me was a blur except for Danyon. He was in stunning and almost overwhelming clarity. I could see the pores in his skin, individual hairs on his head. I could see the sinew of his muscle definition. His color was brighter, the shiny parts of him were shinier, and the dull parts were duller. I could see individual threads that made up the material of his shorts and the individual fibers in the twine bracelets around his wrists and in the ones that were metal I could see tiny dents and miniscule dots that made overall slight variations in color. I was supposed to do something, what was it? Oh, right, breathe.

Breathe. Breathe.

With each breath I took, my field of vision expanded. Only Danyon remained in this strange, crisp, clarity. The rest of the world looked normal which, compared to Danyon, now looked unimpressive and bland. Breathe. I finally found what I was searching for when the image of Danyon split into two images, he was making a decision, this was my gift.

He was deciding whether or not to move a rock about the size of a basketball. One of his images decided not to move it, that image picked up something that looked like a pile of clothes next to it and put that pile on the tent. The other image decided to move the rock. But moving the rock unearthed a tent pole precariously lodged in the dirt. The rock was holding it down and when it was moved the pole sprung up and smacked Danyon on his chest and face. He dropped the rock to cover his eye as a reflex after it was hit. I saw a red welt immediately rising in the flesh on his bare chest. Dots of blood came to the surface. He was walking around, Poppy panting and anxiously circling him, was concerned for his pain.

Brekwyn was at his side within seconds, coaxing him to put his hand down and show his injury. He did and I saw a fat, full, shining wet droplet of blood ooze over the edge of flesh torn on his cheekbone just below his eye. The droplet gingerly slid down his face leaving a trail of blood behind it, the trail leading the way for more blood to follow, a tiny river of it, dripping into oblivion off the edge of his chin. All the while Danyon's other image peacefully and painlessly went about piling our belongings into the tarp, which was once our tent.

I had to go back to the level of my reading before this one and see which choice Danyon made. What would his fate be only minutes from now? I pulled back one level and closed that imaginary second set of eyelids, finding myself still ahead in time but back to the place where I would see what Danyon decided to do. I came out of my reading when I saw him lift the rock.

Chapter Thirty-Six

Breathe. Consciously, I brought the sights and sounds of the world around me back in with excruciating slowness. I allowed myself to adjust to each of them before I brought in the next. Breathe. I realized that this was the way to get out of a reading without being struck half dead with raucous noises or glaring brightness. I still had to keep my eyes closed for longer than I would like to because the sun was just so damn bright. It felt like each time I came out it was a little bit brighter than it was when I went in.

When I was finally able to open my eyes, I was fascinated to realize that Brekwyn and Danyon were still deciding what their course of action was going to be with the piles of stuff in front of them. When I was doing a listening exercise, time in reality would pass by far quicker than time in my other reality. But in an actual reading, it was as if no time had passed at all. In a reading, my alternate reality was infinitely quicker than actual reality, the one you live in. Interesting.

So here I sat, knowing what was going to happen. I also knew that if I wanted to, I could change Danyon's course of action. I could interfere with his path and he would go unharmed. So the question became, what would be my choice?

I continued to watch them in silence. They didn't look at me or acknowledge me, for all I knew they thought I was still in this reading. The two of them sorted out two pieces of tent that were the largest, each laying their piece on the ground. What should I do? Brekwyn was piling the garbage on his piece and Danyon was piling the salvageable things on his. Maybe I would tell him about the rock. Brekwyn would probably think I was the hero if I did.

I was about to intervene when Brekwyn said, "Danyon, this was a great idea. We'll be able to carry these on our backs, nothing will be left behind." He smiled at him, there was clearly love between them. "I don't know what we would do without you and your cleverness here."

Oh give me a break. Anyone could have figured out how to make two scraps of tent into tarps to carry this crap in, this wasn't rocket science. I found myself getting angry, I was jealous of Danyon and his perpetual happiness, getting praised all the time. Why did he deserve all of this? He needed a little dose of reality and a smack in the face and chest with a metal pole would show him what life was really like, what my life was really like.

I stewed in my anger and moments later when Danyon approached the rock I thought that maybe I should just tell him that moving it was going to result in an injury but I didn't. Let him feel something that I felt, let him suffer like I've suffered. Maybe Brewkyn would see that he wasn't so great, he wasn't so much better than me if he was stupid enough to move a rock that was holding down a pole.

He bent to pick up the rock, my pulse quickened. His hands grasped the rock, his muscles tensed, my pulse quickened even more, he lifted and unearthed the metal pole. The pole swung with rapid aggression slicing through the air as it moved and just as it was about to smash into Danyon, instead, it smashed into the outstretched palm of Brekwyn who stood staring at me. What was that look on his face? It wasn't searing pain from the whack of the pole, no, it was anger and it was directed at me and I felt the ground below me start to rumble.

Chapter Thirty-Seven

"Are you okay?" Danyon tossed the rock to the side and immediately went to assess Brekwyn's hand. Brekwyn said nothing. He only stood with his eyes closed, breathing away his anger. "You saved me from that pole! It would've hit me right in the head!" Danyon was smiling from the idea of being rescued even though he was genuinely concerned about Brekwyn. Since he was focusing solely on Brekwyn's hand, Danyon was oblivious to what was happening with me.

I should tell you that my first thought was to run for my life. But Brekwyn heard that thought just like he heard me thinking about whether or not I should stop Danyon from moving the rock and getting hit by the metal pole. So when I thought about running, a root from the tree that I was sitting under almost immediately wrapped around my left ankle. I was going nowhere. I could only sit in silence and wonder what the hell was going to happen next.

I'm sorry, I thought. But would that really be enough?

Brekwyn loosened his vice like grip of the pole revealing a blood red line across the palm of his hand, which Danyon set about wrapping in a ripped piece of cloth.

"I'll be fine Danyon, thank you for your concern." He smiled gently at him, his anger mostly passed now, or at least suppressed enough only to be present in a small furrow of his brow.

"That was crazy," Danyon said, hyped up and bouncing, "I had no idea that was going to happen, I didn't even see the pole."

"Nor did I," he took a really deep breath, "but Aurelious did."

Danyon frowned like he was trying to process what Brekwyn said, then turned to me when he did, "You saw that was going to happen?"

I didn't answer. Danyon started to walk over to me. I stood up, stumbled because of the root around my ankle then straightened myself awkwardly and still a bit off balance.

"Did you see that was going to happen?" he asked again.

I reminded myself that I didn't tell him on purpose, that I wanted him to know what it felt like to live an imperfect life if only for a second so I straightened up and puffed out my chest trying to convince myself that I should stand by my decision.

"Yeah, I knew it was gonna happen." I folded my arms across my chest.

"Could you have stopped it?" he asked, his eyes revealing that he didn't want me to say yes, so I stood even straighter.

"Yeah, I could have," I smirked.

Danyon looked confused, he had his hands out to the side, palms upturned, "Then why didn't you stop it?"

"Because I didn't want to."

"Why not?" He raised his voice and came toward me.

"I had no reason to stop it." I raised my voice back and felt my blood start to boil. I wanted to fight him. I wanted him to feel the pain, my pain. I widened my stance to secure my balance with my free leg and waited for him to take one step closer. As he did I summoned my strength and shoved him, hard, in the chest.

He was taken off guard as he stumbled, but didn't fall, backward and the look of confusion on his face only intensified. He had never been shoved before. I had plenty of experience being where he was but not a lot of experience being the one who did the shoving. I was sweating and panting. Poppy started growling at me. Danyon came toward me another time, quickly, so I shoved at him again. This time he didn't get confused, he got mad, and he shoved me back.

I didn't expect it to be so hard. Now more off balance, I stepped backward with my free leg. He shoved again, this time even harder. He was much stronger than I anticipated. I fell to the ground and he jumped on top of me.

The force of his body knocked the wind out of me. I tried to push him off me. He tried to push me down further. I swung at him but he blocked me with little effort. He was agile. I was awkward, held in place by a tree root like a dog on a leash. I grunted and shoved and he did the same. Rocks dug into my side and the backs of my arms. His knees started to bleed.

Poppy's growling intensified and morphed into aggressive, angry barking. I saw birds flying in circles in the sky above him, squawking and screeching. Squirrels jumped from branch to branch, tree to tree. All around us the forest was alive and agitated, creatures everywhere reacting to the puzzling, dangerous and painful situation their human friend was in.

He pulled his hand back to punch me. I looked in his eyes. He didn't want to hurt me. He had no idea what this emotion was that was causing him to have this reaction.

His body shifted, he was ready to strike, I turned my head out of instinct because I knew that a blow to my cheek bone would hurt him almost as much as it would hurt me and would do less damage then a blow to my nose. This was one of the things I learned growing up.

I was about to close my eyes and brace for impact when a vine sprung up from the ground, wrapped around Danyon's wrist and yanked him backward. He tried to get up but the vine had his arm pulled too close to the ground. Seeing my opportunity I scrambled to my feet but fell over again as the root that held me captive shot further up my leg. We were both bound in place by some element of the Nature that surrounded us. Brekwyn stood silently by, watching all of this happen.

"The reason that you should have stopped it is so that I wouldn't get smacked in the head with a metal pole!" Danyon yelled, realizing that ours was to be a battle of words again.

"You deserve to get smacked in the head!"

"No one deserves to get smacked in the head that makes no sense!"

We were screaming at each other, Poppy was panting and circling around Danyon, Brekwyn remained motionless.

"I have been smacked in the head more times than I can even remember. Do you know what that feels like?" I didn't allow him the chance to answer, "No you don't because you've had this perfect life." I felt tiny vessels in my throat snapping as I yelled, I felt my face getting redder and hotter. "All you do all day is run around with no shoes on and climb trees and talk to animals. Who lives like that? No one really lives like that! This is a fantasy and you've led a fantasy life while I was stuck in a place where I didn't belong, getting smacked in the head! I wasn't supposed to be there. I was supposed to be here running through the freakin' woods, having the goddam time of my life!"

"So it's my fault that this was how I grew up and that was how you grew up?" The veins in his neck bulged in the effort it took for him to yell, I suspect yelling wasn't part of his everyday life. "You were in the wrong place Aurelious, we all know that, we've always known it, but that isn't my fault!" He struggled against the vines, dirt grinding into his shorts and clinging to the blood on his knees.

"I'm not an idiot Danyon, I know it's not your fault." I was still yelling but with less passion, I would lose this argument because I was wrong, I should have told him about the pole. I lay down on my back, catching my breath. I rubbed my filthy hands over my face.

"So you wanted me to get hurt for no reason?"

"No, I wanted you to get hurt because I've gotten hurt!" I tossed my hands above me as if I was yelling at the sky, the trees, the birds, anything. But as soon as I said it out loud I knew it was ridiculous. "I wanted someone else to feel what I felt just for a second, to trade places just for a second. Just for a second I wanted to be the one who felt good while someone else felt bad." I shook my head and covered my face with my arm in defeat. Neither of us said anything for the next few minutes. The animals quieted and a calm came back over the forest.

"Please let him go Brekwyn," I finally said, my voice was hoarse from yelling, "if he wants to hit me, you should let him, I deserve it."

The things that held us captive fell to the ground and reconfigured themselves back into their camouflaged place in the Earth. Danyon came toward me, I readied myself for the pain. But he didn't hit me. Instead he put his hand out to help me up.

I looked up at him, the look in his eyes was serious but it wasn't hurtful or judgmental. I put my hand in his.

"I'm not going to hit you because I actually don't think you deserve it and I'm not comfortable with the idea of hitting someone," his voice was peaceful and in that moment I saw why people loved him because he was kind, just like Brekwyn. "I mean you were definitely a jerk though." And then I saw how he made people laugh, because he was clever and carefree, just like, well, just like himself.

"I'm sorry I didn't warn you. I won't do that again," I said, and I meant it. Because in reality, I didn't like how I felt when I decided to let him get hurt. I felt like what I imagined the Inglore to be and that was not who I wanted to be.

"You made Poppy upset." He gestured toward her with his head.

"Sorry Poppy," I said with exaggerated remorse and a small eye roll.

"Um, she can't understand you. You're just a Reader."

He laughed at his own humor and I knew it was okay to join him in the laugh. We laughed, because Poppy couldn't understand me and in reality it's crazy that she and all other animals actually can understand Danyon. And we laughed because he managed to lift the dead weight of my jealously and stupid action, or inaction, by bringing us back into this new reality that I really needed to learn to appreciate. And we laughed because I wasn't 'just' a Reader instead I was The Reader and I couldn't possibly understand the magnitude of what that meant and probably never would. And as we laughed I noticed one thing that stood out in my mind.

Brekwyn wasn't laughing.

Chapter Thirty-Eight

I knew the look on Brekwyn's face. I'd seen it on many people that I've observed. He was mad. But he wasn't mad at me like you would expect. He was mad at himself because he let my malice affect him far deeper than he was comfortable with. He felt like he lost control, only temporarily of course, but even that instant was too much for his liking.

Brekwyn had been in control his whole life and now I was here testing him, pushing his buttons, driving him to the brink. This was what I wanted when I first met him, but now that I knew him, now that I knew that this life existed, I didn't want him to change and what's more, I wanted him to like me. I just didn't seem to know how to stop screwing up.

Danyon gestured with his head that I should talk to Brekwyn and then returned to the work of sorting out our stuff. Danyon held no grudge, what was done was done. We came to some sort of understanding and were moving on from this point forward. Reluctantly and sheepishly, with my head down and ready to be reprimanded, I approached Brekwyn.

"Brekwyn I..." He put his hand up to silence me.

He took a deep breath and put his hands on his hips, "Aurelious, the choice you made was yours to make. I cannot say that I'm not disappointed in your decision or the way you felt about Danyon who has been kind to you as we all have. I do however understand your feelings. I understand where they come from. I've felt them within you and can, therefore, empathize with you." His face seemed to relax a bit, "I also feel that you've turned a corner, you've released a bit of the hold that your childhood with the Gadje had on you. You're ready to move forward. This is a positive step, I just wish Danyon was not almost a casualty in that process."

"I'm sorry about that with Danyon," I said softly, very embarrassed. I glanced at Danyon out of the corner of my eye. He was cheerfully going about his work. He seemed like he was frequently distracted with all of his looking around but then I realized that he was actually just engaging with the animals around us.

This was fascinating to me and I felt myself getting drawn in by his behavior. I felt my head and body turning almost like a reflex so I could observe him fully. But then I remembered that I was already engaged in a conversation, a penance, with Brekwyn and forced myself to look away. I would have to get back to Danyon in the future. He was someone that I had to figure out, but for good reasons this time.

Brekwyn had a small smile on his face, "You see, he is quite an interesting character isn't he?"

"Yeah, I guess he is." And I smiled a little bit too. "Um I'm also sorry that I upset you that much." I crossed my arms over my chest remembering the rumble of his anger that I felt in the ground beneath me before. "I didn't want to make you loose control."

"I didn't loose control," he said quickly, "but I could have. That's something that I have to work out on my own because I have no intention of loosing control. Not for anyone."

"I guess I have a way of pushing peoples buttons around here." I thought about my interactions with Anira too.

"Yes, well for different reasons, I assure you," he patted me on the back, "let's get back to work."

It would be scary if Brekwyn ever lost control based on the way he was able to move the Earth around me but also because of the look that I saw on his face. It was literally instantaneous but it scared the hell out of me. I know Brekwyn hoped that he would never lose control. I know that he hoped he would never have to access that darker side of himself. But this is really just the beginning of this story, we have a long way to go and one can only hold onto certain hopes for so long before having to let them go. Forever.

When we finished sorting out our mess Brekwyn said, "Aurelious, one of the things you'll learn about being a Gypsy is that you always have to be ready to adapt."

"I've been adapting my whole life," I said.

"Excellent," he said with a smile. "Boys, I think it's time for a change of plans."

Danyon started bouncing, Poppy started wagging her tail.

"What are we gonna do?" I asked.

"We're going to leave." And with that he put as much as he could carry onto his back, we did the same, and we left the woods.

Chapter Thirty-Nine

Our walk back was long and quiet but I knew we were getting close to the village because I started to see things like clothes and papers in the woods. We collected what we saw as we walked and by the time we came out into the clearing, our arms were full. We just stood there for a few minutes, silently surveying the damage.

Brekwyn took a deep breath, an audible sign of concern.

"Why did he do this Brekwyn?" Danyon asked looking completely dejected.

"He's determined Danyon and he was angry when he didn't get what he came for." The Inglore sounded like a monster.

I felt sick to my stomach. We stood there bearing witness to so much destruction, it was incredible and it was really all my fault. I know there was no point in saying anything because Brekwyn would have just told me it wasn't my fault and that we were all in this together, patting me on the back in the process. But it was my fault and I didn't want a pat on the back or to be placated. If it weren't for me being here, none of this would have happened. None of it. I wished for my laptop so I could say how sorry I was for all of this.

There were clothes strewn everywhere, there were broken dishes on the ground and furniture that looked like it was just picked up, twisted into some kind of modern art form that I was too uncultured to appreciate and then thrown aside. There was a broken lawn chair in a tree. Some of the trailers had broken windows and doors that were either off or hanging by broken hinges.

The destruction seemed to be indiscriminant.

"Our family comes up tomorrow," Brekwyn broke our stunned silence, "let's make their homecoming a bit more welcome."

We spent the next several hours piling up broken things. Wood went in one pile, glass in another, metal in another. Maybe one of the coolest things I had ever seen was when we were finished piling up the debris, Brekwyn walked around to each pile and, with the flick of his hand, set each pile on fire. Sometimes he didn't even look at what he was doing, he would walk by a pile and flick it on fire without so much as a glance in its direction. The even cooler thing was that he wasn't doing it to show off or impress me; sometimes he didn't even know I was watching. He was just doing his thing.

The fires burned with different intensity, the metal fires were so hot that I couldn't stand near them without feeling my skin getting redder and hotter to the touch. But we didn't stand around watching these things burn, instead we continued on with our work. The salvageable items were piled up outside of the trailers near where we found them. When the rest of the tribe came back they would sort through the piles and take what was theirs. Brekwyn was confident that that wouldn't take too long for them to figure out.

The sun had set on our day, this long and tedious day. I was on the outskirts of the village looking in as the fires were finally burning themselves out. I have no idea where the remnants of the fires went, the ashes, the liquid metals, none of it. I suspect Brekwyn flicked something and made them disappear while I was searching for any residual evidence of the Inglore's wrath.

Exhausted, I slowly made my way back toward Anira's trailer and stumbled when I kicked something I hadn't seen on the ground.

"Stupid Inglore," I said under my breath and angrily picked up my obstacle. It was a book, the cover was partially hanging off and it was covered in dirt. I wiped it off as I walked and when a stream of particularly bright moonlight appeared in my path I looked at the title.

I wouldn't need to ask whom this belonged to or find a salvage pile to put it in. I wouldn't throw it in a fire either, although earlier in the day I might have considered it.

"Danyon," I said when I found him a minute later, "I think this is yours." It was The Magician's Nephew, the first book in the Chronicles of Narnia.

He smiled when he saw it and held it close to his chest like I often did with my laptop, "This one is my favorite," he said.

"Mine too," I smiled back.

Danyon had an amazing life filled with adventure and people who loved him and weren't afraid to show it. But they loved him because he loved them too so he deserved their love. And his life was amazing because it was just amazing and adventurous and why shouldn't he have that life? Because I didn't? No, he deserved it and he should have, just like I deserved, just like I should have it. And I would have it. So I didn't need to be jealous of Danyon, I would be happy for the great things he had and I would learn to see life through his eyes, as well as the other Gypsies here. I would have a great life and people would love me and somehow I would love them.

I went to sleep that night in the bedroom that Anira prepared for me when I first came here. I would be there in the morning. From this point forward I would have friends and family and the Inglore, with all of his might wouldn't be able to separate us. In the future I would come to know that I was, in fact, correct about one of those things.

Chapter Aurelious Forty ;)

You would think that after all I experienced with the Inglore that I wouldn't be able to sleep well that night. However it was as if I was being rocked like a baby in the loving arms of my mother, I imagine, and I slept like a rock. Maybe my sudden blanket optimism lulled me into a false sense of security because I didn't even dream about him and I actually woke up ready to take on the day.

If I was the type of person to hum a tune, which I wasn't let's be clear, that would be what I was doing when I woke up that next morning. And if I wasn't so observant I might have been completely oblivious when I walked out of the trailer into the blinding sunshine and, after allowing time for my eyes to adjust, saw that we were in a completely different place.

What the?

We were still surrounded by trees but this was not the same forest. It was actually easier to tell that then you would think. The paths that were near Anira's trailer in the other forest were not here, the trailers that were positioned around hers were not the same as the ones that were around hers now and, there were only a few of them. The majority of the trailers were not here at all.

I turned around and looked for human life that would have an explanation for this. But no one was here. I was so disoriented that I wondered if I was dreaming. Just when I was getting used to all of this, just when I made up my mind to be a real part of this they up and change my surroundings. I mean, I was used to waking up in a different place then the day before but I usually went to sleep in that different place.

"Hello?" I called out.

No response. Oh no, what if the Inglore got me and I didn't know it? I felt my face get hot and my heart beat faster. I was about to start running around like a mouse in a maze when behind me I heard, "Hello."

I whipped around and breathed a sigh of relief. It was Anira.

"What?" I just held my hands up with a look of exasperation on my face all of which clearly asked '*where are we?*'

She smiled, "Didn't Brekwyn tell you that it was time to leave?"

"No," I thought about it, "well he said it was time to leave but I thought that meant it was time to leave the campsite where we were training."

"Well that too but no, it was time for us to really leave." She held a bouquet of wild flowers up to her nose and inhaled. "The Inglore was too close and too persistent, we needed to change locations and throw him off your trail for a bit."

She was still talking about how we traveled during the night and how the rest of the tribe would be coming when they restored the Earth back to the way they found it before they took up residence there, blah, blah, blah but I wasn't listening anymore. I was so mesmerized by looking at her. I stayed in this reality though, now that I knew what was happening to me, and forced away the blurriness that tried to creep into the edges of my vision. I wanted to touch her.

I knew she could feel my desire when she looked up at me. She had the same hungry look in her eyes. She wanted me too. But that look quickly turned to alarm and she held up her hand to ward me off as I started to approach her.

"No Aurelious," she said although we didn't exchange any words about how I was feeling.

"Why not?" I asked softly and continued my approach until her hand was pressing into my chest. I felt the tingle and instead of pulling away I pushed in more.

"You feel that don't you?" I asked her.

"Yes," she barely whispered it.

"What does it feel like beyond that tingle," my voice was low and raspy.

"I don't know."

"Don't you want to find out?"

"Yes," she said it as she breathed out.

"Then why do you tell me 'No'?"

"Because it isn't right yet?"

"What isn't right?" I leaned my head toward hers and inhaled, she smelled clean and lemony. I ran my finger along her bare shoulder, her skin was soft and smooth like I imagined it would be.

She shuttered, pushed me away and took a step back, "This isn't right yet, it's not the right time, you aren't feeling it yet."

I took a deep breath, "I'm pretty sure I'm feeling it and I'm pretty sure you're feeling it too." I put my hands in my pockets and went to stand in the shade cast by her trailer, the sun felt a lot brighter here for some reason.

"What I am feeling and what you are feeling are two different things," she put her hands on her hips, she was annoyed by me. "Trust me, I know."

I rolled my aching eyes, "Yeah, you know, which is why I'm not trying to pretend that I'm not feeling something for you but what it is, I have no idea because I've never felt it before."

"You're feeling lust." So my lustfulness must have annoyed her. I looked at her hands on the perfect smooth curve of her hips and imagined my own hands there.

"So what's wrong with that?"

"Nothing, it's totally natural. But until you feel what you're supposed to be feeling then this," she pointed back and forth between the two of us, "isn't going to happen."

"And what am I supposed to be feeling?" I leaned against the trailer thinking I was way cooler than I actually was.

"Love." She tugged on one of her curls, which meant she went from feeling annoyed to feeling insecure. I preferred annoyed, because I didn't want her to be insecure about anything.

I sighed, "You know that I don't love anyone." I felt a little ashamed that I didn't seem to share the Gypsy ability to love so freely.

She smirked, "You will." She started to walk toward the steps to go into the trailer.

"How do you know I will?" I stayed where I was in the shade.

"Because I know who you are."

"Yeah, yeah, I'm the Reader, but what does that have to do with love."

"I'm not talking about you being the Reader although I'm glad you've finally accepted that."

"So what am I then?"

"My soul mate." She took a deep breath and looked at me with love, hope, and something else in her eyes and then quickly went inside before I could see what that other thing was.

"That's not possible," I said to myself. But was it? I mean if I believed all of this other crap, should I believe this too? And what was that other thing that I saw in her eyes, it was familiar? Sadness?

Chapter Forty-One

"What do you know about Anira?" I asked Danyon as we explored our new surroundings with Poppy leading the way.

"Pretty much everything I guess." He shrugged.

"She's beautiful," I admitted.

He glanced at me with a disgusted look on his face, "She's okay."

"No, really she's beautiful." I looked off into the distance, "I have seen a lot of girls in my life and she is probably the most beautiful girl I've ever seen."

"That's not saying much for the Gadje." He smiled and pushed me.

I laughed, clearly Danyon had more of a sibling relationship with Anira even though they weren't related. A consequence of growing up together I guess.

"She told me that she was my soul mate." I looked at him to see if he would be shocked or think this was a joke or something. But he didn't even miss a beat.

"Yeah, I heard you might be." He looked up into a tree at a bird just landing in it's nest, quickly feeding it's ravenous babies.

I stopped short, "What do you mean?"

He looked back at me, "After she met you that time in the park, both she and Brekwyn said they felt the connection you two had."

"And that makes us soul mates?" I crossed my arms over my chest, "Why doesn't that just make us, I don't know, attracted to each other?"

"First of all, gross I have no idea how anyone could be attracted to her like that, and second of all, a soul mate is a soul mate. It goes deeper than just attraction." He looked at the bird again as she took flight to find more sustenance for her growing family. "At least that's what we're told. Isn't it the same for the Gadje?"

"No, I don't think soul mates are a real thing." I watched him looking at the nest and tapped him on his shoulder to refocus his attention. I saw people do that to him a couple of times so I figured I'd try it, he looked back at me like this was normal so I guess it was the right thing to do. "I mean if soul mates were a real thing there wouldn't be so much divorce."

He shrugged again and we started walking, "Maybe it's just a Gypsy thing."

"So what am I supposed to do if she's my soul mate?"

"I don't know, I haven't met mine yet but eventually you get married."

I choked on my saliva, he laughed, "Not yet. When you get older," he patted me on the back to get the choke out, "but you can have some fun in the mean time. Just feel what you feel and learn to like things like moments and feelings."

I looked at him when he said that, and without thinking about what he said he ran over to Poppy to see what she was digging at in the ground. I stood watching him for a minute. I thought he was kind of an airhead but maybe he wasn't. I mean that was kind of a profound thing to say. Wasn't it?

"I'm gonna do a reading," I called to him.

"Okay, just let me know if a tree is going to crash down on me or if I'm going to fall off a cliff and die," he joked.

"No guarantees," I laughed back. Look at me, joking around with my friend. Look at me having a friend.

I did three readings with Danyon as my subject in the next several hours that we spent together. The readings showed little things, everyday decisions that you probably wouldn't be interested in all the details of. The details aren't important, what was important to me was that I could get in and out easily and more quickly. I was never tired anymore when I did it. I didn't feel nauseous. I was accepting what I could do. It was becoming a part of me. Just like they said it would.

Anira was there when we got back to her trailer. I hugged her partially because I was desperate to touch her once I saw her and partially because I wanted to see if she would let me. I inhaled her clean lemony scent and felt the soft waves of her hair on my cheek. She let me hug her for a second, and I could feel her breathing me in just like I was breathing her in.

"Ugh, that is disgusting," Danyon groaned, Poppy snorted and walked away.

"Disgusting?" Anira said, pulling away from me and putting one hand on her hip. One hand meant that she wasn't really annoyed she was just pretending that she was, so I learned. "Danyon would you like me to make you cry like a baby in front of everyone, cause I can do that remember?" They were teasing each other.

"Anira, would you like me to ask that bird to poop on your head, cause I can do that remember?" We all had a good laugh at both of those images. Laughing, now that I knew how to do it and had people to do it with, was becoming really fun. I could get used to this.

Chapter Forty-Two

The rest of the tribe arrived at this site a few days after we did. In those few days, I moved into Brekwyn's trailer because he heard some thoughts I was having about Anira and almost threw up cause my thoughts were a little um, dirty, um, sexy I guess I could say. Sorry, but it's the truth and as much as I tried to not think that way I literally couldn't help it. So he thought it would be better if we didn't live together. It was a good idea for me to move but, just so you know, I'm not a pervert and I wouldn't have done anything with her that she didn't want to do. But playing house was getting kind of confusing.

I followed Brekwyn around when I wasn't hanging out with Danyon and Anira or practicing my readings. I learned about different aspects of Gypsy life like how tradition was so important to them and even as the times changed around them they did their best to keep their way of life alive. Land was scarcer than it used to be so it got harder and harder to find places to settle for their brief or extended periods of time. Gypsies loved to throw a festival in which dance and music was an important part. They loved the Earth and were a very spiritual people. This tribe was rooted in love and kindness but not all Gypsy tribes were the same.

There were tribes that loathed the Gadje, specifically the Inglore's tribe and they often went out among them to try to mess with them in some way. But I'm not clear how or what they would do, no one here seemed to really know the details. This tribe didn't have a lot of interaction with the people outside the Gypsy world except for those, like Anira's father, who went to sell the tribes goods in the cities and towns.

There was something that all Gypsies believed in and that was that they were charged with taking care of the Earth. So they planted seeds of plants, fruits, and vegetables to nourish people and the soil, Brekwyn always had seeds in his pocket 'just in case'. They brought needed water in the form of rain and so many other things but they could only do so much because they had to remain undiscovered so their work had to be subtle. The greater job would be getting the Gadje to change their behaviors and do their part to take care of the Earth since there were so many more Gadje than Gypsies. Oh yeah, please do your part to take care of the environment cause Gypsies can't do it alone anymore. Thanks.

I learned a lot about those that I was closest with. For example, I learned that Danyon never wore shoes unless and until it was really cold outside and he often slept outdoors, under the stars. No one thought twice about either of these things, it was totally normal. Oh, and he didn't wear a shirt too often either. Poppy trailed or walked beside him wherever he went. They were always together and on the occasion that she stopped to sniff something and lagged behind or chased a scent he always waited for her without even thinking about it. Sometimes you would see them by themselves, communicating in some secret silent language, he would laugh and she would jump around. This was probably the most connected friendship I had ever seen between anyone, and it wasn't even between two people.

Everyone loved Danyon. It probably had something to do with his huge infectious smile or that he was always happy and openly loving to anyone. He was very affectionate and touched people a lot, giving a hug or putting an arm around someone's shoulder or patting a little kid on the head. He would hold the hand of a girl, not in a romantic way though, or the arm of an older person. If a child fell near him he picked them up and held them until they stopped crying which was relatively quick because he would whisper something to make them laugh or Poppy would come over and slobber on their cheek. He was a little mischievous, playing jokes or tricks on people but whenever that happened, the target of his good natured humor would usually roll their eyes and smile in an *Oh Danyon* kind of way and when he left someone's presence they always had a smile lingering on their face.

I came to understand that Danyon was never alone. If he and Poppy went off by themselves into the woods he was still with Poppy and if per chance Poppy wandered off, there were other animals going about their business around him so there was always someone or something around that he could communicate with and that often wanted to communicate with him. Sometimes I saw him and I assumed that he was deep in thought but it could have been that he was silently communicating with a small something I didn't see. I imagined it was always noisy in Danyon's head and that he touched people to help him focus on that person he was with. And people would often touch him to bring his focus back on them. You never heard anyone tell him to 'concentrate' because the reality was that he was concentrating, it's just that there is always twice as much for him to concentrate on then there ever is for you or me.

I don't think Danyon had ever experienced real sadness or disappointment or loss. But even though his outlook on everything seemed generally sunny, you couldn't mistake his carefree and positive disposition for ignorance. He may not have experienced the hardship of life outside of his Gypsy tribe but he was smart and often said the most profound things when you least expected it and when you most needed it.

There was no doubt about Brekwyn's leadership in the tribe. Although he was humble and tried to down play his importance it was so clear that he was revered by all, almost worshiped by some. Not worshiped in a way that people would fall at his feet or cry when he approached like he was a rock star and his people were screaming fans, but in a way that people believed every word he said. He could have said that the sky was falling and people would have run for cover without bothering to look up to see if it was true.

He, however, never abused his position in the tribe. If anyone asked him a question he carefully thought about his answer, he never spoke without weighing the impact of what he had to say.

It was a seamless process that went on in his mind so there weren't long pauses in his conversations but his thoughts were evident, at least to me when I watched him and I must confess, I watched him a lot.

I should point out that although he could probably tell everyone what to do about everything, he rarely did. If someone asked a question or if a puzzling situation arose, he would often redirect to the person or people he was talking to and in a round about way have them answer the question or solve the problem, kind of like he did with Danyon and the tarps at the campsite. When you have someone around who is as gifted as he is, you could get lazy with making decisions, always deferring to him. He did not allow that to happen.

Brekwyn made everyone feel that when he was with you that you were the most important person in the world, like everything else faded away and it was just you and him. He treated everyone the same way from the youngest child to the oldest adult and even the teenagers trying to see where they fit in the world, like me. Someone always needed him and he always made time for whomever that person was and for whatever the reason was that they needed him. He never complained and I never saw him look angry, except for that time or two with me.

Anira was the person I sought out in a crowd. I found that if I was not with her then I was wondering where she was. She preoccupied me more often than I thought anyone could. When I was practicing my training, my mind would wander and I would try to find her in the world that I was reading. We spent a lot of time together but I hadn't practiced my reading on her yet. Yet.

She mesmerized me. Her beauty was palpable and it ran as deeply as the blood in her body. She was an emotional person but never confusing in her emotions, never needlessly dramatic. In fact she didn't like drama and would try to calm any situation that seemed to be going in that direction.

She was emotional in the sense that she felt everyone's feelings as part of her gift but also in that she loved deeply, she cared deeply, she feared and she laughed deeply. When she was serious, she was very serious and then at the time when the situation really needed it, she was funny. Don't get me wrong she could be lighthearted and sarcastic too, especially with Brekwyn and Danyon.

Each day I found myself getting more and more attracted to her physically. But she kept her distance that way, knowing that my feelings were more superficial, convinced that someday soon that would change. She was patient. I wasn't. Occasionally I must admit that I found myself wondering what would happen if I manipulated her by using my gift. What if I changed her decision and made her kiss me? Or more than that? But I said before that I wasn't a pervert and wouldn't do anything with her that she didn't want to do. But what if I never fell in love with her like she thought I would?

My days were filled with training and learning to be a friend and a Gypsy. I had more to learn than I could've imagined so the days went by pretty quickly. I rarely thought about my previous life anymore. One day, seemingly out of nowhere, I realized that I had forgiven the Gadje for the childhood that I had and I let that childhood go. The Gadje who raised me were nothing more than a memory that I locked away.

Each day I laughed more than I did the day before. Each day I felt myself caring more about the comfort and well being of those around me. Each day I became more like these people and less like the person I used to be. Each day I grew happier and healthier and more attached to this tribe and this way of life. My family. This felt like my family. Finally I made human connections and the value in that, for me, went far beyond anything that I could adequately express.

But my nights were different. All of the peace and calm that I felt during the day was overshadowed by the darkness and despair that haunted my dreams. Every night I battled for my life, for my freedom. I was chased or cornered or found myself in darkness, unable to find the light. All by a faceless man who only revealed himself in maniacal laughter or feelings of treachery and evil.

I never burdened my new Gypsy family with my nightmares

and convinced myself everyday that they were just that, night-mares relegated only to my subconscious but each night I found myself sleeping less, willing myself to stay awake for as long as I could in the hope that my sleep would be peaceful. It never was. I convinced myself that my nightmares would never come to fruition. But I had been wrong about things before and deep down I knew that the Inglore was not far away.

Chapter Forty-Three

I woke up early. Inevitably I always woke up earlier than I wanted to. Here waking up was just a way to end my nightmares. But waking up before most of the rest of the tribe was good because it gave me time to practice reading whatever unsuspecting person was also awake and it gave me time to process everything without the intrusion of someone hearing my thoughts.

I also woke up early because the early morning sun wasn't as bright as it would be later and for some reason, being in the bright sunlight was becoming sort of unbearable. Just stepping outside meant that I would need to let my eyes adjust for a few minutes. And that adjustment included searing pain, incessant blinking, and a lot of tears. But not crying tears, remember, just watering eyes. Even after they adjusted it just wasn't great. I found myself constantly squinting and looking for shade to stand in. I also started spending more daylight hours indoors which helped but I knew it was a sacrifice for my friends because being outside was a part of their life, especially Danyon.

This morning I decided to enlist Danyon to help with my process, as usual. He liked doing it and it gave us a chance to be outside together.

The village was quiet. No one was really moving about. The birds were just waking up and the dew remained on the leaves and grasses at the border of the woods around our village. I made my way over to Danyon's trailer to see if he was awake yet. I didn't know where to find him but I figured this place was somewhere to start.

I called his name softly outside his trailer, "Danyon?"

No response.

I directed my voice up the ladder in the back of his trailer thinking he might be asleep up top, "Danyon?" I called in a bit of a whisper.

No response.

I didn't want to knock on the door because I suspected I would wake his family if I did. So I looked around more, he probably wasn't inside anyway, he rarely was. I went to the edge of the woods and figured I would just call out softly in that direction. "Danyon."

No response, just the scurrying noise of an animal through the old dried up leaves on the ground. So maybe it was too early. I walked by Anira's trailer and it was quiet there as well, signs of sleep. I could just wait outside here for her to come out when she woke up.

I wondered what she looked like when she slept. She never locked her door, no one here did. I could just open it quietly and sneak inside. Then maybe, I could see what she looked like. Maybe I could wake her up, slowly, gently. Maybe when she woke up we could...

"Hey, I heard you were looking for me." It was Danyon, no shirt or shoes as usual, just purple long shorts. Yeah, I'm calling them long shorts cause that's what they were. And of course he had on all of his accessories like bracelets and anklets and that coin perpetually woven into his hair. They all wore jewelry all the time. He had pine needles in his messy hair, a little dirt on his side, and the look of just waking up on his face. He was chewing on a sprig of mint.

"Sorry did I wake you up?" We were talking softly.

"I was already waking up. I don't sleep late," he said as we sat down in one of the outdoor chairs that somehow managed to survive Inglore's last temper tantrum. His voice was hoarse and deep from sleep.

"Who told you I was looking for you?" I wondered just realizing that he had said that.

"A rabbit heard you calling my name. They don't understand you but they know what my name sounds like. So I guess when she heard you calling for me and she knew where I was, they always do, she came to get me." This was among the strangest things I've had to process since I've been here and I've had to process really strange things.

I noticed that he didn't ask why I was looking for him. It seemed like it didn't matter what I wanted. He would be there anyway, because we were friends.

"Do I move around when I'm in a reading?"

"No, you're really still, it's like you're in a trance," he explained. "It's a little creepy actually."

He yawned and stretched his arms above his head.

I smiled at his honesty, "Do you think people would notice me doing a reading?"

"In the way you've been doing it, yeah. Because you're sitting or standing straight but totally still like in the middle of everything with the world going on around you."

"I have to think of something else, some way to make myself inconspicuous."

He looked casually behind him when he heard an animal scoot by in the woods. He smiled and nodded at it. I thought he wasn't paying attention to our conversation but of course he was, which I realized when he said, "Maybe you should lean up against something. Make it look like you're just thinking." He tilted back in his chair and ran his hands through his hair, shaking out the pine needles as he felt them then just let his arms rest on the top of his head.

I thought about it and nodded, "That's a good idea, let's try it."

The door to Anira's trailer opened and out she stepped looking mouthwatering. This morning she wore a dark blue top that gathered and ended around her ribs. There were no sleeves but little ruffles around the arm holes and the neck and also around the bottom by her ribs right underneath her, ...don't look there Aurelious. Her skirt hung low around her hips. It was a mix of colors, dark blue, greens, and yellows. She was barefoot.

The chain around her belly accented her small waist and the curve of the top of her hips. The gold of the chain glistened against her sun kissed skin. Her hair was wet in some places but starting to dry and curl around her perfect face.

"Um good morning weirdoes hanging out outside of my home." She smiled at both of us.

"We're hungry," Danyon said smiling his trademark huge smile.

"That smile isn't going to work on me Danyon," she said with her hand on one hip.

"Please make me something," he pretended to beg.

"You're lucky I like to cook," she snorted. "I'll make breakfast while you two set up out here to eat."

"No problem," Danyon said popping out of his seat and rubbing his hands together.

Anira was turning to go back into her house when she noticed I hadn't said anything, "Are you okay Aurelious?"

I couldn't stop staring at her, "Yeah, I'm just really hungry." But it wasn't for food. I smiled a wicked smile and winked at her.

"Oh here we go," she said in mock disgust and walked into her house trying unsuccessfully to hide her smile.

Chapter Forty-Four

"Ugh, gross," was Danyon's response to my now completely unabashed attraction to Anira. "So how about practicing that reading?" He was deflecting my attention, which was a good idea or else I would probably accomplish nothing.

"Yeah, where should I stand, somewhere out of the way I guess?" We looked around and decided that I would go by the end of the trailers near the edge of the woods, which was only a few feet away. I was definitely not away from the action but not quite in it either.

"Who are you going to read?" There still were not too many people around and none that were in one consistent spot.

"Anira I guess. I'll read her when she comes out again. That would mean that I would have to get in quickly since I don't know when she is coming out or how long she'll be outside before she goes back in."

I leaned up against the side of the trailer and put my hands in my pockets to prepare to look like I was just thinking. I heard the movement in the trailer that indicated Anira was heading toward the door so I closed my eyes and breathed in deeply. I was there in an instant. When I heard the door open I filed the trailer sound away, the only one I had left besides my own breath, and I pushed forward. I felt the instantaneous rush and I opened my eyes.

Anira was walking down the steps with a pitcher in one hand and some cups in another. Breathe. She stepped off the bottom step and said something to Danyon. Then she looked in my direction, with a nod and a small smile. She looked at Danyon again and said something and they both laughed. She looked down at the ground. I followed her gaze. There was a small ball on the ground in her path to the table. I pushed forward to see the decision she would make about this ball and opened my eyes again.

Her image split. Breathe. One of her moved the ball aside with her foot and set the pitcher down on the table. The other picked her foot up to step over the ball. As she moved forward and her foot came down she caught her toes on the bottom of her skirt. She stumbled forward and as she did, she splashed the liquid in the pitcher up on her shirt and neck. Danyon quickly got up to help her. She didn't fall, just stumbled. I could tell that he laughed and she kind of did too. I pulled back to see which choice she made. Breathe. She would end up wet with her choice, I should tell her.

I brought the sounds back in slowly and waited with my eyes closed, not wanting to feel the pain from the sunlight. I heard the door.

"Where's Aurelious?" she asked Danyon.

"He's over there doing a reading."

This was when she looked in my direction and smiled, happy to see that I was practicing which meant that I had fully accepted what I could do. I went to open my eyes to tell her to kick the ball aside but when I tried they stung severely and started watering a lot.

"Anira, kick the ball aside, don't step over it, you'll get your foot caught in your skirt," I bent over and pushed the palms of my hands into my eyes. I heard her put the pitcher down on the table and a moment later she and Danyon were at my side. I needed to sit down, so I sat where I was with my eyes still sealed shut.

"Aurelious!" Anira was frightened I could feel it.

"I'll be okay Anira," I assured her. She made a conscious decision to allay her fears. "It's the light, it hurts my eyes when I come out of a reading." I blinked more and more until I was able to open them, "Actually they pretty much hurt whenever it's sunny like this."

Danyon and Anira looked at each other and frowned. Perplexed they looked back at me.

Danyon said, "But it's cloudy today, really cloudy. It's going to rain soon."

"It is?" I squinted and tried to look up at the sky to see the clouds but it was pointless. Now even a cloudy day was too bright. "Why is this happening?"

"It's because of the color of your eyes," Brekwyn said coming up to us from around the trailer.

"What about the color? It's never been this much of a problem before," I said.

Again, Danyon and Anira looked at each other like they were confused, this time it was Anira who said, "Aurelious when was the last time you looked in a mirror?"

I thought about it, "I don't remember."

"I think you should go inside and have a look," Danyon said.

We stood up and staying in the shade, we went inside to Anira's bathroom. The three of them watched me from the doorway as I looked in the mirror. Without turning on the light I should add.

"What the?" I couldn't believe what I was looking at. Brekwyn told me that my eyes would get lighter as my gift developed but this was crazy. They were so many shades lighter than they used to be that I could have been a different person. It was literally like looking at someone else's image. The rim that outlined the iris was still the same dark blue that it always was but inside that outline the blue now looked like crystal tinted with turquois. They looked wet and bright, like glass, or like a smooth Caribbean sea. 'Crystal blue eyes' is how someone would describe them. I didn't hate it.

I looked back my friends. They were all smiling with excitement at this new revelation that I just discovered.

"Light eyes are more sensitive to the sun, that's why they have been progressively getting more painful. The lighter they are the more sensitive they become. The lighter they are, the more advanced your gift is," Brekwyn explained.

But I wasn't paying attention to what Brekwyn was saying about that, I was thinking about how they looked, "They don't look so bad," I said trying not to sound like I was too impressed with myself.

"They're cool!" Danyon said and started bouncing.

"Beautiful," Anira said. You heard that right? She said my eyes were beautiful.

Like me, neither of them thought about what Brekwyn said either, but maybe we should have paid more attention to him. Sure they looked cool but they also revealed who I was to anyone who was looking for me. The Reader's curse.

Chapter Forty-Five

"Why do we call him 'the Inglore'?" I asked Danyon and Anira when we were sitting on top of Danyon's families trailer one evening a few days later.

They both looked at me like they were confused so I clarified, "I mean why don't we just say Inglore, what's with the 'the'?"

"He's kind of more of a thing I guess, less of a man," Anira explained, "because he's so powerful and because he's a prophet."

"But Brekwyn is the same as he is and we don't say 'the Brekwyn'," I said.

"Yeah but Brekwyn's a part of our family, we've known him forever so to us he's more regular than the Inglore is," Danyon offered before looking over the edge of the roof to communicate with Poppy who was down on the ground and not too happy about it. "Plus, he hasn't unleashed his full power. Who knows what will happen then. Maybe then people will call him 'the Brekwyn'."

We laughed at the absurdity of the thought.

"The music is starting," Anira said, dancing around while still sitting.

I smiled at her, I couldn't help but smile at her, " So I guess it's time to go then?"

"Oh, yeah," Danyon said bouncing up and going down the ladder.

"After you," I said to Anira.

"Why thank you," she mocked me.

There was a festival tonight. I think it was a festival just for the sake of having a festival. We hadn't had one since we were at this new location. Actually we hadn't had one since the night that the messengers came and by now that was more than a month ago.

We stopped by Anira's trailer to get food that she made during the day and, of course, to get the tambourines.

"I should learn how to play these things," I said tapping one on my hip. "There I think I pretty much just taught myself everything I need to know." We all laughed again.

"Every good Gypsy needs to be able to play the tambourine!" Danyon said, bouncing which meant that he was excited and wanted to go or do or say or anything that excited him.

"Really?" I asked, "Is that like a thing?"

"No," Danyon snorted and shook his head, "you're too gullible."

"That's the thing that isn't true?" I said, "And yet I believe that you can talk to animals?"

We continued with our friendly banter as we made our way to the festival. Of course it was in full swing when we got there, I've come to understand that once the music starts, the festival is in full swing.

Anira went off in a different direction to put the food down and talk to some of the other Gypsies. Danyon and I walked over toward Brekwyn who was telling a story to a group of children.

"This is one of my favorites," Danyon said.

"What's it about?"

"The Gypsy King, of course, the little ones always want Brekwyn to tell them stories of the Gypsy King."

"There's a Gypsy King? I thought there wasn't any like formal leader of the Gypsies."

"Oh, there isn't," Danyon confirmed. "These are just stories that have been past down for generations. This one's almost over, it was about the Gypsy King slaying a dragon and saving all of the Gypsies."

The clapping and cheers from the children let me know that the story was over and the Gypsy King had won as Danyon explained.

As soon as the story was over Danyon gave me a smirk and ran over by the musicians to dance. Did I mention that he loved to dance? Well let's face it, they all loved to dance and celebrate and laugh.

There always seemed to be something for this tribe to celebrate and the feeling was infectious. As I looked around at the crowd I noticed that everyone was enjoying something. Whether it was conversation, food, drink, or dancing, whatever it was there were smiles and laughter everywhere. There was a fire too, in the middle of it all there was a fire that lit up the night and kept those who weren't dancing warm in the cool summer air.

I found Anira dancing with a group of little girls. She had her arms above her head and she looked like she was belly dancing, moving her hips from side to side. The little girls were copying what she was doing. There was a routine to this dance and it kept in time with the music. The moonlight shined on her shoulders and her long wavy hair. She was amazing.

She was wearing all white tonight. Her shirt was that same style that showed off her beautiful stomach, it was a pretty common look for the young women here. Her white skirt was long and flowing and moved with the dance as she did. She had her coins around her ankles and bracelets, too many to count, around each wrist. She didn't wear a scarf around her head to-night. Instead she let her hair hang loosely around her face and neck, down to the middle of her back. Every once and a while one of the gold hoops in her ears would catch the light of the fire, making it look like she was sparkling. Sometimes someone would walk by and try to talk to me but I had no idea what they were saying, I could only watch her. Her smile made me smile. And then I felt it.

Chapter Forty-Six

It was as if I had the wind knocked out of me. My heart started to race. I started sweating. I was suddenly completely overwhelmed. And it was all because of Anira. I realized in that moment that all I wanted to do was make her laugh and smile, I realized that if she was sad I would do anything to make her happy, if she was sick I would do everything to make her well and if she got hurt I might die because just the idea that it could happen actually made my stomach turn. If I had to spend one day without seeing this girl, it would be the worst day of my life. Oh my God. I loved her.

I couldn't wait another second. I had to be near her. I didn't care about whom she was dancing with or who saw me or who thought I was weird by walking into a pack of dancers. I grabbed her hand and turned her around to face me.

She had a huge smile on her face from the dancing and was ready to dance with me until she felt it. The smile faded. We stood just looking at each other, letting the music move the people around us. The air was thick and warm. Everything around me started to fade away but I resisted. I would stay present.

"It's about time." She smiled again but this smile was different. This smile was sexy as hell.

"Come with me," I whispered into her ear, inhaling her haunting scent as I did.

She didn't respond, she didn't protest.

I took her into the woods, our path lit only by the bright full moon above us. We didn't speak until we stopped walking. She leaned her back up against a huge old tree. I moved in toward her, resting one of my hands on the tree next to her head while the other gently smoothed one of her curls.

I leaned my head toward her neck and inhaled again, "You know you smell like lemons?" I told her.

"Must be my soap," she said barely above a whisper.

"Only you smell like this." I inhaled again. "It's ingrained in my memory."

She didn't say anything but I felt her breath on my neck. It was warm, each breath getting quicker but deeper.

"I've never seen anyone as beautiful as you, just the thought of you takes my breath away," I said.

"You were amazing from the first moment I saw you," she responded.

"You saved me and you didn't give up on me. You knew what I didn't know. You saw what I was too blind to see."

"Aurelious," she said but I stopped her.

"But I'm not blind anymore." I moved my face in front of hers, our lips practically touching.

"Anira," I breathed, "I love you."

"I know," she whispered.

I looked at her in the moonlight. Her mouth was soft, slightly opened as if she had something she wanted to say. Slowly I moved my head toward hers. I watched as her eyelids grew heavier the closer we got to each other. Her lashes fluttered on her cheeks. I touched my lips to hers, softly, gently, inhaling the sweet, lemony fragrance of her. Her lips were soft as I pressed mine against them. I felt her hand on my cheek.

There was no sound around us. The only thing I heard at that moment was my heartbeat. The rest of the world stopped. When I pulled away and looked at her she kept her eyes closed for just a moment longer before reaching her fingers up to her mouth, resting them on her lips.

"Aurelious, I've loved you since the day I was born." There were tears in her eyes.

I smiled and rested a hand on the soft, smooth curve of her waist and I kissed her again. And then again. She tasted sweet and warm. With each kiss I willed this moment not to end.

But it did end, when we heard the sound of someone running through the woods towards us. "There you are." It was Danyon and Poppy. "Come back to the festival, it's important." He was out of breath but as soon as he said that he turned to run back so we followed without asking questions but remembering what happened at the last festival.

As we neared the edge of the woods we could hear the sounds of excitement. There was something bigger than the end of a story or a Gypsy dance happening. Everyone was gathered in a crowd, I jumped up to try to see what the excitement was all about but I couldn't see. Anira did the same but with the same outcome.

"Here, stand on this Anira." Danyon had a chair in his hand and a huge smile on his face.

She didn't hesitate but leapt right up onto the chair. I watched her as she saw what the commotion was about. Her hand went to her chest as if she had to catch her breath. Tears sprung to her eyes again, immediately spilling over and rolling down her cheeks.

"Daddy."

It was almost like it came out on her breath, it was quiet but I am certain that the world could feel her say it.

The crowd parted and this man emerged. He had a kind face and straight brown hair that had some flecks of grey mixed in. It was a full head of hair that looked like it needed a haircut, casually pushed to the side. He had a scruffy beard. It wasn't long, but looked like he hadn't shaved in a week. His eyes were both soft and intense at the same time, if that makes sense. His mouth was interesting and when he smiled he didn't part his lips to reveal his teeth, instead the measure of his joy was evident in the intensity of his eyes. He wore a white shirt with the sleeves rolled up to the elbows. His pants were dark colored with a red rope belt around his waist. He was in good shape. Slim but strong.

He came directly to Anira, as if noticing no one else and without saying anything he grabbed her up and hugged her. She hugged him back. Then in the blink of an eye, the girl that I finally fell in love with became someone I hadn't met yet. She became a daughter.

Chapter Forty-Seven

"Let me look at my girl," he said to her softly as they pulled apart from their hug. He held her face in his hands. "More beautiful than anyone should have a right to be." He had a thoughtful look on his face.

"I missed you so much Daddy." Her tears fell harder like she had held them in since the day he left.

"I know my girl. I looked up at the stars every night and was comforted to know that they were shining on you too. I looked to the sunrise every morning and gave thanks that it would keep you warm," he whispered to her and she hugged him harder.

"So much has happened. I have so much to tell you," as if realizing that they weren't alone in the world, she turned to me standing beside her. "Daddy, this is Aurelious."

He looked at me intently. "So, what I've had heard is true," he said seriously. "The Reader is here."

"Yes, he's here," she said to him, smiling at me then smiling back at him like a proud child showing their parent an award they'd won.

He took a deep breath and I saw something in his eyes but I didn't know what it was because it was so quick and then just as quickly he smiled back at Anira. She didn't notice that something, what was it?

"Aurelious, I'm Callay, and I'll be happy to know you." He smiled, just like Anira did, and then he put his arm around me in a hug, "I think we have a lot to talk about too, you and I?"

Anira's smile grew even bigger so, for her I said, "Yes sir." Which was totally unnatural because I've never called anyone sir before but I wasn't exactly sure what to say. I focused solely on feeling happy for Anira, which she would've felt, but to her it could've been that I was happy to meet Callay. And I was, but I was also curious, what was that look?

"Sir?" Danyon said coming up next to me, mocking me just a little for my sudden uncharacteristic formality, "That's hilarious!"

"Danyon my boy, have you been keeping out of trouble?" He rubbed his hand in Danyon's hair affectionately.

"Never!" he exclaimed with a proud pose followed by a typical Danyon smile and laugh, Callay laughed too. Danyon kind of reminded me of Peter Pan, the thought made me laugh with them.

"Callay, welcome back my friend!" Brekwyn said as the two shook hands and then hugged.

Brekwyn turned to address the crowd. "Welcome home to all of our weary travelers. This is a wonderful day for our tribe to have our sellers home with us at last. A perfect night for a celebration."

It was just then that I noticed there were other men I hadn't seen before who were dressed like Callay and standing with their arms around their loved ones listening to Brekwyn.

"We have a lot to tell one another, stories to share about our travels, and introductions of a new member of our family to be made." He winked at me. "Tomorrow we'll talk about more pressing matters but tonight we celebrate!"

Music started again as did the dancing. Later, I watched Anira dance with her father, her head resting on his chest as he held her and swayed, and every once in a while a lonely tear rolled down her cheek.

Chapter Forty-Eight

So all of a sudden I loved Anira and because of that revelation, everything changed. I loved Gypsies, I loved Danyon and Brekwyn, I loved the trees, I loved the smell of the dirt. You name it I loved it. Experiencing love for the first time is unbelievable. Most of you probably don't realize this because you've likely loved someone and someone has loved you since before you could realize what love was so it's natural part of your existence. But I experienced it for the first time when I was old enough to feel how different and amazing it was.

It was the weirdest thing I'd ever felt. I'm not even kidding and you know by now that I've been in some really weird situations recently. The feeling is so consuming that it didn't allow room for the Inglore to haunt my dreams that night of the festival and because of that I got a great sleep and woke up excited. I bounced out of bed like I was Danyon and I ran right out the door intending to go over to Anira's trailer but was struck blind by the light of the sun. Damn it.

I was forced to retreat back into my darkened room to figure out a solution or at the very least, wait until she came over here. Then I remembered that Callay was home and maybe it was better that I gave them some space. So what did I do? Nothing. For the first time in a million years, I laid in my bed, stared at the ceiling and day dreamed. If I had my laptop I would be writing feverishly but since I didn't, I thought feverishly instead. And all of my thoughts were good and happy. I hoped, I planned, I smiled to myself at the amazement of this life I had and I cherished the thought of it all.

After an hour or more, my thoughts were interrupted by the

murmur of voices outside. I perked up thinking maybe it was Anira or Danyon coming for a visit. I opened the door to my room and listened in the kitchen to see who was outside.

I could hear a few men talking. I recognized Brekwyn and Callay's voices but not the others. There was something different about Callay's voice. I hadn't noticed it the night before which is surprising because it would be something I would typically notice right away. I can't say for sure what it was. There was just a hint of something in the way that he pronounced his words. I wouldn't say he had a clear and discernable accent or that he had a speech impediment, really I just couldn't put my finger on it and when I tell you it was extremely slight and totally vague I'm not exaggerating. It was hardly noticeable and maybe wouldn't be noticeable at all to someone else, but I picked up on it and filed it away in the 'hmm that's interesting' folder in my brain.

They were talking about me. It was obvious by all of the times they said 'he'. I didn't plan to eavesdrop but my curiosity got the best of me, surprise, surprise, and I listened.

"Is it true that there have been visits from the Inglore?" one of the men I didn't recognize asked.

"Yes," this was Brekwyn's voice, "but we avoided the path and kept him safe."

"But you didn't avoid his path entirely," this was Callay, "he still managed to infiltrate the village and cause damage."

"He damaged property but our people were all safe."

"Thanks to the insight of the Fortune Tellers," Callay said. I listened harder to see if I could decipher what I was hearing in his voice.

"Yes, thanks to Telera and Megana," Brekwyn was talking more pointedly. There was tension in his voice. If I could see him I know there would have been a little line in his forehead.

"Brekwyn forgive me," from another unrecognizable voice, "but is our family really safe? I mean the Inglore found him before, what's to stop him from finding him again? And then what kind of danger are our loved ones in the next time we cross paths? Surely he could be more destructive next time."

"We'll stop Inglore from finding Aurelious. This is our job, he's a part of our tribe," Brekwyn said this like it should be obvious.

"You're right," this from the first man, "he is a part of our tribe, a part of our family. We'll protect him like we protect all others."

"And if that means we have to move again and again, with less time in each place?" the second man asked.

"Then we move," Brekwyn said with confidence.

"So be it," the second man said, seeming to now agree with my fate according to Brekwyn.

"I think we need to be more thoughtful about this," Callay said just when I thought my position here was safe.

"What are you saying Callay?" Brekwyn asked.

"He's a target. Inglore will not stop until he gets what he wants."

"So we live according to what Inglore wants? I for one will never live my life under the influence of Inglore's erratic, selfish and destructive behaviors and I will not have my tribe living in fear. We are a strong people. We live our best according to Gypsy law and tradition. If Inglore chooses not to live that way then that's on him but we will not cower or give in to him just because he throws a temper tantrum like a spoiled child. We will continue to live as we always have and Aurelious will be a part of this life, he deserves that. He belongs with us."

"Does he?" Callay asked, "Does he belong with us Brekwyn?" Now it was the inflection in his voice that was more disarming than whatever it was that I heard in his speech. So Callay wasn't convinced that I belonged here.

I could hear Brekwyn sigh, "Yes, Callay. He belongs with us."

"I question this as Callay does," another man spoke up. "We're a peaceful tribe, violence is not in our nature. But it appears to be heavy in the Inglore and I, for one, don't want our family to be put in his path."

"Donheil, I appreciate your input but you assume that having Aurelious here means that we will automatically evoke the wrath of Inglore," Brewkyn said to the digger, now I recognized his voice.

"It's already happened Brekwyn," Doheil said, "it's naïve to assume it won't continue to happen until he gets what he wants. Naïve and irresponsible."

"I have never put this tribe in harms way or for one second been irresponsible with anyone's life," Brewkyn said more emphatically. A breeze kicked up, blowing the curtain in front of the open kitchen window.

"Surely that's correct but you haven't been yourself lately, since you found him something is different. You're preoccupied with his training, with where he is, with whom he's with. You're preoccupied by making sure he isn't alone in the woods, that he's always in someone's sight." I didn't know that. "At your request, I've had to follow him underground in case he needed to be hidden. This isn't a normal life Brekwyn, this isn't your normal life." Small, fat drops of rain pinged against the metal roof of the trailer.

"I care for all of our tribe," Brekwyn growled.

Donheil didn't seem to get the hint that he should cool it, instead he said, "Not the same way you do for him, it's as if you're obsessed with him."

Thunder rumbled in the distance. This was not good I had to get out there. Something bad was going to happen. I ran to the door and burst out it only to be stricken blind by the brightness. I staggered back against the trailer to where I knew there would be shade and blinked until I was able to open my eyes.

Brekwyn and Donheil stood facing each other. Callay and two other men that I hadn't seen before sat around a table with an umbrella in the middle of it, not sure what they were witnessing.

"I've searched for him," Brekwyn pointed at me as he spoke through clenched teeth, "I have searched for him for months, rummaging through the dregs of Gadje society. And I found him. I found him!" he yelled and the ground below Donheil's feet started to shift. "I sacrificed everything and I did what I was supposed to do." Donheil started to sink into the dirt, "Do you expect that I should throw all that away?" But Donheil's gift was that he could move dirt so I watched as he focused on the ground below his and pushed himself back up by quickly filling in the hole that Brekwyn was creating.

Donheil wasn't backing down, "If it means keeping our family safe then yes, give it up, give him up, give him to the Inglore and we can continue on as we always did before!"

In a flash Donheil was up to his waist in a hole and just as quickly, rocks came flying from everywhere piling around him. He couldn't move rock and as good as he was at moving dirt, Brekwyn proved that he was far better.

The line in Brekwyn's forehead was deep, he was practically snarling, almost animalistic, "He is not a commodity, I will not trade him for your comfort! And if Inglore finds him and Inglore enslaves the Gadje do you think we will ever have peace? Do you not see the bigger picture? A world of slaves is a world that's dead, it has no future!" The wind raged, ripping the umbrella up out of the table and tearing the fabric off the metal frame. Callay and the other men jumped back from the flying debris. But the umbrella didn't land instead, in mid-air, it turned on it's side and started to revolve like a propeller, the metal spokes whipping around like a deadly weapon inching it's way toward Donheil's head.

"Brekwyn, enough of this!" Callay yelled to him over the resounding wind. A massive crack of thunder was Brekwyn's response.

"I will not now, nor will I ever put our family in danger, Aurelious is a part of that family. And I will do all that I can to protect the Gadje, to save this Earth the right way. How dare you suggest otherwise!" he continued to yell at Donheil.

The digger frantically moved the dirt outside of the ring of rocks so they would tumble toward it and he could get free. It seemed like a logical plan until a bolt of lightening hit the ground in front of him. The sound was deafening and the ground shook so violently that we all stumbled or fell, but not Brekwyn. My ears were ringing, I couldn't hear what he was saying, I could only see his mouth move. Everyone was holding their ears and trying to get to their feet, dirt was flying all around us.

I coughed and spit and wiping my eyes, I saw something in the distance. Something small. It was coming closer. It was Tanent. He was running, running toward Brekwyn. I held my hand up to tell him to stay back but he didn't see me. He was crying and calling Brekwyn's name. He witnessed what was happening and was desperate for Brekwyn to stop. He was so scared. He reached Brekwyn and grabbed his arm. But Brekwyn didn't realize it was a little boy that was trying to stop him and as a reflex, in all of his fury, he whipped his arm to the side sending Tanent sailing through the air, hitting against the trailer and collapsing in a heap on the ground.

Enraged and ready to continue the fight, Brekwyn turned to meet his attacker head on. Instead he saw Tanent's tiny body and everything, maybe even time itself, stopped.

Chapter Forty-Nine

There wasn't a sound in the forest. Not a sound in our village. Nothing moved. Everything was still. Until the reality of what just happened resonated in us.

"Tanent!" Brekwyn yelled and ran over to his little body, skidding on his knees beside him.

"Don't touch him Brekwyn!" Callay called running after him, "We must first alert the healer to see if he can be moved!"

The two men I didn't recognize ran off to get the healer.

"Oh Callay," Brekwyn looked at him, in shock, completely dismayed, "what have I done?"

Donheil crawled out of the ground, stumbling to his feet and staggered backward until he slumped against the table. He was barely able to function, completely incapable of processing what he just witnessed.

None of them understood it, but I did, I'd seen people lose it before and Brekwyn had lost it. He spent every ounce of his energy for his whole life keeping himself under control when it wasn't really in his nature. Just like it wasn't in Inglore's nature either. Nature cannot be controlled, no matter how hard anyone tries; eventually it rears its beautiful, perilous head. And Brekwyn and Inglore, with all of their powers and abilities, were Nature.

"He's alive," Callay said softly but it did little to reassure Brekwyn.

I did the only thing I could think of at that moment, as out of place as it may seem, I slipped into a reading, desperate to find out something about Tanent.

When I came out only a second later, I too tried to reassure Brekwyn, "I saw him," I said putting my hand on Brekwyn's shoulder, "you can pick him up. He's gonna be okay."

He picked Tanent up and cradled him in his arms. And as he rocked the little boy, he cried. And it was the only sound in the world.

It wasn't long before Tanent woke up, he was groggy and scared and as soon as he saw the tears on Brekwyn's face he too started to cry. But through his tears he reassured Brekwyn that he was okay. And within another minute, what appeared to be the rest of the tribe came running to see what had happened. It was a terribly dramatic scene; there was a lot of crying. But not one person was mad at Brekwyn, not even Tanent's parents. It's almost as if the tribe was waiting for this to happen or at the very least aware that some day it could.

Before long Tanent was even laughing. But Brekwyn wasn't. Something changed in Brekwyn's face. Something in his eyes was different. But only I noticed because I was the only one who watched him slip away and into the woods.

Chapter Fifty

Sure no one was upset with Brekwyn but people still didn't know what to do. There was a lot of talking, a lot of commotion, and a lot of confusion. And the reality is that it was all because of me so I decided to man up and address the crowd.

I climbed up onto the table to get everyone's attention, "I'm afraid this is all my fault," I began, "see this all started because of me. Not just what happened a few minutes ago but what's been happening for the last few months. I know that things have changed for all of you and for many the change hasn't necessarily been better. For that I'm sorry. I was quite broken when I came here but the love, care and understanding that you all showed healed me. For that I will be forever in your debt." I took a deep breath and smiled at Anira and then at Danyon.

"I know that the Inglore is looking for me and that puts all of you in danger. The right thing for me to do would be to leave so you can all be safe but I don't want to leave. You've become my family. Danyon has become my best friend and I fell completely in love with Anira." I tossed my hands up in the air and a tear rolled down my cheek, not from the brightness outside.

"I don't ever want to leave this place but that isn't for me to decide. I leave it to you. And don't worry, I understand if you want me to go and I won't harbor any bad feelings if you do because you have done more for me in the last month than anyone ever has in my whole life. Brekwyn withstood my terrible attitude and defiance, he stuck with me, he believed in me and made me become the person that I was born to be and all of you made me better.

"So I'll go for a while so you can decide what to do with me. But please understand that no matter what happens, if there's a fight to be had, I will fight for your side. I will never do what the Inglore wants me to do."

I came down from the table, hugged Anira and Danyon and walked off to find Brekwyn. Completely unaware that I just made a promise I couldn't keep.

Chapter Fifty-One

B rekwyn stayed in the forest for two days. He didn't speak or acknowledge my existence though I know he knew that I was there. I stayed near him but didn't bother him. Instead I paced back and forth, desperately wondering what the tribe was going to decide about my future. It was like torture.

"We are not always born into the places we belong." Callay came up from behind me and, quite frankly, scared the shit out of me. "Some have to journey, but when they find their place it becomes clear that they are where they were always meant to be and with the person or people they were always meant to be with." Callay's penetrating eyes did not leave me when he talked. "You're welcome here Aurelious. We'd like you to stay."

I exhaled so hard it was as if I'd been holding my breath for the last two days, "But what about the Inglore?"

"Well, Inglore is Inglore no matter what. We'll deal with him when the time comes." He smiled slightly with his mouth but more intensely with his eyes then squinted and said, "But I'm going to keep my eye on you. You and my daughter."

I felt my face immediately get red. Thank God he can't read my mind about his daughter. Sheesh.

"Brekwyn," he called, "come now, it's time to come home."

And to my complete surprise, Brekwyn stood up and came over.

"Better now?" Callay asked with a hand on his shoulder, "Re-focused?"

"Yes," he smiled slightly, "thank you my friend."

Wait, that's it? It's that easy?

Brekwyn smiled at my thoughts, "There have been occasions growing up where I had to re-focus my mind and my energies. Being alone is the best way for me to do that. Well, I'm usually alone." He smirked at me.

"Huh," I said, "and all along I was thinking that if you unleashed all of your power and became *The Brekwyn* that like everything would be totally different for you."

"It probably would," he agreed, "but I don't know because I haven't done it. What you saw, that wasn't my full power."

Oh shit.

Oh, by the way, we partied really hard that night. And by 'partied really hard' I mean, danced, ate, drank (juice, really they don't drink alcohol here), and well Anira and I made out, a lot, in the woods where no one was watching. It was awesome. All was right with the world.

Chapter Fifty-Two

"Ahh, here come your traveling companions," Brekwyn said to me when we were sitting outside of his trailer having breakfast a few days later. Anira, Danyon and Poppy rounded the corner when he said that.

"Traveling? Who's traveling?" Danyon asked, Anira and I were equally perplexed.

"Well, Aurelious has a problem to which there is a solution but the solution is not here," Brekwyn said. He tapped his finger on his eye, narrowing down which of my many problems he was referring to, it was the one with the light and the eyes. "The solution is in a little town about three miles down the road on the north side of the forest. Anira you're familiar with how to get there." She nodded, "So, I think it would be a good outing for the three of you to have today."

"To go into a town?" Danyon started bouncing. Poppy started panting. Oh, right, Danyon had never been away from the tribe before.

"Yes, I spoke with your family last night Danyon, and we feel that this is an experience that you must have at this time. The world is not all like it is here. Here is safe and comforting. Out there can be the same but it can also be challenging. It'll be good for you to get a small taste of what's out there," Brekwyn told him, I suspected it was for a bigger reason, I would come to understand that reason later.

"Ahhh, I am so excited!" Danyon hugged Anira really tight while she laughed and then he did the same to Poppy. "Let's go, I'm ready!"

We laughed at his enthusiasm.

Brekwyn chimed in with his voice of reason, "My friend, one of the things you will learn today is that when you go into a Gadje town you have to wear a shirt and shoes."

"Shoes? A shirt?" Clearly he didn't think that was reasonable. "But it's not even cold out."

"True," Brekwyn reasoned, "but when you're going into their world, you have to follow their conventions, at least in terms of actually wearing clothes."

"Okay, I'll go find my shoes. I can find a shirt no problem. Come on Poppy! Isn't this exciting?" She started to jump at his side as they headed off to find Danyon's elusive shoes.

"I'll come with you," Brekwyn told him and I heard him say, "About Poppy...." before they were too far off for us to hear anything else. I suspect this would be the moment that he learned another lesson. Poppy wouldn't be able to come with him on this adventure.

It wasn't long before they returned. This was the first time I had seen Danyon with a shirt and shoes on, he looked uncomfortable and I could be wrong but I think the shoes were making him limp a little. Telera was with them.

"Danyon, please remember the things that I told you. Listen to Anira and Aurelious, they have been to town before," Telera seemed worried, letting her son go away for the first time, no matter how little time that would be, was probably a difficult thing for her. "Remember that I love you and that we will all be here for you when you get home." I thought that last part was kind of a strange thing to say, kind of ominous, but I wasn't a mother so what did I know? She was trying to smile but the smile didn't reach her eyes, I wasn't sure that Danyon noticed.

"Brekwyn, where are we going when we get to town? How will we know what we're looking for to help Aurelious?" Leave it to Anira to focus us all back on our mission.

"You'll find a store called Pete's Variety. It's on the corner of Main Street and Old Factory Avenue. Main Street is what the road off the woods will turn into. There are some rundown buildings in that area. Don't be distracted or draw attention to yourselves. Stay focused and come directly home after you have accomplished your task," Brekwyn advised.

"Will Pete have what we're looking for?" Anira asked.

"Yes, it is called sunglasses," he snickered.

"Are you kidding me?" I asked. How stupid was I that I didn't think of that? Brekwyn and the other men that had come by started laughing. "I thought it was gonna be some magic Gypsy voodoo thing."

Now everyone was laughing including Danyon and Anira, I swear I thought Poppy might have laughed a little too but that would be weird, right?

"Make sure you get a pair that you like because you're going to be wearing them a lot, maybe get a backup pair in case one breaks," Brekwyn said before he added, "and by the way, Gypsies don't do voodoo." Followed by a pat on my back. I shook my head and smiled, joke was on me with all of that.

We were ready to leave as soon as Anira changed from her Gypsy style into jeans, a t-shirt, and sneakers like she was wearing when I first saw her. The three of us were excited for our adventure, excited enough to only listen to the advice and words of wisdom half heartedly.

"Remember Aurelious," Brekwyn said, "do not make yourself obvious. Even among Gadje your eyes stand out, they're memorable. Don't give people the opportunity to remember them. And, one more thing, do not practice your gift out there, you don't know who will be watching you. You aren't ready yet."

"Yeah, I got it," I said but I wasn't really paying attention. I was too anxious to go on this adventure with Anira and Danyon.

I should have paid attention.

Chapter Fifty-Three

It didn't take us as long as you would think to get into town. That probably had a lot to do with the fact that Danyon was practically running. There only seemed to be one thing that he had a problem with when we left and that was not having Poppy with him and then explaining to her why she couldn't come. But he was able to push those feelings aside when we were through the woods and focused on the journey ahead.

"I see it. Up there. Do you see it?" Danyon's first glimpse at what you would think of as "civilization" at least compared to where Danyon came from. I learned along the way that he had seen glimpses of towns when the tribe traveled from place to place but since they traveled at night he wasn't able to see much and most of the time he was asleep. The purpose of traveling at night was because so many trailers in a caravan like that would attract a lot of attention and attention was not something that these Gypsies were interested in.

"Yes," Anira said gently, I think she was trying to keep him a little calm but not take away his excitement, because I was feeling pretty calm myself. "I see it."

"Danyon, when we get up there you have to walk on the sidewalk and stay off the road so we're out of the way of cars," I advised, we were starting to see more and more traffic the closer we got to the town.

"Okay, my mother said the same thing," he laughed and bounced.

Once we were officially on Main Street, which just meant that this is where the town started on the road we had been walking on for three miles, Danyon couldn't get enough. He wanted to look at everything. It was fun to explain to him what kinds of things each of the stores sold. Anira and I pointed things out in the windows, I added stories about when I was in a store like one that we were standing by or about an experience I had with an item displayed in the window. We decided that we would look at the stores on this side of the road on our way to Pete's then cross the road and look at the stores on the other side on the way back so he wouldn't have to miss anything.

I really liked watching Danyon look at the Gadje. He tried to make it look like he wasn't staring which was pretty funny because he wasn't very good at being inconspicuous. He was captivated by skateboards. The clothes and shoes fascinated him too, as did the make-up that many of the girls were wearing. He didn't really understand the make-up because he didn't feel like it enhanced their beauty as I explained was the intention. I had to agree, I don't know if it was something about the town we were in but the make-up was too colorful and too heavy. Then again, maybe I had just gotten used to people looking like what they actually look like here in my Gypsy tribe.

Pete's Variety was easy to find. Once inside, the challenge became picking out the two pairs of sunglasses that I liked the best. With the advice of the two fashion critics (who knew?) we found some that were comfortable, dark enough, and pretty cool at the same time. Hey, if I was going to have these things on my face all day I better look good in them, right? Of course, you should be aware that the decision on which sunglasses to buy did not come until after we all tried on the ones that we thought were the most ridiculous, and maybe a hat or two at the same time.

Danyon was also totally enraptured by the whole idea of paying for goods, everything was new for him and I loved watching it through his eyes. I was so happy for the day he was having, this could have been one of the best days of Danyon's life. It wasn't until we left Pete's and were half way down the other side of the street that things started to change.

I was pointing out a television set that was in the window of a small appliance store. I looked back to see Danyon's excitement but instead he looked like he was somewhere else, he had a confused look on his face, like he was just staring at the window without actually seeing it.

"Danyon, are you okay?" I asked.

Anira turned to him when I said that, "Danyon, what's wrong?"

"Something's wrong," he said, and he started looking around. He got more frantic, his expression both worried and determined. "Something's wrong." He started to walk down the road in the direction we were headed, feverishly looking around. He was looking for something.

"Danyon what is it?" Anira asked. Her own expression worried.

"They're crying. They want to get out. Where are they?" He put his hands over his ears like something was hurting him, "Where are they?" he voice was louder.

"Who, who are you looking for? Tell us so we can help you," I said, as he broke into a slow run, we did the same to keep up with him.

"Ah!" he yelled and stopped running, bent over and covered his ears again. "They're babies, they're trapped and they want to get out!" He stood back up again and scanned the area. I could see it in his face when he spotted what he was looking for. Anira and I both followed his eye line and then him as he ran to the window of a rundown pet store.

As soon as he got there he knelt down to face the four puppies in the window. They all had their front paws up on the glass trying to get to him, their back paws balancing on the rails of the metal crate that was their bed, their prison. There was blood on the rails and the window. Their feet were being cut. He was talking to them in a language that was silent to us.

"I have to get them out. They're in pain, they're hungry." He was determined as he went to the door of the shop. It was locked. He tried pulling hard on the handle. The door wouldn't open. He banged on it. No one came. The sign in the window revealed that the store wasn't open at this hour, even though it was the middle of the day. He became more frantic.

"Danyon, we have to go," I told him.

"I cannot leave them here Aurelious. They're desperate to get out, it's terrible for them in there." He looked from me to Anira, pleading for help with his eyes.

"It's closed, no one's here, we can't do anything about it," I tried to explain. "Let's just go."

"We can't just go!" he yelled. "I have to get them out!"

"Shh," Anira hissed, "there's a guy across the street looking at us."

We all knew that we weren't supposed to draw attention to ourselves but Danyon didn't care, he was focused and driven to free these animals.

"I don't care, Anira," Danyon barked back and banged on the door again.

"Danyon stop this, this is a Gadje problem we have to leave!" Anira urged.

"It's not a Gadje problem, it's an animal problem!" he yelled at her, agony written all over his face. "Ahhh!" he yelled again putting his hands over his ears.

His eyes were wild. He went to the window, slapping it with his hands looking at every inch of the building to see if there was a way in. He looked around him. His expression went from agonized to determined as soon as he saw the large metal garbage can on the sidewalk. He ran over to it and quickly picked it up like it weighed little more than a feather.

"Danyon, no!" I shouted, running over to him. "You can't do this! It's illegal, the cops are gonna come here and then how do we explain this. Think Danyon!" I gripped onto the garbage pail. He wasn't thinking about consequence, he was only thinking of saving the animals. He himself was an animal right now, just as his gift dictated.

"Let go Aurelious!" he screamed back at me while still moving forward, his body positioned to smash the garbage pail through the window.

Anira grabbed a hold of it also. We both pulled back, the metal mesh burrowing into the flesh of our fingers. But in his rage he was stronger than we were, we were merely a bump in the road. I let go of the pail. The unexpected shift in resistance made him off balance and as soon as it did I tackled him to the ground. Anira pushed the pail aside and into the street and then jumped on top of Danyon, struggling to get free from me, legs flailing, arms swinging wildly until we could pin them down too.

"Look at me Danyon," I said right up in his face. "Look at me!" I caught his eye, he stared at me and I watched as his rage and determination vanished, replaced by sadness, helplessness. "We can't do this here, we have to go," I said softly, my own soul growing increasingly despondent at the sight of my friend breaking into pieces.

Tears came to his eyes when he was hit by the realization that he couldn't help them.

"Can I be of service here?" A man's voice came from above our positions on the ground.

"No, thank you," Anira said quickly, neither of us taking our eyes off of Danyon, "we're just leaving."

"Are you sure there isn't something I can do?" he asked again.

His intrusion annoyed me. We didn't need his stupid help. Driven by my empathy for Danyon's pain and fueled by my own adrenaline, I leapt up.

"She said 'No, thank you'." I growled.

"But surely there's something..."

I got right in his face, the look in his eyes changed the minute he saw mine. I know they were startling but he didn't look afraid or disgusted, he looked excited.

"You want to do something? Why don't you get your people to take care of this situation?" I pointed to the window of the pet shop.

"Yes, I would say that this is a situation that my people will have to be alerted to." He smiled the strangest smile as if the two of us were talking about different things.

"Good," I spit out, "stupid Gadje."

"Aurelious," Anira said as soon as I said the word 'Gadje'. I turned to them, both were standing now, "Let's go."

There was no more conversation, we left immediately, all of us knowing that we had just done things that we shouldn't have. I looked back at the man. He was still standing in the same spot. His legs were crossed at the ankles, one hand was in his pocket and the other was flipping a gold coin, which somehow managed to land right back into the palm of his hand even though he wasn't looking at it. The tips of his short, spikey, dark brown hair vibrated in the small breeze that kicked up. His strange smile never waivered.

Something bothered me about that man, why didn't he seem confused when I called him a 'stupid Gadje'? Surely Gadje themselves didn't know what that word meant. I cleared my mind as much as I could. I wouldn't focus on this man that I was sure I would never see again when my friend was in such pain. Danyon needed me and I would be there for him.

Chapter Fifty-Four

We led him away each with an arm around him. Once out of town we sat down on the side of the road and he cried. He cried for the animals in the window and he cried for the feeling of helpless that he had never experienced before. Anira cried for him.

Getting back to our village took longer than it did to get there. We walked in silence most of the way. As soon as we stepped off the road and into the woods Danyon took off his shoes and his shirt. There was no point in having them on anymore, no point in pretending he was anything like the people who lived in the town we just came from. And once in our village, there was no big celebration for this homecoming, no one gathering around us to hear about our trip, no one asking Danyon about how much fun he had.

As we got closer to Danyon's trailer Poppy came running toward him. At the sight of her he fell to his knees. At the sight of him, her ears went back and her tail went down. He buried his face into hers and cried again. Telera, Megana, and Brekwyn all came out of the trailer together. They said nothing to Danyon but Brekwyn offered him a hand which he took as he stood up. With what looked like heartbreak in their eyes they all went back inside, this time with Danyon and Poppy.

Telera, Megana, and Brekwyn knew that the Danyon they had sent with me to get sunglasses was not the Danyon that they would get back when we returned home. Telera's tears and sentiments this morning before we left suddenly made sense. This was a part of Danyon's future that Telera or Megana had seen, they knew it was going to happen and it needed to happen which was why they told Anira not to change his emotions. They were preparing Danyon to feel helpless, a feeling he had never felt before, but one I suspected he would feel again.

Chapter Fifty-Five

I realize what love is. Love is a deep appreciation. It is an awakening of senses. It is kindness and gratefulness. It is empathy, reverence, and happiness. Love as it turns out, is everything good multiplied by a million. But there's a down side to love and I found it.

So, the problem with love is that when you feel it for someone and that someone is in pain then you're in pain. When they're sad then you're sad. When they want to cry then you want to cry. When you love that means that you care and when you care, well, things are much more complicated.

Part of me wished that I could go back to the days when I first came here, the days when all I allowed myself to feel was indifference or even disdain because if I did then it would make this thing that happened with Danyon much easier on me. But the greater part of me had been in this life long enough to have been changed completely by it, so going back to indifference was no longer an option. Feeling bad for someone you care about and not being able to help him is horrific.

It was three days before I saw Danyon again. Each day I would go to his home but each day Telera or another member of his family would say that he was not ready to come out. This is probably the most time he had spent indoors in years.

Anira and I spent a lot of time together and I was getting to know this different side of her, as someone's daughter. She loved her father so deeply and he felt the same about her. I would see them laughing with each other like they were friends then I would see her listening to him like he was her teacher.

Callay was well loved and respected by all the members of the tribe and it was clear that he felt the same about them. But there was something about him that I couldn't put my finger on.

He looked over his shoulder a lot. Not like Danyon looking at an animal scurrying or flying by. No it was more like he was looking for someone or waiting for someone to appear. He seemed to be always protecting himself from something, like he was keeping something hidden away. But like that nuance that I picked up in his voice, I don't think anyone would notice this about him either. There was something that Callay didn't trust. I mean besides me. But I just couldn't figure out what it was so I filed the thought away and tried to convince myself that it was nothing.

It was probably hard for him that his daughter's soul mate turned out to be me, especially with all the baggage I came with. So I spent as much time with him in those few days as I could. I wanted him to get to know me and I certainly wanted to get to know him. We were definitely both trying to figure each other out but I don't know if it was for the same reason.

There was one thing that I was able to make entirely clear. I was completely in love with Anira and I would do everything I could to protect her. Fortunately he believed this about me because, let's face it, his daughter was an empath and if I wasn't feeling that way there would be no hiding it.

Early on the morning of the fourth day after our return from town, Anira and I decided to walk down to the lake. It was starting to take longer to warm up as we were approaching the end of the summer. So we sat close to each other, my arm around her shoulder as she snuggled into me to keep warm.

"I miss Danyon," I confided.

"I know you do, I can feel that. I miss him too. I wish I could've helped him."

"I'll be alright," Danyon said from behind us. We both turned around quickly, he was so quiet we didn't hear him coming but we got up right away and hugged him as if we hadn't seen him in a year.

"How are you feeling?" I asked him.

"Better, different I guess but better," he looked different. There was a spark that he had which seemed to be missing. He seemed more serious.

"Did you sleep out here last night?" Anira asked picking a small stick out of his hair.

"Yeah, I needed some air. It felt good to get back out," he looked off toward the lake, lost for a moment in his thoughts.

"Do you want to talk about what happened?" I asked him.

"I talked a lot with Brekwyn, my mom and my grandma. They helped me to understand what I was feeling and why I was feeling that way." He shook his head like he was disgusted, something I hadn't seen him do before. "I thought it was going to be different. I liked seeing all of the things that I saw but they're so different from us. They don't hear those babies screaming for help, they don't even notice them. Gadje." He practically spit out the last word.

"They don't know that what they're doing is wrong Danyon, find it in your heart to understand that," Anira pleaded with him.

"You don't have to be able to communicate with animals to know that they should not be living in metal cages that are cutting their feet until they bleed," he said this with a quiet forcefulness which seemed much more effective than if he had shouted it while stamping his foot.

"You're right," I told him. "But not everyone is like that, some people are fools but many are good and kind and just like you, if they saw what we saw they too would be doing something to get the situation fixed." There were good Gadje, a lot of them and when I finally released the bad ones from my life I was able to remember that. I had seen them from a distance and knew that were many more good ones than bad.

"Aurelious please, they had to have seen it. How could they

not, it was right there in the window, right on the street," he spoke the truth and I had no explanation that could offer any consolation, he wasn't stupid, he knew what he was talking about.

Danyon took a deep breath, "Let's move on from this. I don't want to talk about it anymore, I need for it to get out of my head." He looked at me and smiled, the smile wasn't as big and bright as the one I had known until now but it was a start, "You look good in those sunglasses. How are they working out?"

The three of us with Poppy by Danyon's side walked along the bank of the lake, "It's so much better. In just these couple of days I've really gotten used to them, I don't go out of Brekwyn's trailer without them. So I've been able to practice more and I feel pretty good about what I'm able to do." The sunglasses had made my life considerably more comfortable. I didn't wear them at night because I didn't have to, obviously, but I kept them on all day to save me from the stinging pain of the light.

"Have you been practicing a lot?" he asked me.

"Well without you bothering me all the time there was nothing else to do but practice," I joked to lighten the mood. It was working.

"Glad I could help," he laughed.

"Of course with you not around Danyon, that meant that when he wasn't practicing he was bugging me." Anira gave me a gentle shove.

"I don't know Anira, you look pretty kissy face. You probably loved it!" This was from Danyon so now it was him that got a shove from her and not quite as gently.

We all laughed at that, kissy face, only Danyon could say that and get away with it. I almost didn't notice a gentle breeze that blew. It was just a quick little breeze, nothing out of the ordinary but it hit my spine in a weird way and sent a shiver down it. And before I could think about it any further, it was gone.

Chapter Fifty-Six

The one miracle of my life, okay you're right there have been a lot of them, so one of the miracles of my life was that I stopped having nightmares about the Inglore. They stopped the night of the festival when I realized that I was in love with Anira. I had myself convinced that the two anomalies were connected. That is until my nightmares came back.

The first one left me in a pool of sweat and panic when I woke up. I was being chased like I usually was. I turned around like I usually did. And where there was usually darkness or the face of some evil player from my past, this time there was a man standing there in full view. But the man wasn't chasing me. Instead, he was in an alley leaning up against the wall. Where had I seen that image before? Do you remember?

Every nightmare ended the same way, a stranger in an alley leaning up against the wall. He never approached me. His expression never changed. He just always looked.... interested. I can't even be sure that it was him that was chasing me. But my fear was always present in the nightmare. Who was that man and who was causing the fear?

Every morning I forced myself to forget my nightmares, forget the man. He was no one, just a Gadje. I told myself that over and over until I could ignorantly will myself into believing it. And by the time I got out of bed I no longer thought about him because I couldn't. If I did then someone may have heard what I was thinking and he would've known what I did and what I said in the Gadje town, which was exactly what I wasn't supposed to do.

Danyon was starting to become his old self again. I was happy to see the return of the spark that I feared he had lost. His recovery took my mind off of my nocturnal anxieties. I noticed more of a serious side of him, more of a thoughtful side, but that essence of him that made him totally unique and beloved was coming back.

Things were changing in the tribe as well. Did you know that Gypsies actually had to do schoolwork? Not schoolwork like you have to do but they have lessons where they learn about Gypsy history and culture. They learn about geography, which is good because they never stay in one place forever. They even have to learn math like measurements and algebra, they learn about currencies both from here and other countries. They learn how to read.

I was watching them from a distance one day to see what they looked like when they learned. But I didn't stay long. I felt compelled to go inside Brekwyn's trailer into my room and stay there. I didn't allow myself to think about why I felt that way. So I read a book and willed myself not to think.

Before we went to into our separate trailers to sleep at night, Anira and I would take a walk in the woods just around the perimeter of the trailers. This was a bittersweet time for me because I loved being with her, especially when we were alone like this, but I knew that the end of our walk meant the onset of my nightmares.

"What are you worried about?" She looked at me. The moonlight illuminating the beauty of her face marred with worry.

I took a silent deep breath and forced myself to think of something other than my pending dreams so that my worry wouldn't be so evident to her. I smiled and kissed her on the cheek, "I'm just not looking forward to the end of our walk." It wasn't a lie, technically.

I took her face in mine and leaned in to kiss her more deeply. I loved the sweet, warm taste of her mouth. How did I ever live without kissing before?

I pulled back when I felt a chilling breeze run down my spine.

Again, it was instantaneous but I felt it. By now I was good at dismissing things and focusing only on what I wanted, like my new found happiness and time with Anira. But something didn't feel right out here, something didn't feel safe. So I forced my mind to think only about kissing her and led her back toward her trailer.

"I think it's time to go in." I smiled at her. "I don't think your father would be too happy with me if I kept you out any longer."

"Oh, so that's what you're worried about," she said as she hugged me in close as we walked. "He likes you, don't worry so much about him."

Well the jury was out about that but I didn't respond. Instead I kissed her goodnight and she walked inside. Then I jogged back to Brekwyn's trailer, though I didn't know why I felt the need to hurry. After all, I'm sure that the shadow I thought I saw out of the corner of my eye was nothing. It was nothing. It was nothing.

Chapter Fifty-Seven

Twice a week Danyon, Brekwyn, Anira and I, and Poppy of course, would take a walk to a remote part of the woods, not far from the road actually but not close enough to see it or hear any cars driving by. We would have something to eat and drink and we would talk to each other about totally miscellaneous things.

We talked about life things. We talked about how we felt and how we could use our gifts to do good in the world. We even talked about relationship things but in a serious way, Danyon never used it as an opportunity to make a joke about Anira and me. We listened to what Brekwyn said and we all listened to what each other had to say in response. I looked forward to these days, we had had five of them already and all were excellent. I didn't have a nightmare for the last three nights. I felt like whatever cloud was virtually hanging over my head which I was forcing myself to disregard had finally dissipated. So I felt great on the day of our sixth class and had no reason to think that this class, this day, would be any different from the others.

We were walking, oblivious to the world around us. We were laughing at an exchange between Danyon and Anira that was caused by Anira tripping, but not falling as she pointed out, over a log that we stepped over every time we came here. It wasn't until we got to our usual clearing that my world, as I had come to know it over the last several months, changed completely. It started with the sound of something flying past my ear followed by Brekwyn grabbing his neck and falling to his knees.

"What?" I was confused, was he joking?

"Brekwyn?" Anira was immediately in a panic as she ran around to the front of him to see his face. "Brekwyn?" she called again to him in horror.

He stared at her as he went from his knees to a sitting position. His face was blank as he pulled a dart out of his neck and looked at it as we did. What was happening?

He looked to me, only to me, "Be good Aurelious," he struggled with the words as he started to lie on his side. "I will find you." His eyes were closing, "Be good."

I didn't know what to say. I looked from Anira to Danyon who was holding Brekwyn's head. He was just as confused as I was, "What is this?" he asked terrified, "What is this?" louder this time.

"Aurelious," Anira physically took my face and turned it to hers. "Run."

"What?"

"Run!" She yelled.

"No, I have to help him!" I was so confused.

"Leave Aurelious, now, run!" Danyon yelled.

But it wasn't just the fear and confusion and desire to help Brekwyn that made me stay there, it was the sudden wind that knocked us over and held us down. It was like a punch in my side that took my breath away, but I recognized it. I had felt that wind before back when I was just starting my training. The Inglore hadn't forgotten about me, he was here and I was caught.

Chapter Fifty-Eight

Within seconds we were surrounded, the wind keeping us in our places, it wrapped around each of us so controlled, so fast that we couldn't move. But everything came into focus when four men dressed in black bound our hands with plastic ties. They were Gypsies clearly, but different from the ones in our tribe. Once our hands were bound the wind stopped, it was eerily silent. I kept my head down, not making eye contact with the men, my glasses had fallen off in the commotion and I didn't want them to see my eyes.

I looked around with my head still down and saw that they had tied Brekwyn to a tree with the same kind of plastic ties but he was completely unconscious from whatever was in the dart. Clever Gypsies, plastic was a Gadje made product, there were no natural elements in it so Brekwyn, if he was conscious, would not be able to manipulate them and break free. Danyon and Anira had their ankles tied as well as their hands. My mind was racing as I was trying to devise a plan for how we would escape this. But when I brought my lowered head to the front of me again, I noticed someone new had come and he was standing right in front of me.

"Look at me Reader," he said gently. He had an accent, the same one that his messengers had the night of my first festival. "There's no point in hiding your eyes from me. I know who you are." He inhaled deeply through his nose, "I can smell you from a mile away." He spoke softly, which surprised me. Part of me didn't want to look at him just for the sake of being defiant but my curiosity would not be overruled this time.

I looked up slowly though, memorizing every inch of this monster that had been taking up space in my mind for months. He wore black combat boots and jeans, white jeans with a black rope belt. There was a silver chain around his hips, lower than the belt, and another that looped from the front of his hip to the back on his left side. He wore a white t-shirt. He had silver rings on each of the fingers and the thumb of his left hand like Brekwyn had on his right hand. He wore a stack of silver bracelets on each wrist. His shirt had a v-neck that revealed a thin, black, necklace and the edge of a tattoo that was on his chest. His hair was long, really long like past his shoulders by about five inches, it was as dark as Brekwyn's, so dark that it looked blue in places but unlike Brekwyn's hair, his was pin straight. The sides of it, above his ears were shaved but you might not notice that at first. The only color on him was the thread that was wound around a section of his hair on the inside in the back only revealing itself with a certain movement just like the shaved sides. His skin was a little lighter than Brekwyn's or Danyon's or Anira's, but so was mine, the color was more like my color. He had a small silver hoop in each ear and an even smaller silver hoop through his right nostril.

His face. It wasn't what I expected. I thought he was going to be older. I thought he was going to be ugly. But he wasn't. He looked only a few years older than Brekwyn I guess, maybe in his thirties. And his eyes they were as black as one other person that I knew and that was Brekwyn. I wondered at that moment if he knew about the similarities in hair and eye color that he and Brekwyn shared or if Brekwyn had known this, or was it just me in my observant ways that noticed it?

He was smiling at me, "You've been busy Boy. I see Brekwyn has taught you well. Not well enough though. If he had taught you better then you wouldn't have pulled that little stunt in the Gadje town and drawn so much attention to yourself." He shrugged and winked at me. "But it was helpful in bringing us together of course, so I thank you for that."

Oh my God, this was my fault. The way I acted in the town, getting in that guys face, calling him a Gadje, it's exactly what Brekwyn said not to do. I led them here. My stomach turned, I wanted to throw up.

"My name is Inglore, I've been looking for you for a long time and I am happy to finally see you."

I said nothing.

Poppy started growling, I looked over to her suddenly aware again of my surroundings, she started to move toward us, all of the hair was standing up on her back, she was bearing her teeth. I looked back to the Inglore. His expression changed from the smile he wore when looking at me to almost a look of boredom, his head cocked to the side after a sigh.

"Please," he was addressing Danyon, "I don't want to hurt your dog. Do you want me to hurt your dog?"

"Why don't you go back to where you came from? We don't want you here!" Danyon said fiercely, Poppy was still moving toward us.

"And I don't want to be here, I just came to collect the Reader and then I'll be off."

"You can't have him!" Poppy started moving faster as Danyon yelled.

The Inglore started to look annoyed, "Here's how this will work. You cannot beat me because I am more powerful than you. Telling your dog to come after me won't work like you think it will because remember, I know what she wants to do. She wants to please you so she will do what you say, but, when I tell her that if she comes any closer that I will harm you then she will be conflicted and need to protect you so I will have no choice but to harm her too. And I don't want to harm you, I don't like to hurt Gypsies and you don't want me to hurt her do you? Isn't she your best friend, part of your family?" Poppy started to retreat, looking from Danyon to the Inglore, wondering what to do, no longer bearing her teeth.

"Thank you," he said to Danyon as Poppy stopped coming forward. "Now, Reader, why don't you introduce yourself."

I wasn't feeling afraid of him, until then I wasn't even feeling anger toward him, this I noticed because all of a sudden I started to feel it and I started to feel it very strongly, the blood rising in my face.

"Now, Anira, why would you make him so mad? You see how lovely he is, why would you want him to feel that way?" He knew her name. That made me feel crazy inside.

"Why don't you stop making him feel like he should like you?" she asked through clenched teeth.

"I want him to be happy. Don't you want him to be happy? " He started to walk over to her, I turned to watch what he was doing.

He crouched by her side and ran the back of his hand softly down her cheek. "So beautiful, Anira," he said as if making the observation to no one in particular. She jerked her face away. I was getting angrier. So was she.

"Look at the flames in your eyes darling," he said to her with that smile again. "For whom do these flames burn?"

"Leave her alone," I growled. His eyes lit up and his smile grew.

"You love the Reader, Anira?" He was almost whispering it to her but we all could hear him, "How lovely. I'm afraid I have to take him with me though, far away from here." He looked around as if disgusted by where we chose to live.

"Untie me Inglore so I can rip your hair out!" Anira lurched toward him. Her anger was almost tangible and so was mine. I tried to get my hands out of the plastic ties, cutting them into my wrists in the struggle.

"Tsk, tsk, tsk, such language from a lady, what would Callay say?" He was toying with her but I welcomed the distraction, I actually thought I would be able to break free and save us somehow if he remained preoccupied by her. I noticed out of the corner of my eye that Danyon was trying to do the same thing I was but his feet were bound too, so as he moved he fell forward and smashed his face into the ground. It did not stop him though as I saw him get himself up and try again, this time with blood running out of the corner of his mouth from the impact on the ground, his face was getting red and sweaty in the meaningless but valiant effort.

"Never utter my father's name or you will rue this day even more than...."

"Hush girl," he cut her off, "don't waste your breath with your petty threats. I'll give you a choice, Anira. Because you love the Reader, why don't you come with us? You choose. Come with us and be with the boy you love or stay here with your family." He knew that he was giving her an impossible choice. I knew what she would choose and I could feel the pain in my chest that matched hers.

When she didn't respond the Inglore changed, he got angrier. "I know how you love him, I can feel it, I can feel your heart breaking because you know he will not be with you anymore. So why don't you come with us? What is this hold that that waste of a life has over you?" He pointed to an unconscious Brekwyn and started pacing around. He was addressing all three of us now, not just Anira. "What purpose does he serve? He has all of this power but he chooses not to use it. He wastes it. Why was it given to someone who refuses to rise to his full potential? Do you know what he could be? He could be amazing but he's afraid, he's foolish. He doesn't think he will be able to control himself if he unleashes his full power.

"That is pitiful and disrespectful to the gift he was given. And yet, here you stay, worshiping him, for what? So you can live in your pathetic dirty trailer in woods right off some Gadje road? With me this Reader will live like a king and you could be his queen," he pointed to Anira, "but instead you will choose to stay with someone that didn't even know I was here in these woods watching you, waiting for you. If he used his full power, he would have known. He would've been able to at least try to stop me."

He crouched down next to Anira again, this time I saw tears in his eyes, "Isn't it sad that your obsession with Brekwyn is greater than your love of this boy?"

Tears rolled down her cheeks, "My love for 'that boy' runs deeper than any love that anyone has ever felt for you!"

"It is not for me to say if that is true, beauty, but never-the-less here you will stay without him," he stood up and turned toward my direction.

"He is just as much a part of my family as Brekwyn and Danyon are!" she yelled at him.

"Is that what you've told him Anira? Is that what that waste of life told you to tell him?" he yelled back at her. She was silent, looking down at the ground and gasping for breath in between sobs. He shook is head in disgust, "Your love is built on a lie. He belongs with me and that's where he shall be."

And with that, he stalked past me signaling to his men bring me along.

Wait, this is it, that's it?

"Come now Boy, it's time to go home."

Chapter Fifty-Nine

"No!" Anira screamed.

"Stop!" this from Danyon.

They both tried to get up, wrenching their hands around in a desperate attempt to get themselves free. I would not go easily, I would fight like they were, with every ounce of strength I had. My feet were not bound so I started kicking at the men who were carrying me by my arms.

"Anira!" I yelled. I could feel the pain and panic rising up in my chest. "Let go of me!" I tried to head butt them.

"No!" she screamed again through her tears, "Brekwyn, wake up! Brekwyn!"

"Brekwyn!" Danyon yelled too as he tried to move toward him on his side.

"Danyon!" I screamed feeling the sting of bile rising up in my throat, the pain in my body making it almost impossible to breathe.

I looked back at them, Anira was sobbing and screaming, trying to get to me but falling over in her attempts to get up.

"Anira I love you!" My heart felt like it was being torn out of my body.

The wind started picking up around us, I looked toward the Inglore to see what he was doing. He was stalking forward quickly and flinging his arms to the right and to the left. I looked in either direction and saw that animals were charging toward us and he was pushing them aside with the force of the wind before they could get too near. Two deer with antlers were tossed aside like they weighed nothing more than paper, the same with a wolf. They were coming at Danyon's orders but it was useless, he too was helpless, again.

"Brekwyn, help us!" I could feel the vessels breaking in Anira's throat as she screamed or were they mine was I still screaming back at them too? "Aurelious! I will find you! I will find you! Aurelious, I will come for you!"

"Brekwyn!" Danyon yelled I looked back and saw that he had made it over to him, he was kicking at him to wake him up. Poppy was barking.

I struggled until I could see them no longer, but I could still feel her, I could still feel the pain. The sound of metal made me turn and look in the direction we were headed rather than back toward Anira, Danyon, and Brekwyn. It was the sound of the back doors of a white van opening. The next sound was the sound of me hitting the floor of the van as I was tossed inside, then the slam of the doors.

I was disoriented. This was all happening so fast. I heard the roar of the engine and felt the van lurch forward as we were jolted over rough terrain and then onto the smoothness of what I assumed was the road. I tried looking around to get a better view of the men. Three of them were in the back with me. The fourth and the Inglore were in the front. I recognized one, the man from the alley, the man from the town.

"I don't like him looking at me with those eyes," one said to the others with the same accent as the Inglore.

"Put that sack over his head," said another, and his suggestion was accepted. The bag smelled musty, I coughed which got the attention of the Inglore.

"Take that sack off his head, he's not an animal," the Inglore said to them and immediately the bag came off.

It was then that I caught a glimpse of the sky out of the back window of the van. It was getting darker and darker with each passing second, shades of blackness swirling around shades of gray interrupted only by bright, massive bolts of lightening. I could see the wind whipping, the trees bending and straining to stay rooted. The air pressure in the van was changing from the forces of nature colliding outside, my ears clogged and popped so violently that my head started to hurt. A piece of hail the size of a baseball smashed through a back window sending shards of glass everywhere but just as quickly as the glass flew in, it flew back up and into position in the door with just the flick of the Inglore's hand. I began to feel a different kind of fear, one that wasn't my own. Someone here had the same gift as Anira and they were scared.

"Give him this," I heard the Inglore say before I felt the prick of a needle in my arm. Immediately my head started to feel heavy, cloudy, it felt both hot and cold at the same time. There was a buzzing sound from somewhere inside my mind. They drugged me.

The drug worked quickly but it was the last sentence I heard before it took full effect that would carry me through the next part of my journey. It was the sentence that I would remember even if I forgot all else. It was the sentence that I would tell myself at night before I fell asleep. It came from a place of fear, and the knowledge of that fear would be my strength.

All of this I felt when I heard a stranger, one of my captors say, "We've just unleashed *The Brekwyn*."

Epilogue

To say that was a dark day for me would be an understatement, to say that was to be my last dark day would be untrue, really, really untrue. I've spent a lot of time considering how I should tell you my story. Do I just throw it all out there at once and hope for the best? Probably not, I think the better approach to helping you be able to take all of this in is to provide you with the story in increments. I thought maybe if you took a break and were able to think about everything I just told you then you would be sufficiently ready for what comes next. This story doesn't end when the Inglore captures me. In fact, that's actually fairly close to the beginning. A lot more happens, a lot more.

The day I was taken was a milestone. It marked the end of one part of the journey and the beginning of another. It made sense that this is where I give you the chance to stop and take it all in. Should we call it an intermission? I should warn you, the next installment of the story is a bit darker than this one. It's a bit edgier. And I apologize in advance if I seem like a real dick when you read it, kind of like I was in the beginning of this volume. I was happy, finally truly happy with the Baliel Gypsies. But as my life has suggested, perhaps happiness is just not my thing.

For those of you who feel like you don't need or want the time to think about what I've told you so far, I'm giving you a little taste of how the next installment begins. If you need the break then don't read any further, but if you feel like you're ready then, by all means, please proceed.

Aurelious Forty: Volume Two

Chapter One

You know it's going to be a bad day when you wake up with a headache so crushing that you can hardly open your eyes. This day would not be an exception to that. This day was the first day that I woke up in the presence of the Inglore.

I can remember some parts of the journey that he took me on when he abducted me from my family, from Anira the girl I desperately loved, from Danyon my best friend, and from Brekwyn my mentor, friend, and surrogate older brother. Brekwyn was the person who saved me from my nothing life as the Gadje I never should have been. Together with Danyon and Anira and all of the Baliel tribe, they made my new life as a Gypsy more incredible then I could've dared to imagine.

It was midday when the Inglore captured me but shortly after that I was drugged. I would only experience bits and pieces of consciousness in between feeling the sting of the needle in my arm administering the toxin that kept me asleep. I remember seeing darkness and then daylight again. I remember being jostled by the movement of the van that took me away. I also remember smelling salty sea air at some point and feeling rolling movement like we were traveling on the water.

The bottom line is that I had no idea where I was or how long it had been since they had taken me. The only thing I knew for sure was that I felt physically terrible, sicker than I had ever felt. My body was bruised, my head was pounding, my mouth felt like it was full of sand, my throat burned from the bile that rose up in it, and my stomach was nauseous.

But I was no longer in a moving vehicle. I was lying on a bed. At least it seemed like a bed from how it felt without opening my eyes. I pretended to be asleep to avoid another dose of the drugs. I thought I was pulling it off so I was startled by the voice that came from somewhere very close to me, clearly not falling for my act.

"I'm sorry you feel so bad. I don't like seeing you uncomfortable but I think that being asleep made the trip easier for you. There was no struggle, no burden of emotion."

I recognized the Inglore's voice. His accent was distinctive to me now, forever engrained into my brain. He wasn't fooled into thinking I was asleep yet, somehow aware of how I felt, he spoke softly to avoid making my head hurt worse. Why would he care about my comfort after just brutally ripping me from the family that I had grown to know and love? This dichotomy confused me so I could only assume his compassion was false, some kind of ploy to get me to forgive him for what he had done.

I opened my eyes slowly. The room was dim, lit only by two candles, one on a table next to the bed I was lying on and one on the small table next to the chair where he sat watching me. I looked at him and said nothing. He sat forward in the chair resting his elbows on his knees, his head down but eyes looking up at me. He had no expression on his face.

"You'll feel better soon and you'll grow more comfortable here," he said to me. Then he looked away and said to someone I couldn't see, "Give him some broth."

I heard movement from the darkness of what I assumed was a doorway and then a round woman wearing an apron appeared with a tray. On it there was a bowl of broth, a piece of crusty bread, and some kind of drink. I looked at it but made no attempt to receive it. Did he think I was going to eat something after he gave me all those drugs? Did he think I wouldn't assume he drugged the food too? So, like a scorned child, I rolled over and faced the wall.

"It's okay Boy, I understand that you're upset. But in time you'll come to realize that this is where you belong. The food I provide for you is to nourish you, to help you regain your strength." I could hear him getting up from the chair and moving through the shadows. "Come, leave the tray. He'll eat when he's ready," he said to the woman and with that I heard a door open, close, and lock.

Acknowledgements

We never really do anything completely alone. Certainly this is true for me in the journey that this story has taken me on. So for being a part of this journey, I must acknowledge the people who helped me along the way.

Mom, thank you for your support and enthusiasm. Thank you for loving each version of this story and for dropping everything to read them all. Thank you for thinking I could do this and for helping me to believe it.

My sister, Leslie, thank you for your interest, ideas, insight, and foreword thinking about what the heck we were supposed to do with this once the words were on the page. This would probably still be a word document if it wasn't for your help.

Carolyn and Toni, thanks for jumping on board early, for your keen eyes, and motivating kindness.

Alix Reid, thank you for your editing skills and remarkable knowledge about the YA world, and for your willingness to share them both.

Dane at ebooklaunch.com, thank you for bringing Aurelious to life on the cover of this book. Your skills and talents as an artist are extraordinary.

Lisa, remember how long ago this all started? You were there from the beginning, thank you for standing by this.

Michelle, my friend, you've had to listen to way too much chatter about this weird world that exists in the pages of this book and you always made me feel like it was important and relevant. For your patience, support, and encouragement, and willingness to share Emma and her insights, I thank you.

Dad, you told me to do something creative, so this is what I came up with. I hope you're proud of it; I love and miss you desperately but know that you are with me. Oh and sorry for all the bad language.

Beloved, you are the reason I breathe. You are all of the good things that exist in my life. You were the first one to read this when it was just a chapter and it was your excitement that encouraged me to keep going. Thank you for your excitement. I love you for all that you are.

And finally, to those of you who have given of your time to read this story, I thank you from the bottom of my heart. Without you this is all just words on a page, you have made it bigger.

17093285R00143

Made in the USA
Middletown, DE
08 January 2015